A Crafter
Knits a Clue

A Crafter Knits a Clue

A HANDCRAFTED MYSTERY

Holly Quinn

NEW YORK

Copyright © 2018 by Sherry Rummler

Published in the United States by Crooked Lane Books, an imprint of The Quick Brown Fox & Company LLC.

Crooked Lane Books and its logo are trademarks of The Quick Brown Fox & Company LLC.

Library of Congress Catalog-in-Publication data available upon request.

ISBN (hardcover): 978-1-68331-771-5
ISBN (ePub): 978-1-68331-772-2
ISBN (ePDF): 978-1-68331-773-9

Cover illustration by Ben Perini
Book design by Jennifer Canzone

Printed in the United States.

www.crookedlanebooks.com

Crooked Lane Books
34 West 27th St., 10th Floor
New York, NY 10001

First Edition: October 2018

10 9 8 7 6 5 4 3 2 1

Wendy and Jason
A real couple. Who make a real
difference. In a real community.

Chapter One

It was yet another gray and colorless Wisconsin day, and Samantha Kane peeked out the front display window of the Community Craft store, urging the sun to make an appearance. Well, at least spring would be showing up inside—if not outdoors. She turned and lifted her round hazel eyes in search of Carter. She found him perched on the top step of the ladder, stretching a long arm to hang a colorful umbrella from the ceiling. Spring Fling—an annual event and parade held the second Saturday in April, designed to drag the community out of the long winter hibernation—was fast approaching, and Samantha wanted her shop to look seasonally festive.

"Over here, Sammy?" Carter balanced on one foot, hooking the umbrella to its final destination with one hand.

"Sure." Sammy brushed auburn bangs away from her eyes. "Please be careful, I don't want you to fall." She loved that he called her by her childhood nickname. Even though she was fifteen years his senior, they had a great rapport because of his older sister, Kate Allen. Carter's sister had been Sammy's best friend since grade school. When Sammy had returned to the small town of Heartsford, Wisconsin, to attend Kate's funeral, she had realized Kate's store—the town's favorite gathering place, Community Craft—would be closed permanently. The shock of losing Kate was hard enough; the tight-knit community couldn't lose the store too.

Kate and her store had brought everyone together through the selling of handmade goods. Knit items, homemade soaps, handcrafted wooden furniture, wood burned plaques, quilts, hand sewn garments and doll dresses, pottery. *Anything* that was handmade by people in the community was sold at Community Craft. The store even had a section with books for sale, and Kate had held book signings for local authors.

The sales weren't the most important part of the shop though. It was the numerous fundraisers and community efforts that made it thrive. When Jane Nelson fell ill with cancer, local quilters had come together at the store to piece together a blanket to bring her comfort. When Miles Danbury lost his job, people had bought his handcrafted wooden furniture to help him pay his bills. He was never late on his mortgage and, most importantly, kept his dignity. When Bob Dueck's brother went missing, the whole town had met at Community Craft to hand out fliers to start a search team. The knitting group supplied the local hospital with soft-knit hats and booties for the new babies born in Heartsford. Whatever the townspeople had needed, the store had provided.

So, when Kate had died in a freak accident, Sammy wouldn't let Community Craft close. No. She hadn't allowed that to happen. She had taken over the store in hopes of eventually selling it to someone who would keep her friend's legacy alive. Yet three years later, she was still running the shop on Main Street. Happenstance. The last thing in the world she ever thought she'd do was retail. And yet here she was.

Sammy looked up at the high school basketball star, grateful he was on the ladder, so she didn't have to overcome her fear of heights, at least for today. She knew it wouldn't last though. With the basketball team heading to the championships, she'd have to prioritize Carter's help for the next few days since she would only have him for a few hours after school each day. His cell phone buzzed, and after he had secured the umbrella to the ceiling, Carter sat atop the ladder with his legs hanging at length off each side. Sammy shook a warning finger at him to not waste time on the phone. She had a feeling she would be working a few late hours this week to prepare for Spring Fling.

Maybe it was time to hire additional staff. Sammy just wasn't sure she could afford it. With the holiday season over and folks still paying off their Christmas debt, the end of winter was seasonally slow. Carter interrupted her thoughts. He cupped his hand over the phone to shield the person on the other end from hearing. "It's Ingrid. She wants to know if I can come over and help hang a knit afghan in the window."

Sammy grunted aloud. The new neighbor who owned the yarn supply shop a few doors down on Main Street, seemed to think she could call on Carter any time she wanted. Even when it was on Sammy's dime. Carter was so good-natured that he bent to the older woman's demands too often. Since Ingrid had turned out to be the high school basketball coach's long-lost aunt, she had some extra pull over the teen. Sammy wondered secretly if Carter would eventually grow up to become the town mayor like his dad, Mark Allen. Always coming to everyone's rescue.

"Tell her *I'll* be right over. You keep hanging those umbrellas. It looks good. I'm happy you hung one upside down to show the design. Clever work."

Carter grinned at her compliment, showing his newly gleaming straight teeth—his much-loathed braces had been removed just a few days prior.

"I'll be right back." She waved a hand at Carter. The more she thought about Ingrid, the more she fumed. She realized that Ingrid had just opened the yarn shop a few months ago and Sammy should cut her new neighbor some slack. But seriously, why couldn't she hire someone? Why did Ingrid always call on her or Carter for help? Although, she knew that wasn't exactly true. If Sammy hadn't agreed to go over now, half the town would be called upon to fix Ingrid's problems. Well, Ingrid was going to have to wait a bit longer, Sammy decided. If she rushed over right away, what boundaries was she setting? Instead, she purposely visited her office to check a few emails. When the guilt wouldn't allow her to wait any longer, she closed her laptop, zipped on a nylon jacket, and set off through the back door.

The alleyway behind the shop was wide and ran along a large parking lot that serviced the public when visiting the many businesses along Main Street. This time of day, the lot was vacant, except for a dark blue car screeching out of the exit. Where were the police when you needed them? She'd have to mention that to Tim the next time she saw him at the coffee shop. Someone should patrol these parking lots. *Geez*. Thank God there were no pedestrians around. People really needed to slow down. Someone could have been hit by that car!

Sammy pulled the nylon jacket hood up over her head to protect her from the postwinter chill as she trudged across the parking lot toward her neighbor's shop. Evidently, the weatherman hadn't factored in the windchill, as the temperature was nowhere near the fifty degrees he'd promised on the morning news. Maybe it was just the lack of vitamin D that was making her unusually grumpy. It seemed the whole town was suffering from the lack of sun. There weren't a lot of people out and about. Everyone seemed to be hibernating. There was a heavy feeling in the air along with the low hanging clouds. Like it could rain or snow again at any minute.

Sammy opened the back door of The Yarn Barn and called out to Ingrid. She was surprised her neighbor wasn't waiting by the door to greet her. Was she with a customer? But the store was eerily quiet. Sammy was growing increasingly frustrated. She didn't have time to mess around since Carter was only on the clock for another hour. She stomped her feet a little louder as she walked a few feet deeper into the shop. Hopefully, Ingrid would get the hint from her nonverbal signals, but she doubted it. Sammy bumped into a rack filled with fleece-lined knitted socks. *Oh, these are nice and soft.* Mental note, after paying off bills, she needed to stop by and pick up a pair. Spring or no spring, her feet were freezing.

Even after Sammy's slight distraction with the sock rack, Ingrid was still nowhere to be found. Where was she? The smell of hot coffee tickled Sammy's senses. She must be taking a break in the upstairs office. But she noticed a full cup steaming a few feet from the cash register. As Sammy turned to walk behind the counter, she almost tripped over a foot. The color drained from her face. The shopkeeper was on the floor—a dark green aluminum knitting needle jutting alarmingly from her throat. It was obvious . . . . . . Ingrid was dead.

Chapter Two

S ammy didn't have to wait to run into Tim at the coffee shop. Within minutes, he had answered the call from dispatch and was standing beside her in the parking lot behind The Yarn Barn. She watched in numb shock as the coroner wheeled the body of Ingrid Wilson, covered with a black plastic tarp, toward an awaiting van.

"You were the last person who talked with her? What time was that?"

Tim—Sammy's cousin's boyfriend, who worked for the Heartsford Police Department—towered over her. He looked like a professional football player. His uniform fit too snugly on his solid arms, and his wide neck was as large as the outer edge of his head. But as he stood next to her asking questions, it seemed like she was in a fog—her ears barely registered the words coming out of his mouth. An EMT approached as Tim waved his meaty hand closer. "Hey, John, can you take a look at Sammy? I think she's in shock."

Sammy shook her head in disagreement and brushed the EMT aside. "I'm fine. I'm sorry, Tim. What did you ask me?"

Her eyes rose to meet his as she tried to convince him that she was emotionally capable of answering all of his questions.

"When did you talk to Ingrid?" Tim threw his hands onto his hips and waited for an answer. His overrun eyebrows furrowed, making one continuous line across his round face.

"I didn't. Carter talked to her. Oh. I forgot about Carter. He needs to clock out soon. What time is it?" From where she stood in the parking lot, Sammy looked toward the back door of her store and saw a perplexed Carter sneaking a look out the door. He was watching the flashing lights and commotion that had taken over the back alleyway of the businesses. Upon noticing Sammy talking with Tim, the teen rushed toward them. His long legs brought him to rest in front of them in record speed.

"What happened?" Carter's eyes darted around the parking lot in search of answers.

"It's Ingrid . . . There's been an accident." Sammy put a hand on Carter's shoulders to brace him for the news.

"Not an accident. A murder." Tim piped up. "Carter, I understand you were the last person to talk with Ingrid?"

The teens face turned ashen. "I was? *Oh God*, yes."

"Tim, he's a minor." Sammy stood between the two and ushered Carter protectively to a nearby bench. She sat next to him and glared at Tim as he shrugged, stepped back, and then headed toward the yarn shop, knowing he'd stepped over the professional line. She followed him with her eyes as he entered through the back entrance of The Yarn Barn to continue looking for evidence.

"I can't believe it. This is totally not possible. What about

Coach?" The high school basketball coach, Augustine Ellsworth Wilson III, who everyone in Heartsford referred to only as "Coach" was Ingrid's nephew. To lose his aunt in such a brutal fashion would be devastating. Carter folded forward and braced his head in his hands. After a few moments, he lifted his head and turned to Sammy wide-eyed. "She died?"

"I'm afraid so." Sammy rubbed the back of the teen's now perspiring neck. The stress of the situation had won out over the cold temperature causing him to sweat. "I'm just glad I was the one who went over and discovered her . . . and not you."

"But I just talked to her?" Carter said with disbelief.

"I know, honey. I'm sorry. It's crazy, isn't' it?" Sammy continued to comfort the young man until he leapt up from the bench in a panic.

"I have to get to practice. I'm late." He ran his fingers over his short blond buzz cut. "Oh God, this is nuts. Poor Coach. Will Coach know? I can't be the one to tell him." Carter began pacing back and forth in the parking lot. He stopped abruptly and looked down at her. "I've got to get outta here."

Sammy stood and reached to grab him by the arm. "Are you okay to drive? This is quite a shock." She wasn't sure it was the best idea to let him go, but she also knew his personality and that no matter what she said it wouldn't stop him. He would turn eighteen next week. Although she protected him like a minor, he would soon bump over into adulthood. *But Tim didn't have to know that just yet.* Sammy knew Carter had nothing to do with the murder anyway. There was no reason the police should need to question him further.

"Yeah. Yeah, I've got to go now." He headed toward his car and left her standing alone in the parking lot, wondering what had just happened in their sleepy town, and now desperately needing one of those colorful umbrellas that Carter had hung on the ceiling.

The skies opened in an icy downpour and the few people left hanging on the sidelines trying to comprehend the scene before them, ran for cover. Sammy decided to close Community Craft early. Tim would know where to find her if he had additional questions. She sprinted to the back door of her shop, shaking the rain off her jacket as she entered. Immediately, she took the path through the racks of merchandise to lock the front door and change the sign to CLOSED so that she wouldn't have to answer any questions about the murder. News in a small town traveled fast, and she wasn't prepared for the gossip that would circle like a flock of vultures.

The realization that she might have been able to prevent this from happening came swift and hard. If she hadn't gone to check her emails . . . if she had just gone to the yarn shop right away when Ingrid called. The guilt nagged at her heart. She rubbed the ache in her chest as if she could make it go away. She had also narrowly missed the attack herself—if she had gotten there earlier, she might have been involved. The thought made her shudder.

The jingle of the bell on the back door alerted her that someone was arriving. Sammy maneuvered toward the back of the store to see who it was. Tim stood in the doorway, filling the space with his wide shoulders. "Hey, I still have questions for you, young lady."

"I know. I wasn't ditching you. I just wanted to lock the front door. I'm closing early. In fact, I should probably post an update on Facebook so my customers aren't disappointed, showing up to find the store closed." Sammy shrugged off her wet jacket that now clung on to her like an unwanted hug and hung it on a nearby rack. She ran her fingers through her damp, short auburn hair that draped just over her ears. It continued to stay matted to her head, so she gave up trying to look presentable.

"You can't share the murder on Facebook."

"I know that. I'm not going to say anything about Ingrid . . . just that I'm closing Community Craft early."

"Oh, okay then." Tim walked through the door and stood in front of the counter, tapping his fingers on the wooden slab. "Hey, do you want to join me and Heidi for dinner at the Corner Grill? Maybe you shouldn't be alone tonight."

The Corner Grill was the local hangout on the corner of Main Street and Sumner. With a large bar and mini stage, they offered karaoke on Friday nights and local bands on Saturdays. Wednesday, however, was all-you-can-eat pizza night, which usually filled the two-floor establishment.

"Nah. But thanks." Sammy moved past him into the office and quickly logged onto her laptop. "Just give me a sec, okay?" she shouted from the adjacent room. After posting the store closing, she moved back to the main room, behind the counter, where Tim waited patiently, digging at a hangnail.

"Who would do this?" Sammy crossed her arms across her chest. She spoke more to herself than the policeman standing in front of her.

"Anything else you can share? I've got Detective Nash over at the scene now. Have you met him yet?" The Heartsford Police Department had recently retired Stan Oberon, and now there was a new detective in town. From Minnesota. Sammy hoped for his sake he wasn't a Vikings fan. If so, he'd certainly be in trouble, as the whole town bled green and gold. Green Bay Packer fans practiced their own religion in Wisconsin.

"No. I haven't, but I'd heard we had a new detective. I figured I'd run into him sooner or later. Your office is literally one block away."

"I'm guessing sooner. Detective Nash is going to want to talk to you. I'm sure of it." Tim ripped the hangnail off his finger. "Hey! I got it," he smiled victoriously.

"I have to say, it does blow my mind."

"What's that?" Tim looked up from his finger and rested his thick muscular arms on the wooden counter top.

"How someone could be that brazen to kill Ingrid across the street from the police department. Right under your noses. In broad daylight, no less! Now that's insane." Sammy shook her head and uncrossed her arms and dropped them to her sides.

"You didn't see *anything?*" Tim pressed.

"Oh, my God. I just thought of something."

Tim waited patiently for Sammy to share her thoughts.

"There was only one knitting needle . . . used to, uh . . . murder Ingrid," Sammy's face twisted at the memory. "But where's the other one? You know they come in pairs, right?"

"Of course, I know that." Tim said. "My grandmother

was a serial knitter." He winked. "But that's a great point. I'll see if the detective found the other one."

Sammy snapped her fingers. "And there's something else. There was a blue car that took off screeching from the lot."

Tim leaned in closer. "What type? You have the model and make? License plate?"

"No. It was a smaller car? I mean . . . not an SUV. Great. I have no idea except it was blue. Dark blue."

"Don't beat yourself up over it. It's something. How were you supposed to know that car had just left a crime scene?"

Sammy hung her head defeated. "I feel responsible."

Tim leaned over the counter and reached with extended arms to shake her shoulders. "Now, don't do that. This is not your fault."

"I have a bit of a confession." Sammy bit her lip.

This alerted the policeman, and he dropped his arms and stood tall and attentive. "A confession?"

"Yeah. I didn't go over right away when Ingrid called. You know how she is. I mean *was*. Always making people rush to her aid. I waited, and I shouldn't have. If I'd gone over right away, she might still be alive." Sammy sighed heavily.

The policeman relaxed and deflated. "That's all? I thought you were going to confess to killing her!"

"Tim!" Sammy moved around the counter and playfully punched him on the arm. "Seriously?"

"Hey. You were the one that used the word *confession*. Careful the words you use around us police officers," he teased. "Look, I'm heading back to the crime scene. I'm sure Nash is going to want to talk to you. He's taking down the specifics. I'll send him over. Don't lock the back door yet."

Sammy walked slowly with Tim toward the back door. "Tell Heidi hello for me. I'll catch up with you guys another night."

"You sure? You shouldn't be alone right now. Come down to the Corner Grill if you change your mind." Tim waved a hand and was off into the inky wet night.

Sammy shut the door and hung the Closed sign but left the back door unlocked for the detective. Just as she was going to retreat into the shop, the new guy in town made an appearance and knocked on the glass door. Sammy reopened it and held it wide.

"Detective Liam Nash. I work for the Heartsford Police Department. You must be Samantha Kane?"

Sammy wasn't sure what she was expecting, but her initial impression of the detective pleasantly surprised her. He stood tall in a brown leather jacket. Of course, tall was relative. Everyone seemed tall to her; even with heeled shoes, Sammy was lucky to reach five feet. Liam's dark eyes were serious, but his hair was something altogether different, his out-of-control curls refused to stay in place. Tim hadn't told her the new detective was attractive, but then again, he wouldn't. The detective wasn't male-model gorgeous, but he wasn't hard on the eyes either. His defined cheekbones and perfectly sized nose, made him look as if he could have been a J.Crew model. Tim also hadn't said if the detective was single. Sammy stole a quick glance at a naked left hand ring finger. No ring. She wondered if her cousin Heidi had met him yet. If she had,

Heidi would have said something; the matchmaker in her would *not* let that pass her radar. By the look of his features, they had to be close in age, give or take a few years. Was he close to her thirty-three years? Or was he closer to forty? She couldn't quite gauge. Either way, the first impression piqued her interest.

"Come in." Sammy closed the store door behind the detective and led him inside the shop. She turned to him and stood to lean her back against the tall counter for support. "Welcome to Heartsford."

"Thanks. I'm sorry we're meeting on these terms. I won't take much of your time. I see you're closing up for the night." His eyes glanced around the space, taking it all in.

"Yes. Small town. If I stay open everyone will be in here gossiping, and I'm not ready for it," Sammy admitted easily.

"I bet." The new detective turned his attention from the merchandise back to her.

They stood in awkward silence for a few moments before Sammy asked, "What did you want to ask me?"

"I understand you were the one to find Ingrid."

"Yes." Sammy nodded her head in agreement.

"I'm sorry about that. How are you handling it?"

"Well, it's not every day you find a neighbor dead in her store." Sammy thought his questioning a bit strange, but who was she to judge?

"Did you kill Ingrid Wilson?"

"Well, you are direct, aren't you, Detective?" Sammy's hazel eyes narrowed.

"I tend to sense when someone is guilty, and I sense you're

15

not. Not to worry." He rested an elbow atop the counter and leaned in casually.

"That's good. I think. And the answer is no. I didn't kill Ingrid Wilson. She wasn't the easiest to get along with," Sammy admitted, "but I didn't kill her."

"Yes. I've heard that."

"Heard what exactly."

"That she wasn't the easiest to get along with."

"Ah." Sammy was a little relieved someone else had voiced the truth about Ingrid Wilson. It made her feel even worse though, speaking ill of the dead.

"Although you do have a motive."

"*Excuse* me?"

"Well, I'm sure she could sell knitted creations over there just as well as you could over here." Liam Nash eyed the merchandise rack standing next to him filled with knit scarves left over from the winter clearance.

"No. Ingrid sells yarn. I sell her customers' creations." Sammy corrected.

The detective altered his line of questioning. "What can you tell me about Augustine Ellsworth Wilson III?"

"Coach? I can tell you no one calls him by his given name," Sammy chuckled.

"Yes, I've heard that's how he's referred to around these parts. What can you tell me about the coach then?"

"Not *the* coach, just Coach," Sammy corrected. "Not much really. He's been the head coach of the high school basketball team for several years now. He actually brought Heartsford to the championships a few times. A select few students have received full scholarships based on his efforts. He's highly regarded in this town for that. I don't really have a personal relationship with him outside the fact he's the coach, and we were introduced at a basketball practice once. Coach and I might briefly chat or wave in passing, other than that I don't have much more I could say. Why? Is he a suspect? He can't possibly be a suspect? Is it because he's Ingrid's closest relative in town that you're considering him?"

Detective Liam Nash didn't flinch. He just continued his line of questioning.

"Tim mentioned you saw a car speed away but that you only recollect that it was dark blue."

"Yes. Unfortunately, that's true. Other than that, I don't have any further information to share."

"What time did you talk to Ingrid before going to The Yarn Barn?"

"I didn't. Carter did. He's a high school student that works part-time for me. Ingrid called him, but I went over instead; she needed help with something. But it wasn't right away. I had a few things to do in the office first." Sammy bit her lower lip. She would not share with the detective the shame that was coursing through her veins at that very moment because she hadn't gone to the yarn shop right away. She wondered how long it would take to work through that type of guilt.

"Do you recall the time?"

Sammy looked at the ceiling as she searched her memory and noticed Carter had finished hanging the rest of the umbrellas. "If you want an exact time, it would be recorded on Carter's cell phone. Honestly, I'm not sure what time it was. I could text Carter and ask him for you. Other than the phone call, Carter wouldn't have anything else to share as he was here at the store the entire time," she assured him.

"Let me be the judge of whether I should question Carter," he said with bite to his words.

"Of course." Sammy released her back from the counter and stood upright. "Do you take vitamin D supplements, Detective?"

Detective Liam Nash gave Sammy a peculiar stare before turning toward the door. He reached inside his leather jacket and pulled out a business card. "I'll be in touch, Ms. Kane." He handed her the card then slipped out the back door.

Chapter Three

Sammy juggled a brown paper shopping bag and her dark leather purse as she fumbled to unlock her rented Cape Cod. Her furry best friend eagerly met her at the front door. She placed the bag on a side table by the door, dropped her purse to the floor, and fluffed her golden retriever behind the ears. "I'm sorry I'm so late, Bara. I should have taken you to work today." Sammy clicked on his old weathered leash and led him out to do his business.

The rain had stopped, but a damp biting wind remained. "Hurry up, boy," she danced from foot to foot trying to keep warm while her dog sniffed for the perfect spot. Sammy grew impatient and led him to his favorite tall oak, still naked of leaves from the long Wisconsin winter, where he finally relieved himself. She felt bad she hadn't taken her pup for a walk. Often, she would walk to work and bring her prized golden into the store where he'd lazily lay most of the day, spoiled and cooed over by her customers. But today she had driven because she had needed to run a few errands after work. It had been a long and emotional day.

A car parked at the end of the tree-lined road flicked on its lights, turned on its engine, and retreated in the other direction. Had the person in the car been watching her? In the dark, she couldn't discern the color of the car. Now she was just being paranoid. Or was she? She gave a jerk to Bara's leash, alerting the dog that it was time to go inside. Normally, she wasn't the type to be anxious while alone in her neighborhood, but the events of the day had left her on edge. She closed and locked the door, unleashed Bara, and hung her jacket on a wooden peg just inside the entrance. With a flick of a switch, the gas fireplace whooshed to life, bringing instant comfort to her living space. Her dog, as if on cue, curled up on the rug in front of the licking flames. She was so grateful her landlord had converted the fireplace to gas. Ralph had mentioned he had done it for selfish reasons. It was neater and would cause less damage to one of his many properties. But for her, it meant one less thing to do—never having to haul wood.

The sound of Adele's singing rang out from the side pocket of Sammy's purse. *"Hello . . . it's me . . ."* She clicked to answer it just before the music stopped.

"Why didn't you call me?"

Sammy winced and clicked the phone to speaker to free her hands. Her sister, Ellie, obviously agitated from the sound of her voice, waited for an answer. "I guess you heard. Boy, news travels fast. Let me guess . ." Sammy pursed her lips and tapped her finger on the side table. "Heidi."

"Of course Heidi. Why do I have to hear this kind of news from my cousin and not my own *sister?*"

"I'm sorry. I haven't even eaten supper yet." Sammy

leaned her head back and peeked at the antique cuckoo clock that hung on the wall. "It's after eight o'clock, and I'm just getting home."

"I just put Tyler to bed and had to call. Are you okay? I can't even imagine . . . You could have been attacked too. Or *murdered*! What would I do if I lost my sister?"

Sammy allowed Ellie to ramble. She knew from experience to let her older sister unload. Even though she was only two years older, Ellie seemed to take on a protective role. And since giving birth to Tyler, her sister had changed. Her carefree attitude had morphed into over-nurturing parenting, bordering on almost neurotic at times. Sammy wasn't sure if it was due to her mothering of two-year-old Tyler, or rather that their own mother was no longer present in their everyday lives. At first, their parents had been snowbirds, overwintering in Arizona. But as the years went by, the overwintering became more permanent and trips back to Wisconsin became random, leaving the two siblings to fend for themselves until the holidays. At times, Ellie's overreactions and smothering proved to be overwhelming and exhausting. Sammy was more than capable of taking care of herself—thank you very much.

"Well? What do you have to say for yourself?"

"I really don't want to be interrogated right now. I'm hungry. I'm tired. And I love you too." Sammy plucked the phone off the side table, walked over to the sofa that sat in front of the fireplace and flopped into its cushions, curling her feet beneath her.

"Maybe I should come over and spend the night? Or better yet, you should come over here?"

Sammy could hear Randy in the background calling for her sister. "Sounds like your husband needs you. I think I heard him say that Tyler just threw up. No offense, but no thanks. I don't need to catch the flu on top of everything I have to do this week."

"Crap. I have to go." Sammy could hear the urgency in her sister's voice. "Depending on how Tyler feels; maybe we'll stop by Community Craft tomorrow. Doesn't look like he'll be going to preschool."

"Hope he feels better. Good night."

Her sister clicked off.

Sammy pulled her weary body off the couch and away from the warmth of the fire and walked into the small kitchen. She tugged the refrigerator door open and now wished she had gone for all-you-can-eat pizza with Heidi and Tim. After glancing at her empty shelves, she remembered she had left her grocery bag on the side table by the door. When she rushed over to grab the bag, the condensation from the frozen items had wet the paper, and the groceries fell out the bottom of the bag to the floor with a thud. Bara jumped to a standing position and sauntered over to investigate. As her dog sniffed the remnants on the floor, Sammy gathered the groceries into her arms and sighed heavily. She moved to the kitchen counter and dumped the heap of items into a pile.

As she attempted to shelve the can of coffee grounds, she suddenly remembered something. There had been a steaming cup of coffee on the counter close to where Ingrid's lifeless body lay. Directly on the counter above her. And it was a paper cup from the downtown coffee shop, Liquid Joy. She would recognize that yellow smiley-faced paper cup any-where. Had someone brought it to Ingrid? If so . . . who? The cup was still full and steaming with the lid off. And she remem-bered smelling the aroma in the air. But the shock of finding Ingrid's body had made her forget. The simple act of shelving the coffee had triggered her memory.

Either Ingrid had gone to Liquid Joy herself to get a coffee or someone had brought it to her. She decided the former wasn't likely. First, Ingrid didn't do anything for herself, and second, she wouldn't have left The Yarn Barn unattended. So, the killer could have been someone who knew Ingrid and had brought the coffee for her. Was it Coach? It couldn't possibly . . . could it? Or someone else that could have visited the store right before the murder? Sammy decided not to pro-gram her coffee machine for the following day. No. She would be making a trip to Liquid Joy first thing in the morning.

Chapter Four

Fat snowflakes, the size of silver dollars, fell from yet another colorless sky, but failed to accumulate on the ground due to the warmer spring earth. Sammy watched out her front window with dismay and felt compassion for the tiny wren clinging to the bird feeder for dear life. A robin bounced along the damp green grass that was matted with soggy aged leaves— leaves from the previous winter that had never made it to the pile before the first snow. Even the spring bird looked dazed as if cheated into coming back too early.

Sammy turned from the window, to an eager dog standing at attention. "I'm sorry, Bara. Not today. I'm taking the car again." His eyes drooped, and he slumped to the floor in response. She could swear her pup understood every word that came out of her mouth. He understood her better than half the people she knew. Leaving him behind for the second day in a row left a knot in her stomach. *Great. Something else to feel guilty about.*

After letting the dog out to do his business, she gave him a quick pat on the head before slinging her purse over her shoulder and stepping out onto the front stoop, moving carefully to make sure she didn't slip on the icy pavement. At least her car wasn't covered in snow. A few wipes with the wiper blades should be enough to clear it. As she backed out of the driveway, she noticed a silver Honda Civic pulling away from the curb. It wasn't a car she recognized as belonging to one of her neighbors. A sudden chill trickled down her spine, and it wasn't from the cold. Had someone been watching her overnight? Was it the same car as the night before? It was unusual for her neighbors to be up at first light. Usually, she was one of the earliest in the neighborhood to leave home. Especially today, as she was leaving extra early to stop for coffee on her way to the shop. She'd have to ask her neighbors if anyone had company visiting this week who had parked on the road. Another item to add to her list of things to do that day. This paranoia was going to have to stop, she decided. There was no time for it, and it only compounded her already jittery nerves.

As Sammy drove toward Main Street, her car barely had enough time to warm up. She only lived a few blocks from downtown, which made her life easy and convenient. When the weather improved, she would hardly use her car, if at all. Except for groceries, everything she needed was conveniently located downtown. Even the farmers market was close by in the summer, filling the parking lot of the Recreation Center full of produce. It was a place Sammy frequented with pleasure on early Saturday mornings before work. Not only were fresh vegetables abundant but often some of the older ladies sold sugary preserves and baked goods as well.

Sammy parallel parked her car in the last available spot in

front of Liquid Joy. The early breakfast crowd was seeping out of the establishment onto the sidewalk, most complaining about the weather and discussing whether spring would ever arrive. Sammy maneuvered through the patrons toward the coffee bar. She stood in line and noticed a hushed silence following her; eyes traveled in her direction. Maybe it wasn't such a promising idea, stopping by this morning. Clearly, the town was already buzzing like bees in a hive about Ingrid's sudden death. Sammy was sure everyone knew that she was the one who had found Ingrid's lifeless body. And those that didn't know were now waking up to the latest juicy chatter. Sammy placed a weak plastic smile on her oval-shaped face and was relieved when it was her turn in line.

"Busy morning!" She leaned onto the counter top and eyed the frosted pastries under the glass.

"What can I get you, Samantha?" Cara, the blonde barista, eagerly waited to compile her order. Cara's ponytail bobbed as if she had just run a race but her hair hadn't caught up yet.

"Is Douglas here this morning?" Sammy hoped she would get a chance to talk to the owner. She knew Cara only worked the early morning shift and wouldn't know anything about the coffee left behind at Ingrid's the previous afternoon.

Cara leaned back from the counter and searched through the morning rush. "I think he's out back unloading the truck."

Sammy found this odd as Douglas always worked the counter in the morning, due to it being the busiest time of day. She frowned.

"Did you want to order? I'm backing up here." Cara lifted her eyes from Sammy to the growing line behind her.

"Sure. I'll take a coffee and one of those." She pointed to a glazed pastry oozing with raspberry out of both sides.

Cara plucked a parchment paper and lifted the pastry into a paper bag. "Are you okay?" The barista leaned closer to the counter top and whispered to Sammy. "I heard."

Sammy leaned in closer. "Yeah. And it looks like you're not the only one." She rolled her eyes after scanning the crowd. "Can you ask Douglas to stop by later if he gets a minute? It's kind of important."

"You bet." Cara turned and filled the yellow smiley-faced cup, added a dash of vanilla cream, snapped on a lid, then placed it on the counter. She knew exactly how Sammy loved her coffee. Cara knew everyone's preferences.

"I know this might be a strange question, but I have to ask you something weird . . ." Sammy waved the barista to lean in even closer so she could whisper out of earshot.

Cara leaned over the counter and turned her ear for Sammy to whisper in it. "How did Ingrid take her coffee?"

Cara's response showed utter confusion. "She didn't. She was a tea gal. Why do you ask?"

Sammy left the crumpled cash on the counter. "Keep the change." She winked as she gathered her breakfast in her hands and headed out the door, eyes boring in her direction the entire time.

Sammy was happy for the protection her car provided. She realized that her day at the craft shop would prove to be an interesting one. The bold ones in the community would be the first to come and grill her about the incident, she was sure. Did people think she was responsible? That could really damage her business. And Ingrid didn't drink coffee. But someone else did. *Who?* Sammy wished she had brought Bara to work. He would be a welcomed comfort. She glanced at the glowing clock on the dashboard. She didn't have time to go back home and pick him up. It looked like she would have to face her customers alone for today. The fleeting wish that she could run home and hide beneath the bed sheets crossed her mind before she pulled away from the curb and circled around the block to the parking lot behind Community Craft. All was quiet. She took a deep breath before exiting the car with her breakfast in hand. At least she had something sweet in the bag to look forward to. She glanced toward The Yarn Barn and noticed there was yellow police tape blocking the back entrance. An uneasy feeling swept over her. The finality of Ingrid's death was still such a shock.

Sammy flicked on the lights with her elbow upon entering the shop, then went directly to her office and placed her breakfast on the desk. She noticed the answering machine had several messages, which was very unusual. The hawks were already circling, looking for the first bit of gossip. She decided to wait to listen to the messages and instead focus on the work at hand to clear her own mind. In thirty minutes, the store would open, and she had a few things to do before that happened.

The craft room, a glass-enclosed space inside the shop, was a gathering spot to hold classes given by various artists who wanted to pass on the love of their craft. The room was easily viewed from anywhere in the shop and built to entice perusing customers to try their hand at something new. The monthly schedule was tacked to the window, and Sammy was relieved to see no classes scheduled for Thursday. On Friday morning, the knitting group was meeting, and in the afternoon there was a painting class.

Sammy noticed that the room had been left in disarray by the quilting group that had met the previous morning. In all the chaos of the day before, she had missed tidying it up before she left. She pushed in the white plastic chairs so their backs touched the long table, then collected random pieces of leftover fabric and tossed them in the nearby trash can. Something shimmery caught her eye, and she dropped to her knees to peek underneath the table. There was a necklace on the floor. When Sammy picked it up, she noticed the clasp was broken. The chain held a locket; she popped it open with her fingernail and saw a photo of a young woman about high school age inside. Sammy didn't recognize the girl in the aged black-and-white photo, but hopefully someone in the quilting group would, so that it could be returned to the rightful owner. It had to belong to someone in the group because Sammy had vacuumed the craft room the day before and would have noticed it then or sucked it up with the vacuum cleaner. She moved over to the lost and found box underneath the cashier counter and dropped it inside. A quick look at the clock showed it was close to opening time. Sammy moved to the door, flipped the sign to OPEN, and unlocked the front door. The sun shone through the window, hinting that it might make an appearance, *finally*, and for that, she was more than grateful.

Sammy turned back to the office to go check her voice messages, but before she could hit the play button, the tinkling sound of the front door bell distracted her. She craned her neck around the office door and saw that it was her cousin Heidi.

"I can't believe what happened yesterday! I'm surprised to see you're open. I thought you might just close the shop and hang at home today. I think under the circumstances your customers would understand." Heidi rushed to Sammy and tackled her with a bear hug, her solid, sculpted yoga arms practically lifting her off the floor.

"I might close early again today. I'm not sure yet. I'll see how the day goes. Are you on your way to work or just getting off your shift?" Sammy pointed to her shapely cousin who even looked attractive wearing pale-green scrubs underneath her thick coat—the uniform at the hospital where she worked as an ER nurse. Heidi's brown eyeliner perfectly outlined her sage eyes that reflected the color of her uniform, and her cheeks held a rosy glow. Instead of looking like a nurse on shift, she looked like a runway model showcasing hospital wear. Sammy envied her cousin's beauty.

"Don't worry, I'm clean." Heidi knew Sammy hated getting hospital germs all over her. "I have a few minutes before work, but I had to stop by and see if you were all right. Are you?" Her cousin grabbed her hand and gave it a squeeze before releasing it.

"Yeah. I'm fine. Still in shock to be honest."

"I can't even imagine." Heidi shook her head. "I mean, I deal with death and disease at my job daily but for you . . ." Her tone was thick with empathy.

"Yes. For me. The squeamish germophobe." Sammy rolled her eyes.

"I didn't say that to be hurtful."

Sammy knew her cousin didn't mean anything hurtful. Heidi was so kind, she couldn't hurt a fly. She'd even try to nurse a bug back to health. Instead of killing a spider she would pick it up and put it back outside where it belonged.

"I wish you had come to dinner with us last night. We missed you." Heidi's eyes searched Sammy's, looking for a white flag.

"Yeah, me too. I'm sorry. It was a long day, and I just wanted to get home to Bara."

"I understand."

"Did Tim mention if they had any leads in the investigation?" Sammy walked behind the counter and leaned over the cash register to turn it on with a key.

"Now you know he wouldn't tell me even if he did." Heidi placed a hand on her hip.

Sammy hesitated about telling her cousin anything further but then blurted out, "There was a cup of hot coffee on the counter by her body, but Ingrid doesn't drink coffee. I think it belonged to the killer."

"Oh, no, no, no." Heidi shook a slender finger at her cousin. "No, you don't."

"What do you mean? No, I don't. What?" Sammy's pencil-thin eyebrows crinkled in guiltless question.

Heidi leaned close to the polished wooden counter and braced her hands firmly on the side. "I see what you're doing.

You're poking around in the investigation. That's what you're doing."

"No, I'm not," Sammy said innocently. After seeing her cousin's reaction, there was no way she was going to share the possibility that someone might be following or stalking her too.

"I can see it in your eyes. This is not S.H.E. playtime from our childhood. This isn't the case of the missing lunchbox." Heidi waved a finger pointedly. "This is serious, Samantha. This is murder."

Sammy knew what she was referring to. The three cousins—herself, her sister, Ellie, and Heidi—had all formed a fictitious detective agency in grade school. They used the first letter from each of their names to form the name of the agency. S: Sammy. H: Heidi. E: Ellie. Of course, they never really solved any cases. Although they did find a stolen bike once *and* a missing lunchbox. She wasn't sure if that counted as a "solved crime." They even had baseball hats and T-shirts designed signifying the tight club of three.

"I'm not playing S.H.E." Sammy rolled her eyes and decided her best tactic would be to change the subject. "I was wondering if you wanted to go to dinner tomorrow? Just us girls. How 'bout us S.H.E.?"

Heidi chuckled. "You *mean* us three S.H.E.s. I have a hair appointment at four thirty tomorrow. Maybe after?"

Heidi's hair was the color of aged cornhusks and equally as dry. "Are you dying it the same color?" Sammy hoped this change of topic would keep her cousin from thinking she was digging too far into the investigation or from saying anything to Ellie. That's all she needed was her sister to be even more on her back.

"I don't know. What color do you think?" Heidi patted her dehydrated hair with her fingertips.

"I would go with whatever color Tim suggests." Sammy knew her cousin wouldn't listen to her anyway. For years she had tried to convince her to stop coloring it. She wondered if Heidi would have a hair left on her head by the time she was middle-aged. Honestly, she couldn't even remember her natural color anymore, it had changed so many times over the years.

Heidi flexed her back and lifted her endowed bosom to attention. "I think he's more concerned with these girls than my hair."

Sammy eyed Heidi's perky boobs with envy as she had none to speak of. Well a little more than none. Barely more than none. "*Whatever*," she muttered.

A customer entered the shop, and Sammy felt relieved by the interruption. She pointed out the customer covertly so that Heidi would take the hint and skedaddle. Which she did. With a wave of one hand, she was gone.

Chapter Five

S ammy was pleasantly surprised by the quiet morning. She thought for sure the citizens of Heartsford would come rushing into the shop to gossip about the recent murder. But they hadn't. Maybe she hadn't given the town enough credit after all? Or maybe the community was still in shock too. She looked at the clock; it was still morning. *Give it time.* That was the one thing that had taken a readjustment period when returning home to work at Community Craft. When she lived in the city of Madison, she could come and go as she pleased. No one cared about her daily affairs. But if she was being honest, at times she had missed the small-town vibe. Not the gossip, mind you. But the caring attitude of the community in which she lived. The one Kate had created and nurtured. Kate had a way of shifting people's perspective to see the good in others and treat them accordingly. It was a quality Sammy remembered about her best friend and aspired to emulate. Sammy felt guilty for the negative thoughts she'd harbored about her community—that they were *all* small-minded gossips. They might be small-minded, but they were big hearted in Heartsford. Kate had always reminded her of that. God, she missed her.

Sammy hoped her uneventful day would continue.

"Hi-dee-ho, friend!"

Sammy knew the familiar voice that called out, and she turned with a wide smile.

Miles, a regular vendor who supplied the shop with hand-crafted wooden furniture, stepped into the back door of the shop lugging a wooden bench over his shoulder.

Sammy rushed toward him to help with the door. "New merchandise? I'm excited to see what you brought. You officially made my day!" she grinned.

Miles set the bench down as he huffed and puffed from exertion. His smile, along with the twinkle in his eye, was so warm and inviting, it was superior to his oversized frame. No one seemed to notice that his diet consisted mostly of beer, bratwurst, and Wisconsin cheese; each minute the man was a possible heart attack. His belly jutted over his worn jeans like an oversized water balloon.

"I've got a truckful, missy." After adjusting his pants, he winked and jutted a sausage-sized thumb toward the door.

"Let me get my coat. I'll help you lug it all inside." Sammy hustled to the office before he had the chance to change his mind and not let her help. He tended to overtake her with his gentlemanly defiance, but she was more than capable of carrying a few items, even though most of them would likely outweigh her.

Sammy stepped out the back door into the sunshine. "Ahh," she said to Miles as he leaned into the back of his pickup truck trying to reach a hand-carved birdhouse. "Doesn't that sunshine feel amazing?"

"It sure does. Been a long winter, eh?" With dry cracked hands, he handed her the birdhouse, and she admired it with awe.

"Wow. Nice work. I have a feeling this one is going to sell fast." The wooden stump had the raw bark intact, yet the house was carved intricately around an access hole.

He smiled wide, showing coffee-stained teeth, before handing her another. "That's enough for you, young lady," he said. "I'll grab the big stuff."

Sammy knew better than to argue, so she headed for the back door. She set the birdhouses carefully inside and then stepped back out into the sunshine. As Miles moved toward her with another bench, she swung the door wide open. "Boy, it sure looks like you've been busy in the workshop!"

Miles heaved the solid carved bench into the store, and she held the door for him until he set the furniture down. As he moved back toward the truck, he stopped and turned toward the back entrance of The Yarn Barn. "What a darn shame," he said sincerely.

Sammy hung her head in reply. "I know. I'm trying not to think about it."

"I'm sorry. I didn't mean to upset you further, Sam." He laid an encouraging hand on her shoulder and gave a light squeeze. "I did overhear that you found her. Did you see anything? You doing all right?" His tone was sincere. Sammy knew he wasn't trying to pry, he was only asking out of genuine concern.

"I think I'm still in shock."

"I can only imagine." Miles must have sensed she was uncomfortable with any further conversation over the matter. As he turned his attention back to the lift gate on his pickup, he asked, "What do you think of this?" He pointed to the last item in the truck. A carving of a black wooden bear holding a mailbox stood tall and proud. The face was so detailed, it must have taken him hours upon hours.

"It's stunning." Sammy gently touched the carving. She had profound respect for his talent. "I think we should put it in the front display window." By the surprised look on the woodworker's face, she knew he felt touched. Everyone knew the display window at Community Craft was a coveted position. Only the most favored pieces were displayed front and center there.

Miles put his hand to his heart. "I'm honored." He leaned his head forward with a slight bow.

"Well, you've earned it!" Sammy held the door as he lugged the solid carving toward the front of the store, her trailing behind him. "I'll have to move a few things. Do you mind hanging around? I don't think I can get that beautiful bear in the window without help."

"Not a problem." Miles breathed deep after carrying the heavy piece and pulled his falling pants back up into position.

Sammy stepped into the window and began removing the winter display to prepare for spring. "Actually, this is perfect timing. I'm a bit behind so I appreciate the push to move the winter stock. I needed to get the display ready for Spring Fling." She piled the merchandise in a corner to deal with later. Miles didn't have to wait while she found a new home for everything. She tossed the green-and-gold fleece scarves representing the Green Bay Packers' colors that were hanging in the display window into the corner and then waved for Miles to place the piece. "I think you have room now. I can move the rest of the stuff after you're gone."

Miles heaved the heavy carved bear up the one step into the window, and together they turned it to face forward. "Go have a look outside, will you?" Sammy suggested.

Miles stepped out the front door, looked at Sammy through the gleaming glass, and gave a double thumbs-up. He returned and thanked her again for the coveted position before leaving her to complete the window display. Before he left, Sammy asked him to place a price list for the items on the counter, and she would make and place the tags.

As she moved the spring items into the window that would complement the stately bear, Marilyn—the owner of the bakery a few doors down—knocked on the window, startling Sammy. She returned the greeting with an exaggerated wave.

Marilyn stepped inside the shop. "I'm so sorry. I didn't mean to startle you, honey."

"I guess I was just deep in thought with the display." Sammy smiled wide. "How are you?"

"Never mind me, darlin' . . . How are *you*?" Marilyn, still wearing her baking-stained pink apron must have left her eatery specifically to visit and check on Sammy. She put her hand to her bosom, which was as round as her oversized hips.

"I'm okay. Keeping busy." Sammy shrugged.

"I can't believe it, can you? I mean, her shop hasn't even

been open that long. Who could have done such a thing? It's awful. Certainly, not a Heartsford welcome!" The baker fanned herself with one hand even though there was still a chill in the air. Sammy wondered how the woman made it through the humid summers with her head in the oven.

"It's tragic." Sammy agreed.

Marilyn must have taken the hint and realized she wasn't going to get any additional nuts from this particular squirrel. She turned to the door as if to leave but then blurted over a shoulder, "Sad to admit but . . . well . . . I'm sure you're aware . . . not a lot of people liked her."

"Wait," Sammy bit her lip. She wanted more information from Marilyn. Maybe she knew something that could help with the investigation. "No, I really didn't know that," Sammy fibbed. "What makes you say that?"

Marilyn turned to face her. "Well, I heard . . . but don't say you heard it from me . . . that she was trying to get Larry kicked off the school board. And you know Larry has had that position for years. And he's done a lot for the school system *and* the community. And she just waltzes into *our* town and tries to bulldoze people after three months? Well. You just can't do that." Marilyn wiped her hands on her apron and stood defensively.

"Oh. I hadn't heard that." Sammy was afraid to say any more. She knew whatever she said would be breathed like fire on a dry field. This was interesting news though. Could prove to be the motive for murder.

"Well. News on the street is that she wanted Larry off the school board because of his history with the bottle." She raised an imaginary glass to her lips and tipped her head back. "If you know what I mean."

Sammy nodded.

"Well, honey, I have cakes in the oven. I'll bring you back a sample. I'm trying a new double-layer chocolate with strawberry buttercream." Marilyn licked her lips. "I'll let you get back to your display. I just love when you put the new merchandise inside the window. It always looks just *darling*."

"Sounds delicious. Anything from the Sweet Tooth is a welcome addition to my day." Sammy admitted easily. "Thanks."

"Toodles!" Marilyn waved a few chubby fingers and, like a breeze, was out the door.

Sammy finished the window display and gathered the collection of discarded items to organize inside the back storage room, all the while wondering if Larry was capable of murdering Ingrid Wilson. She knew he was considered the town drunk, but everyone seemed to look past his addiction and loved him just the same. Had he gone on a bender and killed Ingrid? Over the school board? It seemed unlikely. Or was it something deeper?

Sammy returned her focus back to work. Most of the unsold winter items would have to go back to the artists to stockpile for the following winter as she just didn't have the extra space to keep it all. The storage room was officially full. She would have to make some calls for pickup if she ever had a free minute.

Sammy was looking for tags to price Miles's latest items and couldn't find them anywhere. She reached under the counter and instead found the curling ribbons that she tied on each paper bag for purchase. Her stack was desperately low, so she decided to replenish those first and then deal with the price tags. The ribbon was bunched and tangled, twisted and knotted. What a mess. She moved the lost and found box on top of the counter to inspect the ribbon stash further. Yep, there was even more tangle hidden behind where the box had been. After wrangling the ribbon loose, she rewound it before she would then cut six-inch strips to tie on the handle of each paper bag. As she was cutting the strips, an elderly woman approached the counter with her purchase. Her curly white head barely reached the top of the long wooden slab. Sammy momentarily stuffed the ball of ribbon aside.

"Is that all for you today? Just the lavender soap?"

"Yes, dear."

Sammy rang up the item on the cash register and smiled at the elderly customer. She placed the soap in a paper bag tied with purple ribbon and waited while the woman dug through her purse looking for payment. Her gnarled trembling fingers opened a long brown leather wallet and she handed Sammy a crisp ten-dollar bill.

As Sammy was making change at the cash register, the woman began sifting through the lost and found box.

"Did you lose something?" Sammy knew her customers and this woman, to her knowledge, hadn't been in the craft room. "This is a lost and found box from the craft room. I usually keep it under the counter, but I was looking for something and set it here." Sammy was about to take it away when the woman stopped her.

"Wait a minute." She put her gnarled hand onto Sammy's so that she wouldn't pull the box away. The woman removed the locket from the box. "This belongs to me."

The woman perplexed Sammy. She knew she'd only come into Community Craft less than a handful of times. And even then, she certainly hadn't been inside the craft room. "I think you might be mistaken?" Sammy tried to be patiently gentle with the woman, but she was adamant.

"*No*! It's mine," she said with certainty and clasped it to her heart.

Sammy didn't know what to make of the situation. The woman seemed so convinced it belonged to her. She decided to gently confront her with a question. "Okay, then. Tell me about the photograph."

The woman handed the necklace back to Sammy. "Would you please open it?" she rubbed her arthritic hands together as if to warm them. Sammy knew it must be impossible for her to open it herself, so she did as the woman asked but waited for her to describe the photo before handing it back.

"It's a black and white picture of my sister Olivia. She died in an automobile accident just after this photograph was taken." She looked intently at Sammy. "I know because I took this picture." She lifted her chin as if to dignify herself.

Sammy didn't know what to say. She was correct. The photo was black and white, but that could be just a good guess. After all, a photo encapsulated in an antique locket would very likely be black and white. "Are you sure? Was your sister alone in the picture?" Sammy tried to trip the woman to see if the woman was fibbing but couldn't for the life of her understand why she would.

"Yes, she's alone in the picture, but she wasn't alone in the car that killed her."

"Oh, I'm so sorry for your loss. Was another relative driving with your sister?"

"No. Ingrid Wilson was driving."

Sammy's jaw fell along with the locket which she instantly dropped to the floor.

Chapter Six

Sammy had no other choice than to hand the locket over to the older woman. As soon as the necklace had touched the palm of her hand, she made a mad dash out of the store quicker than the Road Runner. Sammy would have thought this humanly impossible in her stoop-shouldered condition, but evidently not, as she was gone in an instant. Sammy shook her head in disbelief. *Ingrid was driving a car that killed a woman's sister?*

"Hey! Wake up! . . . Cara said you wanted to speak to me and told me to stop by?"

Douglas, the owner of Liquid Joy, stood in front of the cash register, banging on the counter with an opened palm to gain her attention. Sammy was so lost in her thoughts about the woman and the necklace that, for the life of her, she had no idea when or how he had arrived.

"Is everything okay with you? You look like you've seen a ghost." He readjusted the thin-rimmed dark glasses that framed his long face and scrunched them up on his nose for a clearer picture of her.

"Yes," Sammy shook her head as if to clear out the cobwebs in her brain. "Thanks for stopping in."

"Not a problem. What can I do for you?"

"Were you working the coffee bar yesterday afternoon?"

"Yes and no. You know me. I bounce." The coffee shop owner lifted his thin frame up and down on his toes in demonstration. He adjusted his glasses again, this time with his middle finger. All his bouncing made him look like Tigger from *Winnie-the-Pooh*.

Sammy smiled, "Yeah, I know the feeling. That's how life is—in retail."

"Why do you want to know if I was working the coffee bar?"

"It's about Ingrid. When I discovered her yesterday, there was a full cup of coffee on the counter, and I know she doesn't drink coffee . . . so I was just wondering . . . if you knew who it belonged to?" The words tumbled out like water over a waterfall.

"Huh." Douglas shrugged. "I really don't know. Like I said, I bounce. If you want to know every customer that came in yesterday, I couldn't tell you. We had many." He shifted his weight and jutted out one hip. "And most *do* come in for the coffee. It is, after all, a coffee shop," he teased as he threw out a hand dramatically. "I do sell the best coffee in town."

Sammy smiled and agreed with a nod of her head.

"Did Coach stop in yesterday?"

"Didn't see him. I can imagine he's taking this hard. Heck, his aunt barely got settled into Heartsford, and this happened! What a disgrace."

"I was just wondering if he was around here yesterday."

"What do you mean? You don't think . . . Seriously, Sammy . . . you don't think he killed his own aunt? Come on now."

"No, I don't think that." Sammy shook her head vigorously. "I think the police might think that though."

"Anyhow, I wouldn't worry about it. Let the police handle it. They'll sort it all out. We do have a new detective in town. The taxpayers insisted that Stan be replaced, and we paid to move the guy here. Let him do his job. Wouldn't he have taken the cup for evidence? That is . . . if he thinks it's necessary."

"Yes. I suppose."

"Listen, Nancy Drew. No one liked the woman. It's a shame she passed. Indeed it is. Personally, I was getting pretty tired of hearing the hushed talk throughout my establishment about the havoc she was causing."

Sammy checked over each shoulder for customers and then leaned over the countertop, "Tell me."

"Come on, Sam. I know you're not like that. Gossip is so *not* your thing."

"Okay. You can poke fun and call me Nancy Drew, but I'm the one who *found* her lifeless body." Sammy pointed a thumb to her chest. "Doesn't that make me the number one suspect?" she whispered, yet formed every word. "I'm not interested in gossip. I'm interested in finding out who killed the woman."

"I hadn't thought of it that way." His tone reached a higher octave. "Did *you* do it?"

Sammy threw her hands to her hips; the look on her face was pure contempt. "Seriously?"

46

"Well? You said it, Sam. Not me!" Douglas flicked a finger toward her.

"Never mind," she waved an annoyed hand as if to shoo him from her presence.

"Listen . . . all I know is that tight knitting group of gals would sometimes meet at my coffee bar before classes over here in your little craft room." He pointed to the glass room where crafters gathered. "They *really* had a problem with her. I don't know exactly what the problem was, but maybe you can do your little investigating the next time they have a class," he suggested.

"Thanks for the tip," Sammy said sincerely.

"No problem. I'll keep my ears open too. If I hear anymore chatter, I promise I'll keep you posted." The coffee shop owner nodded and then backed away from the counter and maneuvered through the racks toward the front door, physically bumping into Carter on his way out.

Sammy overhead the two exchange apologies before a flushed Carter rushed toward her in his basketball uniform. "You didn't listen to your messages this morning, did you?"

"Nope. I got sidetracked. Thanks for reminding me. I probably should check them now." Sammy turned her body toward the office and Carter trailed behind.

"One was from me. I was hoping I could take the night off? Remember? You asked me to work after close to prepare for Spring Fling, but I can't. Coach isn't leading an extra practice, but the assistant coach is. You didn't text me, so I thought you were mad at me for asking."

Sammy turned to the teen and placed a hand on his rosy

cheek. "When are you going to learn, you can't please everyone? You're just like your father." She smiled. "Don't worry about it, we still have plenty of time before the big event." She shooed him away. "Go."

He smiled wide. "Thanks."

As he started to leave, Sammy reached for his arm to hold him back. "How's Coach?"

"Haven't seen him," he said sullenly. "Assistant Dave's been working us pretty hard. Says we have to win this championship for Coach. We're going to do it. We have to."

"I'm sure you will. I'll be there to cheer you on. Keep me posted on the game times so I can get Ellie in here to cover for me, okay?"

"I will." And with a wave of one hand, he jogged back toward the front door.

Sammy pressed the play button on the answering machine to retrieve the morning messages she had avoided. "Hey, it's Carter . . ."

She hit the delete key with her index finger.

"It's Ellie. Tyler was up all night but doing better now. I don't think we'll make it into the store today. It's a nap day. Sorry. Hope you're okay. Call me back."

"This is Liam Nash from the Heartsford Police Department. I'd like to speak with you again. Please call me to set up an appointment."

Wonder what he wants? Sammy's heart picked up a few extra beats. *I hope he really believes I had nothing to do with Ingrid's murder. He probably thinks I've avoided him all day. Great.*

"Hi, Samantha, this is Lynn from the Heartsford Credit Union. Stop in when you get a minute. I have a form that needs a signature on the Community Craft account. Somehow, I overlooked it on your refinance . . . We must have been talking too much and I missed it." The banker chuckled "Anyway, no rush, hon, just when you get a minute. I'll need it for the file."

"You have no more new messages."

Sammy decided to address the easiest first and returned Lynn's call, letting her know she would stop in later in the week. The next call took a bit more courage. She inhaled a deep breath and then dialed the number to the police department where they connected her to the new detective in town.

"Nash," he said abruptly.

"Hi. This is Samantha Kane from Community Craft. I'm sorry I didn't get back to you sooner. I just checked my morning messages now." She glanced at the clock and grimaced when she saw how late it was. The clock said five forty-five PM . . . *Where had the day gone? Would he believe she was just checking her messages now?*

"Hello, Samantha. I thought you were avoiding me."

From the sound of his tone, Sammy wondered if he was kicked back in his chair with a pencil tapping on his desk. She watched *way* too many police shows on television, she thought suddenly.

"No. I run a pretty busy business over here." She looked around the empty store and frowned at the unfilled space.

"Do you have time now if I stop in the store?"

"Sure. But try to be discrete if you can. The gossip storm

is starting to build; soon we'll have a full-fledged tornado. Would you mind entering through the back door? You can wait in my office if I have lingering customers," Sammy offered.

"Would you be more comfortable coming over to the station?"

"No, it's okay. I'm just about to close. Can you stop in at six or does that cut into your dinner hour?"

She heard a slight laugh across the phone line, as if she'd said something funny.

"I'll see you soon," Sammy said. She frowned at the headset before hanging up the phone. *What did I say that's so amusing?*

Chapter Seven

Sammy flipped the sign on the front door to CLOSED and retreated toward the back of the shop to repeat the same procedure. She had previously decided she would catch up and stay a few extra hours after their usual six o'clock close every evening. This would allow uninterrupted time to prepare for Spring Fling, as well as a few hours of indulged silence. As she moved closer to the back door, she noticed Detective Liam Nash opening it.

"Come on in," she ushered him inside. "I'm just changing the signs, so we won't be interrupted." Sammy moved past him and locked the back door. The detective waited for her to lead him into the office where she sat at the small desk, and he took a seat on a metal folding chair beside it.

"How's the investigation going?" Sammy closed her laptop so she would not get sidetracked by the growing number of emails. She faced him squarely, giving Liam her undivided attention. "You don't really think Coach had anything to do with Ingrid's murder, do you?"

The detective ignored her line of questioning and instead kept his answer vague.

"Pandora's box I'm afraid. The more I investigate, the more suspects are added to the list." He wiped his hand across a weary face. The corners of his eyes showed a few wrinkles that Sammy had missed at their initial meeting, and scattered white strands randomly peppered his black hair. It only added a more mature allure to his looks. The stress of the job, though, must have taken its toll. She wondered what horrors the detective had seen over the course of his career.

"I was afraid of that." Sammy chewed her lip. "Did you collect the coffee cup for evidence?"

The detective's tired eyes narrowed. "Coffee cup? You remembered that on the scene? You didn't mention it when I questioned you." He leaned forward in the chair, resting an arm comfortably on the desk.

The closeness of him, leaning in on the desk made her uneasy, and she wasn't sure why. Maybe it was the scent of his cologne. The musk stimulated something in her that she thought was dead: attraction. There really wasn't a big pond left to fish in Heartsford. He was new fish. She wondered how quickly his shiny new scales would wear off.

"I remembered when I was putting my groceries away. I think I was in shock when we spoke. . . . I still might be. In shock, that is." Shock or desire at the current moment, Sammy wasn't sure which was the stronger emotion. Was her face flushing? Oh God, please let her face not be flushing.

He nodded.

"So, did you?"

"Did I what?"

"Did you collect the coffee cup . . . for evidence?"

"As a matter of fact, we did collect it." Liam sat back in the chair casually and crossed one ankle over the other. "I don't imagine we'll find anything other than Ingrid's fingerprints," he added flippantly.

"Well, I certainly doubt that," Sammy said under her breath.

"Sorry?" Liam cuffed a hand to one ear. "I missed it."

"Yes. It seems you miss *a lot*." Sammy rolled her eyes. "Ingrid didn't drink coffee."

"Is that so?" The detective shifted in his chair. "Seems to me you're the one with all the answers. I guess I came to the right place to ask questions. You obviously don't trust that I know how to do my job." He pointed a finger at the desk.

"It seems to me," Sammy interjected, "that we're getting off on the wrong foot. Should we try again?" The attraction was morphing to irritation. After all, how inappropriate would it be for her flirt with the new detective during a murder investigation? The timing felt wrong. Sammy knew intuitively she was trying to put out her own flame. She knew herself well. Arguing with him was her strategy for diffusion. Unfortunately, it didn't seem to be working. The man was hot.

The detective smiled wide, surprising her. "You are something." He smirked. "The name's Liam Nash, new to Heartsford." He extended a hand for her to shake. "Won't you give me the warm Heartsford welcome that I've heard the Community Craft store is known for?"

Sammy rolled her eyes and shook his hand, his palm hard

and calloused to the touch. She couldn't help but think Mrs. Brown's sugar scrub soaps would soften them up right quick. Would it be rude to suggest it?

"I did hear that your store is the hot spot for the town. A real gathering place." Liam looked around the office room and waved his hands dramatically. "You should be proud of what you've created here. I've heard nothing but really good things," he added sincerely.

"I can't take the credit. A good friend of mine created it. I'm just furthering the legacy that her blood, sweat, and tears built."

"Ahh. I'd like to hear more about that sometime. Maybe over dinner?"

Liam Nash continually surprised her. That was the last thing she thought would come out of his mouth. The detective was very unpredictable. She wasn't sure if he wanted to see her for business or pleasure. He was a tough read. Something was drawing her to him though. Curiosity? Attraction? Or wanting to solve the murder of Ingrid Wilson? Either way, it didn't matter. Sammy decided to take him up on the offer.

"Sure."

"Let's go then." Liam lifted from the chair, causing a scraping sound on the floor. He then stretched his arms toward the ceiling to crack his back.

"Oh. I can't right now. I have to go home to let my dog out."

"Perfect. We'll pick up takeout and eat at your place." He picked up the phone and handed it to her. "Order up. I'll buy. It's my way of starting us on the right foot." He winked and headed into the shop to browse the handmade products while she made the call.

"But I still have work left at the store to get ready for Spring Fling . . ." She stood and leaned forward over the desk so he would hear her.

He returned and rested his hand on the doorjamb. "I thought you said you had to let your dog out? Never mind the spring thing; tomorrow's another day. You'll get it all done."

"Spring *Fling*, not spring *thing*," Sammy corrected. "And yes, I was going to pick him up and bring him back with me to work after hours. Oh, forget it. Fine, I'll call." She dialed the number for the Corner Grill and ordered a pizza. "What type of toppings on your pie?" She cuffed the phone as she called out and waited for an answer.

"I'm easy. You choose. I'll eat the box, I'm starving," Liam said over his shoulder. Sammy watched as he fingered a local author's book about the farming industry surrounding Heartsford.

"The cash register is still on if you want to purchase something?" Sammy moved out of the office and onto the shop floor after placing the order.

He turned to her. "It will give me an excuse to come back."

Sammy tried to read his expression. He must have done a lot of interrogations in his line of work because all she could read was pure poker face. "Suit yourself." She reached for her lined nylon jacket and, after he reshelved the book, they walked to the back door.

"How about you give me your address? I'll pick up the food and meet you back at your place. It will give you time to let your dog out." He handed her a tiny old fashioned notebook to write her address in, which made her chuckle. Most people would just text it. Or find some other modern technology to use for taking notes.

"Sounds good." Sammy handed back the pen and the pad with her address and waved goodbye in the parking lot, just as Marilyn was bouncing toward her, waving a hand and balancing a pink box in the other.

"Hey, darlin'! Are you leaving early? I thought you were working overtime to prepare for Spring Fling? I told you I had a sample for you. You're my best critic." Marilyn eyed Sammy cautiously. "Was that the new detective? What did he want?"

The baker's eyes moved to follow the back of the detective getting into his car. A silver Honda Civic. *He already knows where I live. That's the car that was on my block this morning.* Sammy couldn't believe her eyes. She did a double take.

"Honey. Did you hear me?" Marilyn was shaking Sammy's arm to get her attention.

"I'm sorry. Thanks so much for the treat. I have to go." She plucked the pink box from the baker who wanted more than gratitude. A stunned Marilyn looked like her face had been slapped, but Sammy kept pace, moving toward her car. "I'll let you know if this recipe's a keeper. But you already know I love *all* your baked goodies," she said as she placed the cake on the front passenger seat and closed the door of her car. Sammy knew this wasn't a gift; it was a bribe to get her to open her mouth for more than just dessert. Sammy gave a wave of one hand through the window and drove out of the parking lot as Marilyn stood and watched her leave.

Chapter Eight

The Wisconsin sun made its final appearance as the day sunk deep into the horizon. Brilliant magenta colored the skyline as if someone had taken a bucket and splashed it with vivid-colored paint. Sammy soaked in the beauty of her surroundings as she led Bara on a short trek down the street to stretch his legs. It had been a few days since they'd had a solid walk and neither had gotten the workout they both needed. Hopefully the upcoming warmer weather would encourage a better exercise routine. Sammy saw Detective Liam Nash pull into her driveway, so she turned and started a light jog toward him with Bara in close pursuit. Liam retrieved the large pizza box, the smell emanating from his Honda Civic tantalizing Samantha's appetite. He then leaned over and gave Bara a pat on the head. The dog wagged his tail and lolled his tongue in response.

"He's a doll. What's his name?"

"Bara." She grinned and stroked her hand down the Golden's back. "He's my baby. How did you know he was male?"

The detective jutted his hip revealing a badge attached to his dark blue jeans. "I'm into details."

Sammy smiled and nodded in response. She was into details too. She wanted to ask him *why* his Honda Civic had already been in her neighborhood and *why* he pretended to not know her address. It left her feeling slightly uncomfortable. She would have to get to the bottom of it. But to avoid getting back on the wrong foot, Sammy brushed it aside. *For now.*

"Come on in."

She held open the door of the house as he squeezed past her. The dog and the large pizza box forced them to bump arms. He tried to remove his shoe using the back of his heel for leverage while balancing the pizza at the same time. Sammy noticed his predicament and removed the large box from his grasp, hurried into the kitchen, and set it on the counter. "What would you like to drink?" she hollered from the adjacent room.

"I'll have whatever you're having." He stayed close to the door as he seemed enamored with her dog and sank to his knees petting the animal.

Sammy leaned into the refrigerator and came out embarrassed. She needed to visit the store again, the minimal amount she had picked up yesterday barely filled the top shelf. "Water? With a squeeze of lemon?"

"Perfect."

Sammy glanced around the small kitchen. She loved the sophistication of the space. The tall white cabinets reached the dark bead-boarded ceiling, giving a cozy feeling of height. The country-style nickel knobs added a muted sparkle. Ralph took pride in his rentals, and it showed in the design. The kitchen's major downfall was that the center island left only a few feet of space in which to maneuver. There was only room for a small table and two ladder back chairs in a corner nook. Sammy wasn't sure she wanted to sit so close to the detective again. She quickly removed the pizza box from the counter and set it on the coffee table in front of the fireplace. "If it's okay, let's eat here . . . in the living room?"

"What can I do to help?" he asked as his attention left the dog and he stood to help her.

"Flip that switch. Please. Let's get a fire going. It's a little chilly in here." She pointed to the switch and then shrugged off her coat. "Can you hang our coats on the peg over there?" Sammy handed him her coat and then quickly moved back into the kitchen. She returned with two glasses of water and a roll of paper towels under her arm.

Liam was sitting comfortably on the couch, with Bara at his feet. Sammy could see that her dog had already taken a liking to the man. That was encouraging. Her dog was a pretty good judge of character.

"Sorry it's so casual." She set the glasses on the coffee table and then handed him the roll of paper towels. "I wasn't expecting company tonight."

"Not a problem. As I told you before, I'm easy to please." He leaned forward and ripped them each a towel, setting his on his lap and placing one on the coffee table for her.

Sammy's face flushed. Did she want to please him? She wasn't sure. Or was he only here to soften her up for an upcoming interrogation? She pushed the thoughts down deep and instead flipped the pizza box open. "Dig in."

Liam pulled at the melted cheese to release a slice from the pie. "This looks amazing." He took a large bite and closed his eyes as if in a dream state.

"Yeah, they make a pretty good pie."

"*Pie*?" he said between bites. "Are you from Chicago? I thought you were most likely born here in Heartsford? Isn't that an Illinois term?"

"My dad is from Chicago. I guess he called it pie growing up and it stuck with our family. Yes, I'm from Heartsford. Born and raised." Sammy smiled before taking a bite of pizza. The cheese melted in her mouth. The pepperoni a perfect combination of salt and spice. He was right. It was delicious.

"Tell me more about Community Craft. I've heard so much good comes out of that store, and I don't just mean merchandise. You mentioned a friend started it? To be exact, I believe you said it began with blood, sweat, and tears?"

Sammy took a deep breath and rested her half-eaten slice of pizza inside the box. "Have you met Mayor Allen yet? Carter's dad?"

"Yes, I've briefly met the mayor? Why?"

"Well, Carter was their oopsy-daisy baby. There are many years between him and his elder sister. Now, I don't think he's so much of an oopsy, but more of a miracle . . . As God knew what was in store for the Allen family." Sammy paused a few moments before continuing.

"Anyhow, the mayor's daughter, Kate, was my best friend in high school. She and I were seriously tight. Wherever you saw Kate, you saw me, and vice versa. My sister and cousin are a few years older, and when they graduated from our school, I was completely lost without them. Kate stepped in . . . sort of replacing them, to be honest . . . and she and I became inseparable." Sammy smiled at the memory. "She was always small-town. Never wanted to leave Heartsford. And she didn't. What she created at Community Craft is so much bigger than retail." Her eyes filled when she glanced at Liam. "It's her work. It's the way she so freely loved. That's what created it. I'm just trying to fill very big shoes." She picked up the slice of pizza and took a bite to keep her from crying in front of the detective.

"I've heard nothing but good things. People talk very highly of Community Craft . . . and *you*."

But Sammy quickly waved away the compliment. "It's all Kate. It's also why I was so protective of Carter the other day, regarding questioning him. He's my adopted little brother now."

"What happened to Kate?"

"Terrible. Kate was in a freak accident. There was a big event planned at a farm just outside town. A fundraiser of course, for something she was involved in. They were going to have tractor races at the event, and she was practicing with some friends and townspeople. Anyhow, she was on a tractor . . . it backfired. When she stepped off to see what was wrong, the tractor rolled on top of her . . . gruesome." Sammy took in a breath and stopped.

"You don't have to say any more. I can see this is upsetting to talk about."

Sammy quickly wiped a tear that had slipped out and then smiled out of embarrassment. After a moment, she took another bite of pizza and didn't stop eating until she hit crust.

Her mind wandered as she chewed. It flipped back and forth like a seesaw until she couldn't take it anymore. After finishing her slice of pizza, the curiosity won out. "Okay. I know you've been in this neighborhood before. I recognized your car when you left the parking lot in town. Care to explain?" Sammy knew her words were coming out sharp. She tried to gentle them, but her attempt was weak at best.

The detective set his pizza slice down in the box to respond before taking another bite. "You are attentive. I'll give you that." He wiped his mouth with the back of his hand instead of removing the napkin from his lap. "What makes you so sure it was my car?"

"Because it was a silver Honda Civic, and there's a bit of rust on the front bumper."

"Nice. You are certainly paying attention."

"Well, I'm sorry. I still feel horrible I couldn't give a better description of the dark blue car that rushed out of the lot yesterday when Ingrid died." Sammy slumped her shoulders. "I'm trying to be more alert to my surroundings." He didn't have to know that, on a good day, she usually *was* alert to her surroundings. Just not the day Ingrid died. Unfortunately, *that particular day* she was in a lack-of-sunshine funk and too caught up in her own head.

"That's good. You should pay attention," Liam encouraged. "Especially now."

"Why do you say that?"

"The reason I've been following you is not what you think."

"You've been tailing me?" Sammy rose from the couch

and brushed the crust and crumbs off her lap to the floor. She was too irate to care about cleanliness. Immediately Bara came and licked them up and put the remains between his paws and started chewing at the long crust.

The detective reached for her wrist and encouraged her to sit back down. Sammy shook her wrist loose and stood defiantly with her hands on her hips, waiting for an apology. He had lied to her, and it was not sitting well.

"Typically, after a victim is found, the perpetrator will follow those closest to the victim . . . to see how much information they know. You could be in danger, Samantha." The alarm in his voice caused her to soften, and she slumped onto the couch.

"You think someone's following me?" Sammy wasn't sure if she was ready to tell him he might be spot on. Had it been it her imagination the other night? Or was that also Liam in his Honda Civic? She couldn't be sure as it was dark at night when she thought she was being tailed.

"Let's just say I've been doing my job. I'm sorry I didn't tell you I already knew where you lived. I didn't want to spread unnecessary alarm, and now I'm afraid I might have." His eyes were soft and concerned.

Sammy wasn't sure what to say, but she didn't have time to respond as they both were suddenly interrupted by a knock at her front door.

"Were you expecting company?"

"No." Sammy rose from the couch and when she reached the door peeked through the peephole. "It's my sister. Can you excuse me for a moment? Go ahead and keep eating without me. I don't want your pizza getting cold."

Sammy opened the door, and her sister almost barged past, but Sammy lifted a strong arm to stop her.

"You're not letting me in? It's getting dark, and it's cold out here." Ellie brushed her wind-blown russet hair away from her eyes. She leaned over Sammy's shoulder to get a better look at who was inside.

"Step outside please." Sammy gave her sister a swift shove, knocking her backward.

"What's wrong with you?" Ellie almost lost her balance and caught herself from flying off the concrete step.

"I have company."

"I know. I saw a car in the driveway. A *date*?" Ellie searched her sister's eyes with deep interest.

Sammy hoped to God that the detective couldn't hear this conversation. She closed the door behind her but didn't pull it tight. "No," she hissed. "It's not a *date*."

"What are you so angry about? I'm here as a concerned sister, and this is what I get?" Ellie pushed her sister lightly on the shoulder. "I'm way over-tired and exhausted because Tyler has been sick. You have the audacity to not return my phone call from this morning? And then, I stop by the store and you left *early*? Which you hardly *ever* do, especially with Spring Fling around the corner. Forgive me for being the concerned sister!" She turned on her heel in a fit of irritation and stomped toward her car.

"Ellie, wait!" Sammy followed close on her heels. "Look I'm sorry. The detective working on Ingrid's case is inside. Okay? Please don't tell anyone he was here. I don't want to become the talk around town, and after my visit to Liquid

Joy this morning, trust me, it's all anyone is talking about. Please."

Ellie stopped midstride and turned before reaching her car. "I want to be here for you. Let me. I'm your sister, and Mom and Dad are worried sick."

"Ugh." Sammy took a deep breath. "Mom and Dad know?" Sammy must not have fully closed the door as Bara nosed his way outside and bounded toward Ellie.

"Hey, boy!" Ellie reached and scratched Bara behind the ears, "At least *someone* is happy to see me."

"Ellie. I am happy to see you. Just not right now." She leaned in and gave her sister a kiss on the cheek and hugged her tight. "Which reminds me, Heidi and I thought tomorrow night would make a great girls' night out? What do you think? Why don't you ask Randy if he'll watch Tyler? Come on, please? The three of us haven't been out together in *forever*." Sammy hoped in begging her sister she could defuse some of the agitation she saw on Ellie's overtired face.

"Fine." Ellie waved her sister off. "Go back to your *date*." She opened her car door before getting one last word in, "I'm still mad at you." Ellie shook a warning finger at her sister.

Sammy mouthed the words through the closed car window: "*It's not a date*." She smiled, waved, and leaned down to pat her pup and then held his collar tight. She watched her sister pull out of the driveway before returning inside. As Sammy and Bara turned toward the front door, she noticed the detective was standing at the screen, watching her with an amused smile on his face. She wondered exactly how much of the conversation with Ellie he'd overheard. He held the door for her as she entered. Bara blew past them and curled himself in front of the fire on his plush dog bed.

"You could have invited her in." Liam sat back down at his original place on the couch.

"Yes. I could have. However, you don't understand how overprotective my sister is. I would have been forced to spend the night at her place after knowing we were discussing the possibility of me being followed. I'm a big girl, thank you. I can take care of myself."

"I see that," he said with amusement.

"Have you finished with the pizza?" Sammy opened the large box to see that a few pieces were now missing.

"I'm good. But you certainly didn't eat much."

Sammy took a tepid piece from the box and raised it to her lips. "One more, but I'm saving room for dessert. I have something special to share."

The detective raised his eyebrows. "And what would that be?" he asked in a teasing tone.

Sammy frowned. Seemingly, he was getting the wrong idea. "Cake," she replied between bites of pizza.

"Ahh," he said in a delighted tone. "You know a way to a man's heart is through his stomach," he added jokingly. She wondered if he had overheard Ellie and now was teasing her.

"Well then, I guess you'll be falling for Marilyn," Sammy said with a quick jab of return wit. She was enjoying the banter between them. He was easy to be around, and she enjoyed his company. Maybe Ellie was right. Maybe this was a date? "Do you want me to put a pot of coffee on to go with the cake?"

"Sounds good to me. Will you drink some this late?"

Suddenly, Sammy was aware the room had begun to darken. She flicked on a nearby lamp to add to the radiance of the fireplace. She certainly didn't want Liam to think she was purposefully keeping the room at a romantic glow. "How about I put on a pot of decaf?"

"Sounds perfect."

The detective trailed her into the kitchen as she finished her slice of pizza. She pressed her foot on the stainless lever to pop open the lid of the Trash can and tossed the leftover crust inside. Sammy wiped her hands on her jeans before opening the cabinet to pull out the can of decaf coffee.

"So, who's Marilyn?" Liam leaned on the kitchen island with a casual ease.

"Your dessert maker." Sammy pointed to a pink box that sat on the kitchen island. "Go ahead and open it. I don't mind if you sample the frosting with your finger." She turned to put the coffee filter in the machine. "Don't tell my cousin Heidi. She thinks I'm a germaphobe." Sammy said over her shoulder. "But she works in the hospital and doesn't understand why walking around in her scrubs after work and touching everything is *not* okay. That's a whole different kind of germs." Sammy shuddered to shake the image from her mind.

Liam removed the tape from the box, pulled the cake from its wrapping, and set it on the island. "This does look amazing." He took his finger and did as she suggested and licked the dollop of pink frosting from his finger. "It's very good. Strawberry, I think?"

"Well. There you go. Now you can go meet Marilyn from

the Sweet Tooth Bakery. Maybe there will be an even deeper love connection, besides cake," Sammy hinted. After filling the coffee pot with water, she turned to him, "You are single, aren't you, Detective? I guess I shouldn't have made that assumption." She placed one hand on her hip and pushed the power button on the coffee machine with the other.

"For the moment." He cleared his throat. "What about you? Tim mentioned you had a bad breakup before you moved back to Heartsford and it sort of put a bad taste in your mouth when it comes to men."

"He said that, did he?" She would have to wring Tim's neck the next time she saw him. "Let's just say my past relationship didn't fit with my current living situation."

"He didn't like dogs?"

"No. He didn't like Heartsford." She pulled two mugs from the cabinet and set them on the island. "Brian was a city boy. Still is. Except now he's married with a baby on the way and looking for a small town where he can raise his new baby."

"Ouch."

"Yep, but I've already shared too much. I'm not bitter. It is what it is. Sometimes things just don't fit, and you certainly can't force it." She reached into the refrigerator and pulled out the bottle of French vanilla creamer. "What about you?"

While Sammy reached for plates and cutlery, the detective explained. "My fiancée died of breast cancer a few years ago. We were engaged to be married and then she shared the news. Brenda didn't tell me she had found a large lump. She went to the doctor without telling anyone. Instead of getting treatment right away, she lived in denial. When she found an additional lump, she finally told me and decided to take on surgery and the chemo treatments. Unfortunately, it was too late. Three months before our wedding date, she died."

Sammy almost dropped the dishes upon hearing such tragic news. She was surprised at how candid he was about sharing his story. "I'm so sorry for your loss." She set the plates down gently on the kitchen island and waited for him to continue.

"I've had a few years to adjust," he walked over to the sink and washed the rest of the sticky frosting from his finger.

Now she knew why the man had early gray. It wasn't only the stress of the job. Hearing his story made Sammy look at Liam Nash in a whole new light.

Sammy wanted to grill the detective further about the murder investigation, but they were having such an easy time together, she didn't want to break the spell. She got the sense that the detective was holding his cards close to his chest, especially when it came to his work. Sammy didn't get the feeling he was going to share with her as much as she'd hoped. Even though she was desperate to pick his brain on whether Coach was indeed his number one suspect, she decided to wait it out in hopes of winning his confidence.

After she had plated the cake, they stood at the kitchen island sharing the dessert. To break the awkward seriousness, Liam said, "Maybe you *should* introduce me to this Marilyn." He rolled his eyes in pleasure. "She's a great baker." He winked. And they both laughed aloud.

Chapter Nine

S oft light filtered through the bedroom window, waking Sammy from a restless slumber. She sat upright in the bed and stretched her arms to the ceiling. Bara welcomed her with tail wagging and kisses, giving her the push she needed to get out of bed. She tossed her blue-and-yellow star quilt aside and swung her feet to reach for her terrycloth, rubber-bottom slippers to avoid the chill of the solid wood floor. Sammy moved swiftly down the stairs with Bara close behind. She could tell from his impatience he was ready to go. She swung open the back door and let him out into the small fenced yard.

Sammy rinsed the coffeepot from the night before and refilled it, but this time not with decaffeinated coffee. Today she would need the full, robust caffeine. As she eyed the pink box of cake, she recalled the previous night with Liam Nash. It had been a long time since she'd spent an evening alone with a man in her home. Even though it wasn't *really* a date, she was enjoying her new friendship. Though he certainly didn't dig deep in his investigation. He hadn't asked her much about the case. The conversation had swayed more toward getting to know each other. Maybe he was just testing her to see if she'd leak information? She pulled a fork from the drawer, flipped the box open and decided to nibble a piece of cake for breakfast. While leaning over the box with a fork in her hand, she decided her time would be better spent with Lynn at the bank, instead of adding bulge to her growing waistline. Her eyes darted to the clock on the microwave to see if that would work. She set down the fork and rushed her morning along.

After a hot shower, fresh whitewashed jeans, and a cotton-white button up, Sammy settled Bara in for the day. With more errands, he would have to stay home yet again. She hugged her puppy tight and kissed his head before skipping out the front door. Her neighbor Mary, from across the street, was out picking her cellophane-wrapped newspaper off the front step in her bathrobe and shared a morning wave and then retreated inside like a turtle.

Filtered light shone through thick clouds, as if the day was trying to decide what kind it was going to be. Sammy looked through the windshield, disgusted. She was tired of the same gray skies. Spring sunshine could not come fast enough. The drive to Main Street took no time at all and Sammy found a parking spot directly in front of Heartsford Credit Union. She stepped out of her car and noticed Carter's basketball coach talking to another man. She wondered if it was a school parent sharing his condolences. Sammy didn't want to interrupt the men so deep in conversation, but wondered if she should have stopped to say something too. Instead, she stepped into the bank and decided if she saw the coach alone on the way out she would approach him. Considering she was the one who found his aunt deceased, it would be the right thing to do. Then she might be able to truly gauge his emotions regarding the loss of his aunt too, which might prove telling. Lynn however, noticed her right away and waved her inside the glass corner office.

"Good morning, Samantha. How are you?"

"Hi, Lynn, it's good to see you. Looking well I see."

Lynn had lost over a hundred pounds and was working hard to keep the weight off. Sammy saw her religiously walking past the front window of Community Craft on her lunch break trying to get in her daily exercise. She also came in and signed up for classes from time to time to try her hand at various crafts.

Lynn gave her a friendly smile. "Thanks. You know how hard I work at it! I appreciate you coming in today. Before I get into the business of why you're here, I must ask, how you are holding up? I heard you found Ingrid. You poor thing! I can't even imagine . . ." She laid a French manicured hand against her cheek.

"Yeah. I'm trying not to think about it."

"I'm sorry to bring it up. Do you think the police know who killed her?"

"I have no idea." Sammy shrugged.

"Well." Lynn took a deep breath and smoothed her long pencil skirt and then took a seat at her desk. She placed reading glasses on the end of her nose and then began to idly shuffle papers in front of her.

Something in Lynn's demeanor gave Sammy pause. "You know something, don't you?" She leaned forward onto the large oak desk with both hands.

"Not *really*." Lynn's eyes darted around the small office, as if she was looking to escape Sammy's grilling.

"Please. If you know something, please tell me." Sammy took a seat in front of the desk to try to appear less confrontational. She waited in silence until Lynn had the courage to continue.

"I just know Harold wanted to rent that retail space for a new hardware store before Ingrid opened The Yarn Barn. He didn't have the funds to back it, and we just couldn't take his proposal. She didn't need a large loan to open. But he did. And . . . well . . . I just know there was bad blood between them." She put her head in her hands. "I haven't told the police yet, and this is driving me crazy. Do you think I should mention it? Or am I overreacting? I can't imagine Harold . . . but . . ."

"Yes." Sammy nodded. "You probably should mention it to the police. If for no other reason than to ease your own mind."

Lynn nodded her head in agreement and then slid a printed form across the desk. She directed Sammy with a pen to where to add her initials, and then handed over the pen to Sammy. "It's just to lock in the interest rate. Sorry again for having to drag you in here for this. I really don't know how this page escaped me."

"No problem, it's nice to have a visit too. We're all so busy these days." Sammy signed the form and slid it back across the desk.

Suddenly, a roaring screeching sound of tires followed by intense yelling and horrific shrieks came from Main Street. Lynn and Sammy made alarmed eye contact before the two leapt to their feet, scrambled through the bank, and rushed out the front door. Carter's basketball coach lay in the middle of the road, a crowd quickly forming around his unresponsive body while someone yelled: "Call nine one one! Call nine one one!"

Sammy noticed Douglas on the sidewalk and grabbed him by the arm to gain his attention. "What happened?"

"Coach was hit by a car." Douglas held one hand to his chest, trying to catch his breath. "Someone ran him down. It all happened so fast."

"Did you see the car?" Sammy shook his arm to wake him from his shock.

"No." The coffee shop owner shook his head violently and then turned to a nearby garbage can and vomited.

Detective Liam Nash jolted out of the front doors of City Hall at top speed. He stopped for a quick moment, locked eyes with Sammy, and then ran out to join the growing circle around the coach.

"Back away!" He waved his hands to enlarge the circle around the unconscious man. "Give him some room." The detective knelt on one knee and quickly checked for a pulse. "He's still with us." He waved the emergency crew closer.

From the corner of First Street, an EMT rolled a stretcher out from the back of an ambulance, and the emergency crew got to work on the coach. The detective backed away from the emergency team to give them space and ran a hand through his wavy curls. Sammy approached Liam and tapped his shoulder.

"This has to be related, if it was an accident . . . the car that hit him would have stopped, right?" Sammy uttered quietly in his ear so only the detective could hear. "You have to believe Coach didn't have anything to do with Ingrid's murder? Right? Especially now," she pointed to the man, who was now on the stretcher, being wheeled toward the ambulance.

The detective's eyes never met hers. Instead, they darted around the scene, searching. "Did you see anything?"

"Douglas, the owner from Liquid Joy, might have seen something, but he seems to be in shock and unable to process what he witnessed. I haven't heard if anyone else saw the incident. Unfortunately, I was inside the bank when it happened." Sammy hoped that the coach would pull through this. Thoughts of Carter flashed through her mind. She wondered how the teen would take this news. Her concern for him grew, and the rest of the basketball team, who would depend on their coach to lead them through the upcoming championship games, as she stood watching the horrible scene playing out before them.

Sammy noticed Lynn remove herself from the crowd and head back into the bank. It must be too uncomfortable for her to watch. Sammy rubbed her arms up and down as she shivered from the slight chill that ran through her. When she turned her head, she noticed the detective had left her side and was talking with Douglas. The color had returned to the coffee shop owner's face, but he still looked completely overcome.

Sammy couldn't believe it. Another crime committed in their small town? Why? This had to be related to Ingrid's murder. Two malicious deaths in the same family? That could *not* be a coincidence. She wondered if Heidi was working in the ER today. Hopefully, she would get more information on the coach's condition and would be able to share the news over dinner.

She watched an unfamiliar, tall, thin-haired man standing alone, observing the commotion from a slight distance. Everyone else in the crowd seemed to be talking with friends or neighbors. He was alone, which made him stand out from the rest. He slipped from the crowd. He had appeared from nowhere. Then disappeared from sight. *Who was he?*

One look at the oversized antique style clock that stood proudly on the sidewalk revealed that Sammy was late opening the store. *Darn it.* She had completely forgotten that the knitting group was meeting in the craft room at nine. After realizing that because of where her car was parked there was no way she'd be able to move it through the current crowd, Sammy decided she would have better luck walking the few blocks to Community Craft and returning to move her car later in the day. When she discovered she didn't have her purse with her, she turned, and her eyes darted over the ground beneath her. She must have left it in the bank; she scurried back inside where Lynn was talking with the manager. Upon seeing her, she watched Lynn pluck Sammy's brown leather purse from a locked drawer and rush to hand it to her.

"Thanks. In all the commotion, I misplaced it. I'm super late. Did we resolve all the paperwork issues? I can't stay now since the knitting group is on their way . . ."

"It's okay. I have everything I need for your file. I'll see you soon, Samantha," Lynn said in a saddened tone. She patted Sammy on the arm as they walked together toward the front of the bank. "Watch your back, okay? I know how you tend to involve yourself. Just be careful. The last thing I want to hear is that something happened to you too."

Sammy smiled at Lynn and adjusted her thick leather purse strap on her shoulder before leaving the bank. *Watch your back?* Was that a friendly warning? For some reason, Lynn's comments didn't bring her comfort; instead, they left her feeling on edge. What happened to the community where people left their doors unlocked and trusted and loved each other? And shared life together? Now everyone was looking over their shoulders. The icky feeling wasn't sitting well with her. As Sammy walked, she texted Carter: I'm here if you need to talk. She figured he would soon understand her cryptic text. It was only a matter of time before the news of Coach's accident would fill the high school hallways. She also sent a text to Ellie and Heidi: Corner Grill—OUR table 7 PM tonight—be there girls! Tonight, she needed S.H.E. if only to pick their brains.

Two of the knitting group participants were standing by the front door of Community Craft waiting for Sammy to open. They were talking and laughing, not a care in the world. Oblivious, no doubt, to what had taken place on Main Street less than forty-five minutes ago; and Sammy wasn't about to tell them.

"Good morning, ladies, sorry for the late start." Sammy placed the key in the lock and opened the door for the two middle-aged women to enter ahead of her.

Annabelle Larson chewed her peppermint gum, working her jaw hard. She swiped wiry red curls away from her eyes with one hand. "I bet you haven't been sleepin' with what happened to Ingrid and all." Annabelle elbowed her friend, Maria Boyle, who stopped and nodded her blonde head, though her hair didn't move. Maria's head, coated in a thick shellac of hairspray, looked as if she was wearing a swimming cap. They both suddenly dropped their amusement and instantly took on a more somber tone.

"I'm fine," Sammy said. She knew there was no other way around this other than to plow right through. "I'm sure you're both saddened by the news. Didn't she occasionally join you for knitting group?"

Maria piped up. "Only twice. She didn't really fit in with our tight group. You know how it is, for newcomers." She added as if that were a proper excuse.

Sammy opened the interior craft room door and they piled in, their bags filled with multi-colored yarns and needles and partially knit creations hanging from their stash. The two rushed to drop their belongings on the table and Sammy decided she would have to make herself available when the rest of the group arrived. Douglas might be right. Someone knew more than they were sharing. She turned and walked out the craft room door and moved to the front of the store to flick the lights on in the shop and turn the CLOSED sign to OPEN and continued through her normal morning routine. Slowly the craft room was filling up and Sammy could hear the chatter and laughter leaking from the room. She decided to work on the merchandise closest to the door so she could listen in. It wouldn't take long before the murder would be the hot topic of conversation. Of that she was certain.

As she took a feather duster and cleaned a nearby shelf to prepare it for merchandise, she strained her neck and reached to be in hearing range of the craft room.

"I guess we're going to have to carpool. It's awful to have

The Yarn Barn closed. It's at least forty miles to find natural skeins of yarn. It's absolutely heartbreaking."

"Yeah . . ." the group agreed in unison.

The knitting group was more concerned with natural fibers than the murder of Ingrid Wilson, evidently. Sammy thought that fact alone was very sad.

"Where's Greta? Should we start without her? Has anyone heard from her?" The boisterous voice of Annabelle bellowed from the room.

Where *was* Greta Dixon? Sammy wondered. She was typically one of the first to arrive. She was also part of the quilting group. Had she come when they met the other day? Maybe she was just having difficulty committing to both with all the family drama swirling around her?

"I heard her brother's in trouble again."

"Ohhh. Nooo. What happened this time?"

Here we go, it's already starting. The gossip train has arrived. How long did that take? All of fifteen seconds? Sammy chuckled to herself. She should have invited the detective to take part and listen in. Although if she had, the group would be as quiet as church mice. She leaned in closer. And then the guilt set in. She was just as bad as the rest of them. Well . . . not really. She did have a reason for eavesdropping. Someone had to find out who killed Ingrid Wilson. And why not her? She held her breath to hear.

"They've had a time and a half with that fella. Drugs. Once they start. Well, poor Greta."

"Her mother has aged about ten years. She looks terrible. All the stress. Well, poor Greta's just trying to keep her family from falling apart."

"Poor thing."

"Yeah, poor girl."

Sammy lost her balance and fell into the room. Served her right. The room at once hushed and all eyes were fully upon her. "Sorry, ladies. Please get back to your knitting. Don't let me interrupt those creative juices. I can't wait to see those knitting formations you all are preparing for Spring Fling." She smiled, trying to gain some sort of composure. As she began to retreat from the room, Sally Jefferson stopped her.

"We're proud of how you're handling yourself through all of this, Samantha," she said from across the table. Her overlipsticked mouth came up in a bow. Heads bobbed in agreement. "It must be just awful with that last image of Ingrid in your mind."

"Actually, I . . ." Sammy put a hand to her heart.

"Yes, dear, tell us . . ." Knitting needles instantly fell into the participant's laps. All leaned toward Sammy, eyes alert, waiting expectantly.

Sammy slowly backed her way out of the room. "I'm great, ladies. Don't worry about me. All good." She smiled. "I have to get to the register." She noticed a few customers forming in line and was filled with relief.

"Wait!" Annabelle Larson chimed in. "Do you know who did it? I mean . . . *who* killed her?"

"No. I . . ." Sammy stuttered. "I don't." She crossed the threshold and turned toward the cash register.

"God, Kate . . . a little *help* here?" she said under her breath to the ceiling as if talking to her deceased best friend was going to save her from the gossip in this tiny village.

Chapter Ten

The day moved quickly and before Sammy knew it, the afternoon painting group had already come and gone. Except for the teacher of the class, Deborah Morris. Sammy noticed her dainty friend, a former professional ballerina, still in the craft room gathering her supplies. She decided to pay her a quick visit.

"How'd class go today?" Sammy tucked her head inside the craft room door to catch Deborah collecting the last of the acrylic paint bottles from the middle of the table.

"It went great as always. I always have an enjoyable time teaching class." After placing the paint in a box, Deborah adjusted a strand of dark black hairs that had fallen from her neat bun with a bobby pin at the nape of her neck.

"Anything we can sell here at the store?"

"Well, I wouldn't go that far," she giggled as she displayed one of her student's creations with a graceful hand. "Does that look like an open rose to you? Or an oversized red cabbage?"

Sammy laughed and then shrugged. "Maybe not. Although, I guess art is subjective."

Deborah placed the piece back on the table to dry. "I do have some spring glassware already painted to bring in. I noticed the display is getting low." She nodded her head toward the display floor.

"Sounds good. I've been so busy getting ready for Spring Fling. You know, the store is usually jam-packed that day and I'm not even close to ready. I really need to make some phone calls and get additional merchandise in here. The winter stuff has to go." Sammy said more to herself than her friend.

"I'd be happy to help. That is if you want my help? With the kids in school now, I'm sort of at a loss for what I should be doing with my time." Deborah looked suddenly out of place as if she didn't know where she belonged. It was obvious she missed her former profession on stage. "Teaching the painting classes is great. I'm just not sure it's enough," she admitted as she removed paint brushes from a mason jar filled with muddy colored water, dumped them all in a nearby sink and began to rinse them off.

Sammy breathed deep. "I just don't know if I have the funds to pay you. With everything going on, though, Carter may be happy to give over some of his hours. He's so busy with basketball, and especially now, being the team captain. Let me tell you, the last few days have been extremely hard on him."

"Oh, I'm sure it has. Poor kid. First Ingrid, now the coach . . . That's a lot to deal with for a guy his age." Deborah agreed.

"Let me talk to him okay? Maybe we can work something out. And it would be fun! Us working together more would definitely add sunshine to my day." Sammy smiled wide. The idea sounding increasingly encouraging.

A new light shone in Deborah's eyes too. "Yes. Please talk to him. I think I'd really love it. You know, I have to work in a creative environment or I'll just die." She suddenly blushed and winced after she caught herself. "Oh! That was not the right thing to say this week. What an idiot I am." Deborah slapped her forehead with one hand. "Sorry for being insensitive."

Sammy shrugged the comment off and tried to diffuse Deborah's concern. "Don't worry about it at all. I know what you meant."

"It really is unbelievable. I never thought we'd have that type of crime happen here in Heartsford," her hand fluttered to her heart.

"I hear you." Sammy sighed.

"Do you think the police know who did it?"

Sammy shrugged. "If they do, they're pretty tight-lipped about it."

"I've heard chitchat from other school parents. Apparently, Larry and Ingrid had issues between them. That doesn't make him a killer. I'm just sayin' . . ."

Sammy nodded. "I've heard that. What kind of issues? Do you know? I mean, why would Ingrid want his school board position? Seems unlikely for a woman that didn't even have kids."

"Honestly? I try hard not to involve myself. The women I volunteer with at the school get into a lot of trouble by insinuating and over sharing. I try and avoid it like the plague." Deborah took the rinsed brushes and set them back inside the clean mason jar right-side-up to dry. She then tucked them neatly underneath the sink in an open cabinet.

Sammy could only imagine.

Deborah glanced at the clock on the wall. "I better get going. Supper doesn't make itself, and I have two hungry boys to feed *and* a husband. I haven't even been to the grocery store yet to get the fixings." She stuffed the rest of her belongings in a canvas bag and tossed it over a slender shoulder. "I'll leave the painted glass by the back door or in the storeroom if that's okay? It's already priced and ready to go on display."

"Okay, I'll get out of your way. I'll talk to Carter and let you know soon. Enjoy the rest of your day."

"Yeah, you too!" It seemed as if Deborah had a lighter skip to her step after their conversation. Sammy was glad they'd had a few moments to chat.

When Deborah returned to drop off the painted glasses, Sammy left the register and decided to unpack the box and display the new spring merchandise right away. It was time she got on the ball, or she wouldn't be prepared for Spring Fling. There was a lull in the store crowds, so no time like the present she decided. Customers expected fresh new merchandise for the event every year, so she needed to stay focused. Sammy unwrapped the glass plates first. Each plate was finely painted with daisies, hydrangea, and roses. Deborah sure had talent. The items were beautiful. Next, she unwrapped stemware that complimented each glass plate. She placed them neatly on a shelf and continued the task until the box was empty. After tossing the empty box in the storeroom, Sammy wandered over to the counter, checked her phone, and noticed

Carter had texted that he wouldn't be in the rest of the week. She would have to talk to him soon. Hiring Deborah just might work out perfectly. She'd have to take a keen look at the budget and just make it work. As she was stepping away from the counter, her phone beeped a text again. It was from Heidi: S.H.E. at 7 our table—you bet. The S.H.E. reference was interesting. Heidi must have news about the coach or something to do with Ingrid's murder. Sammy could hardly wait until dinner to find out.

Chapter Eleven

The dimly lit eatery emitted tantalizing scents as Sammy pulled open the heavy door to the Corner Grill. She maneuvered her way toward the back of the restaurant to the richly stained oak booth where she always met with her sister and cousin. Ellie was already comfortably seated in the corner. She set down her cell phone and waved as Sammy approached.

"Heidi just texted. She's running a few minutes late. She said to go ahead and order appetizers to hold us over until she gets here. Are you hungry or do you want to wait?"

Sammy smiled at her sister. She noticed Ellie had gotten a little rest. Either that, or she had done a great cover-up job with her makeup. Her hair was neatly pulled back, and her lips were perfectly glossed. "It's up to you. How's Tyler feeling?" Sammy removed her coat, hung it on her arm until she slid into the deep bench, and then set it aside.

"Much better." Ellie breathed deep. "Thank God. I couldn't handle another night like that one. It was pretty rough."

"Good to hear. Give him a hug from his Aunty Sammy when you get home." She moved the paper placemat displaying a Wisconsin map and cutlery to the side to give her more room at the table until the food arrived. "I'm glad we can finally catch up. Just us girls. It's been a long time since we all met for dinner." Sammy noticed Marilyn sitting across from someone a few tables over. "Sorry, can you excuse me for just one sec?"

Ellie shrugged and then plucked her cell phone from the table and started scrolling.

"One minute, I promise." Sammy held up a finger as she slid from the bench and made her way over to Marilyn's table. She stood for a moment in awkward silence. "Sorry to interrupt." Marilyn's eyes lifted from the menu. "I just wanted to tell you that your cake was amazing," Sammy said honestly. "Maybe the best recipe yet. It will be perfect for Spring Fling. Not only that, I think you should consider it for the everyday menu at Sweet Tooth. Thanks for letting me be one of the first to try it. I'm honored."

Marilyn set the menu on the table and clasped her hands in delight. "Thank you, darlin', for sharing that with me." She turned her attention to her longtime business partner across the table. Word on the street was that Marilyn was interested in taking their relationship a little deeper than business, but he was dragging his feet. "Isn't that so nice, Benjamin?"

Benjamin placed the menu on the table and turned to Sammy. "It certainly doesn't surprise me. Look what this gal built." He put his hands on his belly that was almost touching the edge of the table. The middle-aged man scarcely had room to move in the booth.

"I get blamed for *everything*," Marilyn waved a hand of

disgust toward her business partner. "Never mind him, sweetheart."

"I don't want to interrupt you further. I noticed you sitting over here and just wanted to share my appreciation for the lovely cake. Enjoy your dinner." Sammy bowed her head slightly and then made a quick escape back to the corner booth. The waitress was standing at the table taking an order from Ellie. Sammy was surprised she'd never seen her before.

"Drink?" Ellie asked.

"Sure, I'll have the same. Glass of Pinot?" The new waitress turned to retrieve the drinks, and Sammy stopped her. "Can we add an order of mozzarella sticks too?"

She added it to the drink menu and skirted from the table. "New waitress?"

"Yeah, I guess so. They sure pack in a crowd here." Ellie switched gears. "Everything okay with Marilyn?"

"Yeah, she gave me a new cake to try. A chocolate recipe with strawberry frosting. Quite good. You should try it. I think she's going to offer it as a specialty item for Spring Fling. I had to thank her."

"You get all the sweet treats," Ellie said with a hint of envy.

"One of the benefits of working in town, I guess." Sammy looked up at the wall. Old-time pictures of Heartsford peppered the walls, giving a reminiscent flair. "I wonder if Grandpa is in any of these photos? I never really think to look when I'm in here. We're always so busy gabbing."

Ellie set her phone down on the table and ignored the nostalgia. "Did you hear about the basketball coach? It's all over Facebook."

"I saw. I was there this morning."

"You were?" Ellie leaned across the table. "How is it possible you've witnessed two tragic scenes in one week?"

"Call it my kind of luck? I guess . . ."

The waitress came and set the wine glasses in front of them. "Sticks will be out in a sec," she said over her shoulder. Before she rushed from the table, Sammy caught her attention, "You look familiar. Did you just start working here?" The girl's highlighted hair and freckled nose reminded Sammy of someone she had known back in high school, but she couldn't place the face.

"Yes, I'm taking a break from college. Not sure yet exactly what I want to do with the rest of my life. So here I am, back with the parents," she shrugged.

"What's your name?"

"Rene Gallagher."

"You must be Gabe Gallagher's little sister?"

Her green eyes widened in surprise. "How did you know that?"

"We went to school with your older brother." She pointed to Ellie and then back to herself."

Ellie chimed in, "Yes all the girls at school had a crush on your brother, including yours truly," she admitted easily, her face immediately flushing red.

Seeing the crowd filling in, the waitress said, "Nice meeting you all. I've got to get back to work before I get fired," she chortled before quickly moving from the table.

From the corner of her eye, Sammy thought she saw Heidi moving toward them. She turned her head and did a double take. Her normally blonde cousin was now a light brunette. It was a welcomed change.

Heidi bounced toward them animatedly. "Whatcha think, girls?" She tossed her head from side to side, letting soft waves fall to her shoulders.

"Stunning," Sammy said. "Absolutely stunning."

"I have to agree," Ellie nodded. "You look great." She took a sip of wine.

Heidi's confident smile widened. "Thanks." She glanced at the table and noted only two glasses. "Where's mine?"

"You said to start without you," Ellie interjected. "Here she comes now," Ellie gave the waitress a wave and pointed to the table. "Can we have one more glass of Pinot?" Rene bobbed her head in acknowledgment and kept moving past them toward another table.

Sammy grasped her cousin by the arm as soon as Heidi slipped into the seat beside her in the booth. "Were you in the ER this morning?"

"Yes, and I knew you would ask me about it. I'm assuming you want to know about the coach from the high school basketball team?" Heidi flipped her hair to one side. "Due to patient confidentiality, all I can tell you is the coach will survive. But he's going to be in a world of hurt for a bit yet. He did get admitted today. He'll be in the hospital a few days . . . maybe more." Her face grimaced and Sammy knew he must not be doing very well.

"I can't believe it." Sammy shook her head.

"Can you believe *she* was there. At another major tragic

event?" Ellie pointed to her sister, and Heidi turned her attention toward Sammy.

"You were a witness?" Heidi asked.

"Not exactly . . . I was inside the bank when the actual accident occurred. Although I shouldn't call it an accident. It was intentional."

"Oh, I hadn't heard that," Ellie leaned in. "You mean someone did this *on purpose?*"

"Yes, Ellie, that's *exactly* what I mean."

The two focused on Heidi when she said, "The new detective was at the hospital this morning talking with Coach, but I'm not sure if he actually knew or saw what hit him. He's drugged up at the moment, so it's hard to say. I don't think the police are looking at Coach as a suspect anymore, especially not after this. At least now the injured man has one thing going for him; he's no longer blamed for his aunt's demise."

"I'm sure Sammy will find out. She had a *date* with the detective last night." Ellie pointed accusingly at her.

"And here we go again." Sammy huffed. "It was certainly *not* a date." She overemphasized the word, but it was still enough to catch Heidi's attention.

"Date, huh? I did get a good look at him for the first time. Kind of cute." Heidi nudged Sammy's arm.

The waitress came and set a plate of steaming mozzarella sticks in front of them.

"Perfect timing. Girls, please stuff your mouths with melted cheese!" Sammy hoped it would take the focus off her and the detective and *whatever it was* that had brought them together last night. She really didn't want to discuss it a minute longer.

"Back to the coach's accident . . ." Ellie said. "I did hear that the assistant, Dave, was vying for his job. These championship games are a big deal. Scouts coming in from the Big Ten schools and all. It's a huge deal. Kids get scouted at these games, and Dave's son is quite the player. Coach hasn't been giving him enough game time either, from what I hear."

Sammy took that bit of information in but stayed silent. She didn't want them to know how invested she was in solving this mystery.

Heidi stole a mozzarella stick from the plate and dipped it in the nearby marinara sauce before taking a bite, and Sammy joined her. Ellie, on the other hand, sat looking at the plate as if trying to decide.

"Have one, before they're gone." Sammy pushed the plate in her sister's direction.

"You guys don't understand. It's not as easy for me to keep the weight off. Especially after giving birth. I'm still not back to my normal weight." Ellie frowned.

Heidi shook her head from side to side. "The boy's two years old! Good God, if that's the case, I'm never having kids."

Ellie shrugged resignedly.

"Do you know how many miles on the treadmill it takes to counteract one of these?" Sammy held up the fried stick of cheese.

"You two are depressing me." Heidi rolled her eyes. "I'm hungry, and I'll eat the entire plate if you guys are suddenly worried about your weight. Sorry. This seems to be a new concept to you two. I've never heard such complaining before. We've eaten these since we were kids." She pointed to the plate.

"That's because you don't have to worry about it, Heidi. You never gain weight. It's disgusting." Ellie huffed.

"Maybe it's because I'm on my feet all day!" she shot back.

"Are you insinuating I'm not on my feet all day?" Ellie's eyes bore into her cousins.

"Girls . . . *Girls!*" Sammy, exasperated, took a bite. "White flag!" she tossed her white napkin on the table. "No more weight talk."

Ellie folded her arms across her chest and pouted. Sammy wondered if she had crossed her arms to help deter herself from reaching out and devouring the plate of cheese.

Sammy changed the subject and focused on her cousin. "What has Tim told you about the investigation?"

Heidi wiped her lips with a napkin to remove the excess sauce that had trickled from the side of her mouth. "I know you guys think my boyfriend is just a big goof. However, he takes his job very seriously and doesn't really share information with me."

Sammy and Ellie exchanged glances. Between the three of them, only one of them saw Tim as professional. They kept their opinions to themselves, but evidently, Heidi knew what they really thought. The sisters often wondered what the couple had in common. But Heidi seemed happy, and that was enough for them.

"He didn't say one word to you?" Sammy pressed.

"He stopped in at the hospital today but didn't say that much to me about the accident, or whatever it was." She zipped her lips with her fingers as if she was closing them shut and tossed the key.

The waitress approached the table, set a glass of wine in front of Heidi and then stood expectantly with a pad and paper. "You ladies know what you want?"

The three exchanged glances and Ellie spoke up, "We haven't even looked at the menu yet, but I'll have a salad with ranch dressing on the side please."

"I'll have a burger with fries, medium well please," Heidi added to the order.

"Same for me," Sammy said. "Not the salad . . . the burger." She winked at Heidi, and Ellie huffed audibly.

Heidi snatched the last mozzarella stick off the plate before the waitress removed it from the table. "I'll be back shortly with your order."

"Thanks," the three said in unison just like they had when they were kids. They all laughed aloud. Sometimes they acted like triplets.

"We need to do this more often," Ellie said. "I do miss you guys. Our lives are way too busy. Sitting here with you both brings me back to our childhood."

"Yeah, and missy over here is playing S.H.E. again." Heidi flung a finger in Sammy's direction.

"I'm not playing anything. This is serious." Sammy set down her glass of wine and her eyes darted between the two. "We have a real problem in this town. And we need to get to the bottom of it. A woman was murdered! Right here in little ole Heartsford!"

"What do we know so far?" Ellie's eyebrows furrowed, and she leaned in closer.

"Oh, no. Not you too." Heidi said. "You guys need to leave this to the professionals. And *stop* the kids play."

"Well, for one," Sammy started, as she purposely ignored her cousin, "there are several people with motive."

"Like who? Spill it. Don't hold anything back," Ellie encouraged.

Heidi just looked at the two of them and shook her head in disgust.

"It could be Larry. Ingrid was trying to get him kicked off the school board."

Ellie waved her off. "That's weak. It's not him. Totally old news. Honestly, I don't think he'd care if he got kicked off. He'd rather be out at the bar anyway."

"Gee, I don't know. Maybe there's more to the school board thing. What's a weak motive to you may not be to him? The school board could be really important to Larry. Who knows? Maybe he doesn't realize the townspeople *know* he's a drunk. Being the school board president makes him look important and well received in the community. That's extremely important to some people."

"What else have you got?" Ellie pushed.

"Harold wanted to open a hardware store, and Ingrid beat his proposal at the bank and opened The Yarn Barn instead."

"Now that could be a plausible motive. I always thought that guy had a screw loose," Heidi cheeped before taking a sip of wine.

Sammy felt encouraged by her cousin's addition to the conversation. "Actually, I found out a really interesting tidbit this week about Ingrid too."

The three all leaned in as Sammy encouraged them to bring their circle closer. "Did you know Ingrid was in a car accident years ago that caused a fatality?"

Ellie sucked a breath. "Now that's big."

Heidi nodded in agreement. "That is big. I didn't know that. How did you find that out?"

"Purely by accident really. Someone dropped a necklace in the craft room, and I had it in the lost and found . . ."

"Go on," Ellie encouraged, but Sammy noticed the food arriving and leaned back in the booth.

The waitress set the salad in front of Ellie. "I'll be right back with your burgers." Rene said and left them in a hurry once again.

Ellie set her salad aside to wait for the rest of the food to arrive. "Go on. You might be onto something here."

"I can't believe you're encouraging her." Heidi flipped her newly coiffed hair over her shoulder with a finger. "This is dangerous. Two in one family?" she hissed to them in a loud whisper. "It's not cool."

"The woman that came in and claimed the locket, I've seen her maybe a handful of times in the store . . . never in the craft room though," Sammy continued. "No way she could commit a crime at her age. I just don't see how she could physically do it."

Ellie leaned on the table and rested her chin on a closed fist. "Who else has a motive?"

"Douglas mentioned the knitting group had issues with her. But I didn't get much from that today when I was eavesdropping." Sammy admitted.

"You need to let this go." Heidi was adamant. "Whoever is doing this in broad daylight in front of the police station has a set of big ones, if you know what I mean." Her eyes were wide, and her manicured eyebrows danced up and down.

Heidi's reference made them all giggle like teenagers.

"Big ones?" Ellie laughed. "Really? You're too funny." She put her wine glass down for fear she was laughing too hard to take a drink, and it would come out her nose. "Heidi's right though, Sam, you should back off. It's dangerous," she added in a more serious tone.

"I can't let it go. I've seen too much, and I'm too involved. You guys don't understand."

"So, who is it? Colonel Mustard in the conservatory with a candle stick?" Ellie mocked.

"Very funny." Sammy gave her sister a dagger look. She wasn't laughing—the jokes were officially over.

Ellie kept at it, "Actually, wasn't it Professor Plum with a knitting needle? Yikes! Sooo . . . gross. It couldn't have been premeditated? If it was, wouldn't they have used a better weapon?"

Heidi nodded in agreement. "She's right about that. If you wanted to kill someone, wouldn't you be better prepared? Like with a gun or something? A knitting needle? It had to be a last-minute hit."

"I can't believe you guys. A woman has been *murdered*. And you're poking fun." Sammy was incredulous.

"Did you hear what she just said? Poking fun? As in poking . . . with a needle. Ha ha!" Heidi's eyes were watering from laughter. Or maybe the wine was hitting her empty stomach. Either way, Sammy couldn't believe the goings on at their table.

"What happened to Ingrid is tragic. If I took the time to think about the fact that there is a killer on the loose in our small town, I wouldn't be able to get out of bed in the morning for fear my sweet baby Tyler would be in danger. Cracking jokes . . . it's just the way some of us cope."

Heidi leaned over and placed her hand on top of Sammy's. "We understand that this isn't child's play. It's dangerous, and you need to stay out of it. How about that?" she said with firm finality.

Ellie nodded. "Heidi's absolutely right, Samantha, and you know it. Let the professionals handle it."

Sammy hated when her sister used her formal name, it made her sound like their mother. Sammy sat back in the booth and decided to remain silent. The two sitting next to her were clueless. Someone had to get to the bottom of this investigation. Even if she had to do her undercover work solo. She was going to find out who killed Ingrid Wilson and why.

Chapter Twelve

Early Wednesday morning, Sammy still couldn't erase the murder of Ingrid Wilson from her mind. She decided the walk to work might help clear her head, but it wasn't long enough. The cloudless morning, a first after many months of gray, caused her to want to extend their walk after reaching Community Craft. After checking her watch, she decided she had time to meander along the river walk that snaked through the downtown area. A volunteer group of master gardeners that met semi-monthly in the craft room of Community Craft handled the landscape along the path that hugged the river. Sammy was extra happy that morning that she had offered the space for their meetings as she noted the bright yellow daffodils with their faces pointed to the sun. The deep purple hyacinths stood proudly beside them for an eye-catching contrast. Soon there would be hanging baskets full of multicolored petunias and ivy along the light posts downtown to prepare for Spring Fling. She would have to compliment the volunteers at their next meeting. They did such an impressive job keeping the town of Heartsford colored with beauty. Sammy tried to focus on the moment and breathe in the serenity around her. Bara seemed to enjoy the extra long walk as he sniffed along the path, taking it all in. It had been a long winter for them both; Sammy even allowed him the slight indulgence of chasing a squirrel. As the leash extended to its farthest point though, she gave a quick jerk of the leather strap to remind him of their journey. He turned his head as if to say, *Come on . . . I was so close,* but then he acquiesced and sauntered back to the path, his furry hips moving at a comfortable pace.

As Sammy turned the corner in the direction of the small covered bridge, Mayor Allen jogged toward her. Dressed in full workout gear, he stopped just long enough to take a swig from his water bottle. Despite his advanced years, and full head of silver hair, he was in much better shape than most his age.

"Good morning, Sunshine Sam," He gestured toward the sun that had finally made an appearance. "Isn't it a beautiful morning?" Ever since she and Kate had been friends, Kate's father had a special nickname that he alone used; he called her Sunshine Sam, and the name had stuck with her into adulthood.

"It sure is, Mayor Allen," Sammy grinned and reached for him as he pulled her into his tall frame for a hug.

"Don't mind the sweat," he laughed as he released her. "It's good to see you."

"You as well. I don't want to interrupt your workout, but I do want to know how Carter has been holding up. He hasn't been working in the store lately because he's been so busy with the upcoming big games. I can't help but feel concerned. Especially after the last few days events."

"It's not an interruption. It's a pleasure to talk with you. Ever since Kate left us, I feel so lucky that Carter has you in his life. I know you don't replace his sister, but I don't know what he would have done without you, Sunshine. Honestly, I don't know what any of us would have done," he added sincerely as he gave her shoulder a fatherly squeeze. "Carter's doing well considering the circumstances. He's deeply focused on working hard for Assistant Coach Dave. They all want to bring this one home for Coach. You understand."

"Yeah. I know." Sammy nodded in agreement. "I'm going to see if Ellie can come by and take over the store, so I can catch a few of the games too. I promised Carter I would. I'd especially like to come on his birthday."

"That would mean so much to our family if you could. Especially Carter. I can't believe our baby is going to be eighteen on Friday." Mayor Allen bent down and gave Bara a pat on the head as the puppy begged for attention. "What a sweet dog you have here, Sunshine," he smiled. "I bet he's great company." He took another swig from his water bottle before kneeling to retie a shoelace that had come undone.

Sammy had no other choice than to take this opportunity to ask him what he knew about the investigation into Ingrid's murder. "Have the police made an arrest yet?"

"No," he responded quickly, "but I sure hope they do soon. The town is really on edge."

"I know." Sammy agreed. She wished he'd said more, but considering his job and standing in the community, she understood why he would keep a tight lid on the issue.

"Nice to see you, Sunshine. I've got to get moving, but

we'll save you a seat at the game. Okay?" He waved and was quickly off and running again.

"You bet." Sammy waved goodbye and continued her walk along the path.

After her encounter with Mayor Allen, her mind began to wander back to her best friend, Kate. What would her life be like now . . . if it hadn't been cut short? She made her way to the covered bridge that resembled a small red barn, she remembered how she and Kate used to come and pick wild-flowers along the river for their mothers on Mother's Day. Or talk about their latest high school crushes. Inside the covered bridge she stopped at the wooden post and ran her fingers through the carved heart inside. KA LOVES GD. She had for-gotten that Kate had been in love with Greta's brother, Gary. The thought made her chuckle. All Kate had talked about that summer was Gary, Gary, Gary. She remembered fondly as she fingered the old carving. And now . . . she wondered if up in heaven Kate knew. That the love of her life, Gary Dixon, had been in and out of jail, apparently struggling with addic-tion problems and causing his whole family stress from the pressure of it all. She silently wondered if Kate's death had furthered his addiction. They had long been long broken up by the time she had passed away, but maybe he never really got over her? A newfound compassion for Gary swept over Sammy. Sometimes things weren't always what they seemed.

Bara nosed at her wrist, removing her from her reverie. "I know, pup. We better get to work." Sammy took the cue from her dog and picked up the pace, heading back toward Com-munity Craft.

Before heading into work for the day, Sammy decided to make a few stops. First, she dropped Bara at Community Craft, so he could rest on his plush bed that sat beside the register. After making sure her puppy was more than comfortable, she headed across the street for a coffee. The early morning rush had passed, so Sammy easily made her way to the counter where Cara stood waiting.

"Did Douglas stop by yet?" Cara leaned in on the counter to speak directly to Sammy.

"Yep, thanks for passing on the message. I'm just here for the caffeine today. I went for a walk this morning. I just couldn't pass up the sunshine." She grinned, feeling the vitamin D from the change in spring weather already taking full effect.

Cara turned to pour Sammy's coffee. "It sure is nice out there," she looked toward the window with longing. "As soon as my shift is over, I'm going to go play tennis or at the very least go for a walk. Too nice to not take advantage . . . In case the weather turns again. You know how bipolar Wisconsin weather can be."

"I sure do," Sammy's eyes wandered around the coffee shop, looking for anyone she knew. Secretly she was looking to see if the new detective was possibly sharing a cup of coffee with Tim. She didn't spot either of them.

The walls of the café, painted a bright yellow, were the same color as the café's signature cups. Large emoji-style smiles were hand-painted on the wall above the coffee bar. Each of their white painted tables held only four chairs, for a more intimate feel. To her surprise, Sammy noticed the woman who had retrieved the lost locket necklace. She had seen this woman only a handful of times before, and now suddenly she was popping up again? Because of a large ficus plant in the line of her vision, Sammy couldn't see who was on the other side of the table.

"Hold my coffee for a few minutes, Cara? I have to use the restroom," she fibbed and stepped away from the coffee line, leaving the barista with a perplexed look on her face.

Sammy maneuvered her way through the tables toward the bathroom but specifically toward the older woman to see who was accompanying her. *Gary Dixon*? What was Gary Dixon doing with her? Who *was* she? Sammy was going to have to figure out the identity of this mystery woman. The question was . . . how? She really wasn't friends with Gary in high school. The fact that he had taken Kate's attention away from her had a lot to do with it. Sammy opened the door to the ladies' room and stood at the sink. Her auburn hair was windblown from the walk along the river. She brushed it from her eyes and combed her fingers through it to try to make it more presentable. She should pay closer attention to her appearance, she scolded herself, instead of looking for trouble. Maybe her sister and cousin were right. Sammy turned on the sink and washed her hands and patted her face with the water. She should just learn to mind her own business. Unfortunately, she knew her curious nature wouldn't allow that, especially when the questions in her mind kept rolling. She wiped her face and hands dry with a paper towel and tossed it into the trash. Hopefully her spare makeup bag was back in her office drawer at Community Craft. Otherwise, her appearance would be rather unsightly for a full day at work.

With her mind swimming, due to all the tragic events, she couldn't remain focused, and that needed adjusting or she wasn't going to be much help to anyone. She exited the bathroom, and as she retreated toward the coffee bar, she noticed Gary and the mystery woman leaving the café. Now she had really lost her chance for a proper introduction. She needed to do some research about that car accident and see whose life had ended that day Ingrid was behind the wheel. Because the accident happened years before the Internet, Sammy doubted a quick Google search would give her the answers she needed. She would have to stop by the library and find out. The history room might contain some valuable information. She had to find out why this older woman was meeting with Gary. It just didn't make sense.

"You all right?" Cara asked as she handed Sammy the coffee that had been sitting on the counter.

"Yeah, I'm fine," she smiled, "Hey, you don't happen to know that older woman who was here with Gary Dixon?"

The barista stood organizing the sugar and napkins on the counter. "No. Why?"

Sammy handed her a five-dollar bill from her pocket and Cara took it to make change.

"She came in the store recently. Just wondered who she was?"

Cara shrugged. "Sorry. No idea." She handed Sammy her change, and she jammed it into her pocket.

"Thanks, enjoy your day. Get out there and get some sun." Sammy smiled at the barista, waved a hand, and was out the door.

Bara greeted Sammy as soon as she was back at the shop. Before opening the store and starting her official morning routine, Sammy headed straight to the office to retrieve her makeup bag with her dog trailing behind. She felt relieved she had left it in the desk drawer. After a quick addition of blush, black mascara, and berry lip gloss she felt much better about opening the door to customers.

Sammy wondered if the detective would make an appearance? He really hadn't asked her a lot of questions about the murder, which she found perplexing. Did he have a unique way of approaching his cases? He was probably trying to be friendly to everyone in town so they would let their guards down and maybe let something slip? In times such as these she wished she had paid more attention in her college psych classes. If she had, she might have everyone's mindset figured out.

Sammy hurried to the front door to flip the store sign to OPEN. As she was unlocking the door, she noticed Lynn walking past at a rapid stride. She stepped outside the door and gave a wave. "Gorgeous morning!"

"Sure is!" Lynn returned the wave and kept pace, not missing a beat. Suddenly though she turned and, walking backwards said, "Hey, thanks for the suggestion. I talked with the police about my concerns. Just so you know, they said they did bring Harold in for questioning. It's sure a weight off my chest." Before Sammy had the chance to reply, Lynn had already returned to a steady pace and was too far away to respond.

Good for her, Sammy thought. *She sure is sticking to the exercise program.* Sammy wasn't sure how Lynn could walk by the Sweet Tooth though and see those mouth watering treats through the window. Sammy wondered if that was why Lynn often crossed the street before she made it to Marilyn's storefront. Sammy also wondered what had come of that conversation with police? Did they think Harold might be their guy? She closed the front door and headed to the back to repeat her opening procedure.

As Sammy was opening the back door, Ellie and her son were approaching. When Tyler saw his aunt, he let go of his mother's hand and started running as fast as his two little legs could manage.

"Aunt-ie Sam-ee!" The little boy with boundless energy came rushing into her arms.

Sammy ran her fingers through his fine reddish-blond curls as she hugged him tightly. "Someone's feeling better!" She ruffled his head one more time before letting go so he could enter the store in search of Bara.

"He's better all right. Back to his old busy-boy self," Ellie said with tired exaggeration.

Sammy held the door as her sister stepped in. Sure enough, Tyler was cuddled up with Bara, petting him tenderly on his back, the two of them very content.

"I thought I'd stop in and look for something to hang in the newly remodeled living room. Randy has the paint job just about finished. You'll have to stop in and see. I think you'll absolutely love the color." Ellie's eyes searched the store walls in hopes of finding the perfect item to use for decoration.

"Are you thinking a painting? Or shelves? How about a wall quilt? What kind of style are you going for?"

"I'm not sure. I think I'll know it when I see it. I came in first thing hoping you wouldn't have many customers this early so you could keep your eyes on Tyler while I shop? You know how he gets into everything, it's hard to stay focused on what I'm doing. Such an inquisitive nature. He must take after his aunt," Ellie winked.

Sammy wanted to ignore her sister's little dig, but she was right. She was losing sleep because of her rampant curiosity. It was impossible for her to let the investigation go, it was borderline compulsive. "Well since you brought up my *inquisitive nature . . .*"

"Oh, boy. What now?" Ellie stopped looking at the merchandise on the rack and gave her sister her full attention.

"Remember that woman I told you about with the locket? She was having coffee with Gary Dixon today at Liquid Joy. I wonder who she is and why she would be having coffee with *Gary*?"

"I don't remember a Gary Dixon. Who is he? Can you jog my memory?"

"He dated Kate for a while. Remember that? Oh, and his sister Greta is a few years older than you and Heidi. She's in here quite a bit. Ring any bells?"

Ellie stood for a moment and then snapped a finger. "I remember Greta Dixon. Doesn't she take classes here? Do you think it's his mother? Or you mentioned she's a bit older. Could it be his grandmother?"

"No, it's not his mother. I know what she looks like. I suppose it could be a grandmother, but I don't remember Kate ever mentioning that he had any other local family. Mom might remember. I'll have to call her and ask."

"Anyway, I thought you were staying out of it?" Ellie lifted one eyebrow and smirked at her sister.

"Of course, I am. Go shopping, check out that corner . . . There's new stuff over there," Sammy suggested the corner farthest away from her so she didn't have to discuss it further. Besides, it would give her time to hang out with her nephew for a bit.

"I'll take you up on that." Ellie strolled to the front of the store in search of the perfect item for her home.

Tyler left Bara's side and ran toward Sammy, almost knocking over a rack.

"Careful, buddy!" Sammy moved toward her nephew to steer him in a safer direction.

"Aunt-ie Sam-ee!" he looked up at her, his round blue eyes big as saucers. "Lol-ee?"

Sammy kept a hidden drawer where she stored large colorful lollipops for when her nephew came to visit. Ellie hated it, which made Sammy love it even more.

"Let's go see." She led him by the hand to her office and pulled out a key to open the locked drawer. After unlocking it, she let him choose from the package. Tyler's hands shook with delight. He plucked a red one from the pile, and after she had helped him unwrap it, straight into his mouth it went.

"Now, you'll have to come sit by the register with me. That's the rule. Otherwise, I take your lolly," she held him with one hand and hauled a chair with the other out toward the cash counter. He obediently sat in the chair kicking his legs back and forth while he sucked on the candy. A large smile was pasted across his chubby rosy cheeks.

Before long, Ellie was standing at the cash register, arms full of merchandise. She was so enamored with her new things she didn't even notice her son, hands sticky with a mouth full of candy. She filled the counter with the items and held up two handblown glass sconces, one in each hand.

"What do you think of these? Wouldn't it look nice with a collection of family photos in between? I'm thinking for the large wall behind the couch?"

"I love that idea." Sammy carefully took them from her sister and removed the tags. "These are just gorgeous, aren't they?" she said as she carefully wrapped them in bubble wrap for safe transport.

"I love these quilted pillows too. I'm thinking of tossing them on the living room chairs. I need to get rid of the winter blah and bring in a pop of color."

"Aren't they great? I love the patchwork, but with the pale floral color, they don't look country. Instead, they're quite modern, don't you think?"

"This is close to the color on the wall." Ellie removed a paint swatch from her purse to show her sister how the patchwork would tie in beautifully with her newly painted room.

"I can't wait to see it when you're finished." Sammy rang up the items at the register, and it was then that Ellie noticed her son with a large ring of red around his mouth. He held his sticky hands out in front of him but still sat obediently in the chair, swinging his legs wildly.

"You didn't."

"I did." Sammy grinned.

"It's not even lunchtime, and you're giving him candy? What are you thinking?"

Sammy's smile widened. "Wait until Randy sees this bill . . . hand over your credit card, lady." She hoped the change of subject would take the heat off her giving Tyler an early morning treat.

Her sister dug into her purse and handed over the plastic card. "Yeah, I overspent. I'm going to have to go back to work soon. A single-income household is hard sometimes."

"Speaking of that . . ." Sammy decided it was the perfect time to take full advantage. "I have a way you can earn off some of that bill. Any chance you can work the store Friday afternoon? It's Carter's eighteenth birthday, and I want to surprise him by catching his basketball game. It would only be a few hours."

"That could work."

Sammy could see her sister's mind working, hopefully in her favor.

"Let me talk to Randy, and I'll call you later to confirm?"

"I would really appreciate it." Sammy placed the filled packages on the counter.

"I know. You've been very good to the Allen family, and I know how close you are with Carter." Ellie scooped up her packages and then moved to hide them behind the counter.

"Hang on to these, I have to go take Tyler to wash his hands. *Thanks a lot.*" She sent Sammy a stern look.

"You are so welcome," she teased.

"Just wait until you have kids. Remember, paybacks!" Ellie said over her shoulder as she lifted Tyler up off the chair and headed directly to the restroom.

Chapter Thirteen

The familiar smell of sweat and foul-smelling shoes greeted Sammy as she swung open the gymnasium door of her old high school. It had been a long time since she had stepped into that space. Her memories of Heartsford High rushed forward almost taking her breath away. Images of Kate kicking her leg and swinging red and white pom-poms as she cheered the team to victory came flooding back. The memory was so vivid, Sammy had to shake her head to return to reality, where she was an adult and no longer in school. The squeaky sound of rubber sneakers hitting the highly-polished maple floor helped sharpen the focus of her mind and return her to the present moment. Sammy breathed deeply as her eyes scanned the bleachers for the Allen family. She noticed the mayor right away, waving a hand to catch her attention. She maneuvered her way through the standing crowd and stepped through the wooden bleachers until reaching a seat to join them.

"You made it right on time." The mayor patted her on the back as the buzzer sounded, making everyone aware the warm-up was over, and the game would soon begin. The mayor's wife, Connie, reached across her husband's lap and gave Sammy's hand a squeeze to welcome her without words in the noisy atmosphere.

"I wouldn't miss it for anything." Sammy smiled wide and then turned her gaze to the team until her eyes landed on Carter. He was laser focused on what the assistant coach was sharing with the circled team.

The mayor leaned into Sammy and pointed out a few nicely dressed men who were standing in the corner. "All our hopes for a scholarship are right there," he said in her ear.

Sammy noticed the scouts that most likely represented some Big Ten colleges. This was an important game. She could physically feel the tension in the room and read it on the players' faces. They were under a lot of pressure. As the team prepared for the start of the game, the mayor pointed out the team's starting point guard.

"Looks like Assistant Coach Dave got his wish, his son's in the first string."

"Doesn't he normally play?"

"Not when the head coach is here. He's usually benched."

The buzzer sounded, and Carter took his spot on the court as the team's center. His height made him the perfect pick for the position. The game began, and it was like watching a wild game of ping-pong, each team equally matched. As the opposing team would score, a collective "*Ohhh*" would rise from the crowd, and when Heartsford had the ball, the crowd would leap to its feet and cheer. The fast-paced game seemed to have everyone's hearts in their throats.

Even with the rush of the game, Sammy couldn't help but think about Assistant Coach Dave and his son's sudden promotion to be front and center in front of the Big Ten scouts. The advantage was glaring. She couldn't help but wonder if there were other kids on the team who might benefit with the head coach in the hospital? As sad as it was, she could see how that could prove to be a motive for injury. Apparently, she wasn't the only one with this opinion. Her eyes caught Detective Liam Nash just inside the door of the gym, standing with his back against the wall. Sammy studied him without being overly obvious. She wanted to know where his focus lay. He seemed to be happy just taking it all in. Although she did notice his eyes taking in the Big Ten scouts too. Without warning, his eyes locked on her and she quickly turned her head in the other direction. She hoped he hadn't caught her staring at him.

Carter had the ball and was close to scoring a basket. After the swish through the hoop, the crowd went wild as the basket brought them back into the lead. Sammy leaped to her feet and clapped along with the others. She was happy Carter was playing well on his birthday. No doubt he'd be scouted as a draft pick, hopefully for Wisconsin. He had confided that it was his number one pick for college. Some of those college players even went on to play in the NBA. Granted, it was hard to imagine her adopted *no-so-little* brother ever living outside Heartsford.

The game was a nail-biter, but the home team pulled it out in the end. The roar of the crowd reached an almost uncontrollable level; the excitement palpable. Sammy knew she would have to hang around while Carter met with some of the coaches and his teammates and she didn't want to steal his attention. As the crowd rushed the court, she noticed the detective slip out the door. If she weren't so far away from the exit, she would have followed him to pick his brain. But there was no way she would fight her way through the crowd, it would have to wait.

Connie Allen caught her attention. "Thanks so much for coming, Sam," she said warmly. Carter's mother was a picture of her son. They had hair the exact same color and the same wide smile. "Mark's already out warming the car for us. We're in a bit of a rush, heading home to order pizzas and get the house ready for the team. Would you like to join us?" Kate's mother exuded hospitality. Sammy always felt loved and welcomed in her presence.

"Not tonight. But thanks for the offer. I have to go relieve Ellie at the store for close."

"Sometime soon then. Don't be a stranger." Connie's gray eyes danced with pride as she took one last look at her son before exiting the gym.

When the crowd dispersed and Sammy found an opening, she made her way toward Carter. One glance and he sprinted over, picked her up, and spun her in his arms. When he finally dropped her back on her feet, Sammy laughed from the excitement of it all. "Happy Birthday! Great game!"

The teen's flushed face was beaming ear to ear. "Thanks for coming, Sammy. I know how hard it is for you to break away from the store. It really means a lot." He slapped her a high five.

"I'm glad to be here and share this moment with you." She reached in her dark leather purse and pulled out an envelope. "Here." Sammy handed him a card. "Just a little something for your birthday. It's not every day you turn eighteen. I'm so incredibly proud of you."

"Thanks!" he said quickly before the team all gathered around him and picked him up off the floor screaming his name: "Allen! Allen!"

Sammy watched with amusement as the team members carried Carter across the floor, his face radiating pure delight. If only Kate were there to take in this moment. Before heading out the door, something seized Sammy's attention, causing her to adjust her vision. She observed the assistant coach, his arm slung loosely around his son's shoulder, talking to one of the nicely dressed men. Yes, indeed. There was no question. He definitely had something to gain by the coach being hospitalized. A full scholarship to a Big Ten school for his son? Priceless. To ensure his son's recruitment had he struck down the head coach? Were the crimes indeed connected? If so, how? Sammy wasn't sure. Sometimes she hated how her mind worked.

After leaving the gym, Sammy realized it was getting late. She called Ellie from her cell phone to apologize. "I am soo sorry. Please don't be mad. The game went a bit over and by the time I wanted to give Carter his card . . ."

Ellie interrupted. "It's absolutely no problem. Don't worry about it. I've closed the store for you before. I think I remember the routine."

"Do you want me to stop by? Or do you have it handled?"

"Totally have it handled. It was quiet in here tonight.

I think the whole town must have been at the game! How was it? Did Carter score a lot of points?"

Sammy was unlocking her car with the key fob and accidentally hit the alarm button sending shrieks of alarm bells into the parking lot. "Oh crap. Hold on a second. Can I call you back?"

"I'll talk to you tomorrow. Don't worry about close, I've got it." Ellie clicked the phone off ending the call between them.

As she was deactivating the car alarm, Detective Liam Nash pulled up alongside her in his silver Honda Civic and rolled the window. "Everything all right over here?"

Sammy's face flushed red. "Yes. Just a minor issue unlocking my car. Nothing to see here." She waved her hands as if to shoo away an annoying insect. "You can move along."

"Feisty tonight I see." He leaned his arm out the window. "I was hoping to talk with you for a moment. I didn't think I would get the chance but since you sounded the alarm for me to find you . . ." He grinned.

"I did *not* sound the alarm on purpose, I assure you." Sammy rolled her eyes and threw a hand to one hip. "What did you want to talk about?" She was a wee bit upset that she hadn't heard from the detective since the night they'd shared a pizza, although she had no clue why this bothered her. But it did. Clearly, her defensive walls were going up brick by brick.

"Do you have time to grab a cup of coffee?" Liam turned his head to check the clock on his dash and then asked, "Better yet, is Sweet Tooth still open? I'm still dreaming about that darn cake. I think I'm hooked." He tapped his fingers on the steering wheel as if to say *hurry up and decide.*

He missed the *cake* . . . not her. Sammy took in a slow breath, still confused at the offer. "Sure. Ellie's closing the shop for me. But Sweet Tooth is only open until seven o'clock, so we don't have much time." She opened the driver's side door. "Although sometimes Marilyn keeps the store open on game nights because the excitement draws a crowd."

"I'll meet you there." He didn't wait for her to change her mind and quickly drove away.

"Men." Sammy huffed. "All he wants is *cake.*"

She couldn't understand her sudden agitation. He certainly hadn't done anything wrong. She was just pissed she hadn't heard from him sooner. He was using her for information. Nothing more. Sammy decided she'd better change her attitude before reaching the bakery. She flipped on the ignition switch and turned the steering wheel in the direction of the lengthy line of headlights leaving the parking lot. After two nineties songs played on the radio and transported her back to another era—and singing inside the empty car at the top of her lungs—she felt much better.

Sammy pulled up in front of the bakery, snagging the last available space on Main Street. She glanced down the road before exiting the car and noticed the darkened Community Craft windows. She was glad Ellie had everything closed tight and had returned home to Randy and Tyler. The Sweet Tooth, as expected, was overflowing with teens in basketball uniforms, and parents, and friends celebrating the big win. The detective was exiting his car and swiftly joined her as she stepped out onto the sidewalk. He rubbed his hands together in excitement. "I'm so glad they're still open. My mouth is watering."

"I guess I should have sent you home with leftovers. I ended up putting the rest of the cake in the freezer."

"Yeah, mine wouldn't have made it to the freezer. I would have eaten it long before I would let that happen."

"That's why men are so lucky. They never have to worry about their weight or what they look like."

"Sometimes you say the strangest things," he shook his head in disagreement. "Guys still have to watch their weight. But it's okay to splurge now and then," he added as he looked down at his trim waistline.

Sammy shrugged before opening wide the bakery door. "After you," she held the door, and to her surprise, the detective walked directly inside. Most men would have said, "*After you*," and insisted on holding the door. But not Liam Nash. She thought about this as they fought their way through the crowd to stand in line. Sammy's eyes adjusted to the pale pink walls of the bakery. They had been repainted but remained the same color as they'd been when she was a child and would come with her mother and sister to have those dreaded *you'll soon be a woman* talks. The thought made her chuckle.

Liam was right, maybe she did say some strange things. Her filter must be broken. The things that crossed her mind usually tumbled right out her mouth. She'd have to pay more attention to that. *Now* that *was a good thought.* She chuckled to herself.

Sammy looked at the length of the line and the remaining seats filling up and made an executive decision. She called Liam closer and cuffed a hand to his ear. "What do you want? How about I wait in line and you go save us a seat? Otherwise, it'll be standing room only."

Liam reached into his pocket and handed her a twenty-dollar bill. "Something sweet and delicious. You pick. I trust you have good taste." He winked and then left the line to sit in the last corner booth.

When she reached the counter, Marilyn's face was flushed from the rush of juicy gossip, and she couldn't keep herself from smiling. "Did I see you come in with the new detective? Care to share, darlin'?" The baker's eyes danced from Sammy back toward where Liam was sitting casually looking down at his cell phone.

"Oh. No." Sammy laughed. "We just ran into each other at the game, and he wanted to ask me something. I'm sure it has to do with the investigation." She waved a hand airily like it was nothing. And it *was* nothing. But she secretly wished it was something.

Marilyn's eyes narrowed. "I heard they're getting close to making an arrest. You'll have to let me know what he tells you."

This took Sammy completely off guard. "You're kidding?"

"No, that's what I'm hearing." Marilyn lowered her voice.

The line backed up because the baker wanted every bit of juicy gossip from every person who stood to wait in line. Before anyone could get any more agitated, Sammy said, "I'll have two chocolate cupcakes with that new strawberry frosting and two milks please." She pointed to the glass case that held every amazing and hip-extending piece of pastry imaginable.

Marilyn placed two cupcakes on a tray along with the glasses of milk and rested it on the counter until Sammy gave her the detective's twenty-dollar bill.

While making change, Marilyn said. "You have a good night, darlin'." She raised her eyebrows in delight. "And keep me posted, you hear?" she mouthed.

Sammy picked up the tray and carefully made her way to the booth where the detective was sitting, being ever so cautious not to drip the milk on the tray. She placed it on the table of the booth and, without removing her coat slid into the red leather seat.

The detective frowned.

"What's wrong?"

"I don't drink milk. I'm lactose intolerant." He moved the milk to her side of the table.

"Oh, gosh. Do you want something else?" *Why didn't he tell her that before she ordered? Did he not say he'd eat anything she chose?*

"Nah," he waved her away and instantly took a bite of the cupcake, closing his eyes in a dream state of euphoria.

"You realize there's probably lactose in that cupcake you're eating," she warned as she pointed to the deep dark chocolate with whipped strawberry frosting, perfectly piped.

His eyes popped open, and he frowned. After slowly swallowing the lump of chocolate in his mouth he said, "I didn't have trouble the other day."

"I'm just warning you. Don't blame me if you have to make a run for it."

Liam began to laugh, and he didn't stop laughing until his eyes watered.

"What?" For the life of her, Sammy couldn't understand what was so funny.

"I'm not lactose intolerant. I'll drink the milk," Nash waved his hand toward himself. "Give it here. I'll take it."

"And you think *I'm* the strange one?" She rolled her eyes. "Choke on your chocolate."

"I'm just trying to get you to relax. You seem a bit, what's the word . . . aggravated?"

Sammy breathed deep. She never liked when someone pointed out her attitude—even when they were dead-on. It was sending her mood deeper in the wrong direction. "I apologize. I have a lot on my plate, and all this chaos happening . . ." She took a bite of the cupcake before divulging anything more.

"I wanted to talk to you because I think this might help you feel better, and I wanted you to be the first to know so you don't have to worry another night." The detective sucked in a breath. "You do have some bags under your eyes. Have you been sleeping?" he said, pointing to her eyes.

Who is this guy? Sammy continued to eat her cupcake. The thought of throwing it at him fleetingly crossed her mind. She stayed silent.

"I take that as a no?" his eyebrows rose. "Anyhow . . . We're getting close to making an arrest and normally I don't share this kind of information but . . ."

"Lower your voice," Sammy hissed as she looked over her

shoulder. "You've never lived in a small town, have you? Marilyn just told me you were making an arrest which means half of Heartsford probably already knows!"

Liam sat back in the booth as if his face had just been slapped. He was obviously shocked. She really needed to work on her approach as he seemed taken aback yet again. It was an interesting self-reflection. Maybe because he was new in town? Was that the reason he was consistently surprised by her words? In a small town like Heartsford, most people tended to look past your personality because they'd known you for years. Was she this pointedly candid with everyone . . . or just him? She was enjoying his company if for no other reason than to psychoanalyze herself.

After a long pause, Sammy addressed him again. "Who?" Sammy softened her tone. "Who are you arresting? I'm assuming you're talking about the murder of Ingrid Wilson? Or did you mean Coach's rundown on the road? Or are you arresting someone for both crimes?"

The detective regained his composure and leaned in across the table so only Sammy could hear.

"Miles Danbury."

Sammy had no other choice than to sit in stunned silence.

Chapter Fourteen

Sammy hesitated before calling Heidi, knowing full well that her cousin's preferred method of communication was text. But she needed information desperately. She finally settled on a text:

> Any chance you can stop in store today? Need to see you.
> Everything okay? What's wrong? Is this a 911?

Sammy knew this would happen.

> Everything fine. Just need to talk.

Sammy hoped this would stop the back and forth and Heidi would make the time to come in. A phone call would only rile Heidi up, and Sammy wouldn't get the information she needed without a face-to-face visit.

> Be right over.

Sammy smiled. "Good," she said aloud.

While she was waiting for Heidi to stop in Community Craft, she went straight to work, unloading new spring merchandise. A fresh box of Lilian Brown's handmade soaps had been dropped off during Ellie's watch. Sammy heaved the large box over to the soap display and made room on the shelves to restock. After she opened the box, the air filled with a welcome scent. As she unwrapped each bar of the new lavender-scented soap, she breathed in deeply; her anxious mind soon relaxed. She hadn't even emptied a third of the box when Heidi came rushing into the store and came over to stand directly at Sammy's side.

"Holy cow. That was fast." Sammy turned and greeted her cousin. She swiped at her hair that had fallen in front of her eyes and tucked it behind one ear.

Heidi jutted a thumb toward the door. "I was across the street having coffee with Tim. He's starting his shift soon . . . so here I am." She displayed jazz hands as if she was about to start a Broadway production.

"Looks like you're just getting off your shift." Sammy pointed to her cousin's scrubs. It was Sammy's absolute pet peeve. Couldn't she change at the hospital or clean up at home first before sitting at a public establishment like Liquid Joy? But today, she bit her lip. She had more important things to discuss.

"Yeah. Long night . . . I'm about ready for bed. How was the game?"

"How did you know I went to the game?" Sammy placed a bar of soap on top of a pyramid that she had created on the shelf.

"Mayor Allen and Carter stopped in the hospital after his birthday party. It was late, but Carter insisted he had to see Coach to talk about the game or he wouldn't feel right. He's such a great kid, that Carter." Heidi leaned a hand on the display to suddenly hold up her weary body. "So, why did you want to see me? Ideas for Spring Fling? How about we consider a fashion show this year? I think that would be right up my alley. I'd be happy to model if you'd like." Heidi puckered her lips and batted her long mascara-dipped eyelashes.

"Actually, I was thinking more along the lines of a fundraiser for Coach to help with some of the medical bills. How is he?"

"Stable. Hopefully he'll be out of the hospital soon. But that's all I'm sharing. Patient confidentiality." She zipped her lips with her fingers and flicked an imaginary key. "I like the fundraiser idea though. Nice thought. I bet the kids from the high school would get involved too."

Sammy took a deep breath and tried to word her question in a way that wouldn't make Heidi zip her lips again. She was about to dive into dangerous waters.

"After the game, I hung out at the Sweet Tooth with Liam Nash," she said carefully.

"Ohhh . . . Do tell! Am I detecting a *love* connection?" Heidi's eyelashes flitted like a butterfly. "This could be so fun! I imagine double dates already! Yes! Yes! Yes!" she clapped her hands like an overgrown teenager.

As to not shut down Heidi's enthusiasm she pacified her a bit, saying, "I'm not sure." If she could lead her a little bit down the trail, Heidi would open up like a flower.

"I think you *like-y* our new detective. This is exciting. I'm glad you asked me to come over. Big news!" Heidi playfully punched Sammy on the arm.

Sammy smiled. "Well, he did confide in me about something."

"Oooh, yeah? What's that?" Heidi moved in close like a co-conspirator.

Sammy lowered her voice. "Miles Danbury?"

"Oh, I know. Can you believe it? I'm surprised the detective shared that with you. He must *really* like you." She grinned as she crossed her arms and rested them on her sizable chest.

So . . . her cousin *was* privy to information, just as Sammy thought. "We have to do something." She grasped Heidi by the arm and shook it as if to wake her up from a coma. "Heidi! I know that man. He couldn't hurt a fly." She pointed to his hand-carved birdhouses that hung on a rack. "He feeds nature, he doesn't destroy it. He's humble and gentle and an absolute sweetheart of a man."

Heidi looked over both shoulders before confiding. "They have evidence."

"Like *what*?" Sammy's eyes centered on her cousin, giving her full attention.

"His fingerprints were on the coffee cup. The police took a DNA swab when they brought him in for questioning. Sammy, the DNA is a match. Miles then invoked his Miranda rights and remained silent. How do you explain that?"

Sammy felt taken aback. She studied Heidi for a moment. She knew Tim told her more than she was sharing. Treading carefully would be her best option.

"So? He brought a coffee over and panicked when he saw her on the floor? People don't all respond to trauma in the same way. Heck, it stunned me, finding her like that!"

"Do you know that for sure?" Heidi's eyes narrowed.

"No." Sammy waited silently hoping her cousin would spill more information. It seemed to be working as Heidi interjected more details before Sammy had a chance to speak.

"They have more than just the coffee cup."

"*What*? Come on now." Sammy threw her hands in the air in disgust. "What more could they possibly have?"

Heidi breathed deep. "Tim's going to kill me. Never mind Ingrid, I'm going to be next for sharing confidential information." She put an imaginary dagger to her throat and cut across.

"I won't tell a soul. I promise," Sammy held up scout fingers. "Liam didn't share what they had on the guy. I was just so shocked at the accusation! Miles *Danbury*? Honestly, I sat stunned like a bird that just hit a window. Please, Heidi, tell me so I can let this go. I have a few other suspects in my mind, and if I can just put all this behind me, I'll feel so much better. Just please help me understand . . . Why him?"

"*You* are supposed to stay out of it." Heidi pointed her finger at Sammy.

"Maybe you can help me if you share with me why Miles is their guy? Maybe *then* I can let my S.H.E. mind sleep and let this go. But I can't if you don't tell me," Sammy pressed, adding a hint of guilt for pressure.

Heidi huffed. "It has to do with Miles losing his job a few years back."

This confused Sammy. "What does *that* have to do with

Ingrid? She's was new to Heartsford and, to my knowledge, didn't really know Miles."

Heidi must have noticed a customer enter the store because she swiftly led Sammy by the arm toward the office for complete privacy.

"I swear if you tell anyone you heard this from me I'll have your hide." She warned with a finger. "My relationship with Tim is on the line here." Heidi cautioned with words sharp and eyes stern.

Sammy waited.

"Miles Danbury used to work for Hanson Brothers Construction. Remember them? They travel the entire state of Wisconsin to follow the workload. They were on the job about thirty miles from here in another town, I can't remember the name of it. Doesn't matter. *Anyhow* . . . Just happened to be where Ingrid was living in a new condominium complex." She took a breath before continuing. "So, they were working one morning . . . Pretty early in the day and I guess, as the story goes, they were disturbing Ingrid when building more units across the parking lot. You know how she *loved* to complain. Well, she called OSHA on the job to run an emergency safety inspection on the contractors. They were ill-prepared, and someone had to take the hit. The Hanson brothers certainly weren't going to, so they blamed Miles . . . which cost him a job."

Sammy let the information sink in. "The Heartsford Police think that Miles killed Ingrid as revenge for losing his job?"

Heidi shrugged. "I guess."

"Here's the problem, though. Why would Miles do a hit-and-run on the coach? You have to think the two crimes are related. I don't believe in coincidences." Sammy shuffled papers off the side of the office desk and sat on the corner, resting her chin on a closed fist.

"Not necessarily. Maybe it *is* just a coincidence? Maybe it's two separate unrelated crimes? It's possible."

"Come on, Heidi. Seriously? Do you really believe that?" Sammy leaped from the desk.

Heidi leaned up against the doorjamb, resting the full weight of her body on one arm. "You know what I don't understand?"

"What's that?"

"How you're getting me sucked into this investigation." Heidi shook her head in disgust. "I'm trying to get you to stay out of it, and now my mind is spinning on the subject."

Sammy smiled. "I think it's time for some S.H.E. don't you?" her eyes twinkled and danced at the thought.

Heidi quickly stood at attention, obviously seeing something outside of Sammy's field of vision. "Oh, hey, Carter! Nice to see you this morning! Heard you were on top of your game the other night. Sorry I didn't get a chance to say congratulations at the hospital."

The teen smiled at Heidi and then squeezed past her and entered the office. "Just clocking in. I'm going to work on finishing that box of soap I almost tripped on as I was walking in the store. How does that sound?"

"Perfect. Thanks." Sammy nodded. "Oh, while you're working on that. I want you to help me think of a fundraiser idea we can do for Coach. To help with some of the medical costs. What do you think of a brat-fry outside the storefront during Spring Fling? Would the basketball team cook if I provide the grill and brats?"

"That's a great idea!" The teen lit up. "Yeah, I like that better than a car wash. We do a lot of those for school. I'll brainstorm who can come from the team while I'm working on the display." Carter smiled. "Love it."

"Awesome." Sammy patted him on the back as he turned to leave the office.

After the teen had exited, Heidi pointed two fingers at her eyes and then back at Sammy. "I'm watching you, girl. Don't get in over your head." She slumped her shoulders. "I'm going home to bed. Hope I can sleep now with everything you filled my mind with. Thanks a lot," she added.

"Yeah, good idea. You go home and get some sleep. I'll have to find a way to talk to Tim or maybe Liam Nash. Do you know when they were going to make the arrest?"

"They want to make sure they have all their ducks in a row. They're waiting until tomorrow. They know the news is going to hit the town pretty hard, so they want to strategize the damage control."

"Okay, I'm on it." Sammy moved over to her cousin and gave her a light push out the office door. "Get out of here. Go get some sleep."

Heidi leaned in for a hug, and Sammy stopped her. "Get those hospital germs away from me." She thrust her lightly away, squished her face, and then grinned. She watched as

Heidi reached up to ruffle Carter's hair on her way out the front door.

After checking her email, Sammy strolled over to Carter who had the empty soap box in one hand, heading directly for the storeroom. She trailed behind him until he dropped the box to the floor.

"Do you want to check out the display?" Carter gestured a long arm out the storeroom door.

"Nah, I trust you did an excellent job," Sammy said. "I need to talk to you about something else I think we've both been avoiding."

Carter interjected, placing an open hand up to stop her. "Before you say anything, I don't want to forget. Thanks again for the birthday card," he said sincerely. "The loaded Visa that you stuck inside is going to come in real handy. I've already decided what I'm going to do with the money."

"And what's that?"

"I'm using it for stuff I want for my dorm room. I still don't know which college yet. But either way, I still need to get a bunch of stuff for next year. So, thanks again."

Sammy was going to miss this boy. He sure was the nicest kid. "You are so welcome." She switched gears. "Which is actually what I want to talk about." Sammy stuck her head out of the door to see if they had any customers. One was lazily meandering through the merchandise not needing immediate attention. She turned her attention back to Carter. "I'm thinking of hiring someone else to work here at the store. Ellie comes in from time to time for emergencies, but with you going off to college next year, I think I want to start training someone soon. But I don't want you to feel pushed out by me moving forward. I'm just trying to free you up for whatever you need. Okay?"

The teen looked down at his oversized feet and slumped his shoulders.

"What's wrong?" Sammy was surprised at his reaction. She thought he'd be happy to have the freedom of fewer hours.

Carter slowly lifted his head to meet her eyes. "I don't know." He took a breath to steady himself before speaking. "Giving up working here is like losing Kate all over again."

Suddenly, Sammy understood. "Oh, Carter." She could feel the wave of grief swiftly washing over both of them.

"As stupid as it sounds, sometimes I think I'm going to look up and see her here. And sometimes, even when I don't see her, I *feel* her here." He shook his head and then ran a hand over his growing buzz cut.

Sammy nodded. "I get it."

"I know you do. That's why I don't know what I would have done without you, Sammy." Carter's eyes began to fill, and he sucked it back, refusing to let his emotions overtake him. He moved outside the storeroom, slammed open the back door leading to the parking lot, and stepped outside into the fresh air.

Sammy didn't follow him. She respected the private time she knew he needed.

Chapter Fifteen

After another night of restless slumber, Sammy woke early the next morning to a misty, gray day. She rolled over and groaned. She couldn't remember the last time she'd slept well. She thought the crappy weather seemed appropriate though, as she showered and dressed in a simple black dress for Ingrid's memorial service. She wondered when she had last worn heels as she squeezed her toes into an uncomfortable two-inch pump. Yes, they accentuated her legs, causing her calf muscle to bubble. But, in her opinion, it definitely wasn't worth the pain. She kneeled on both legs and tossed random shoes from the closet floor searching for an alternative but came up empty. She sat back on her heels in frustration. Her only other formal wear consisted of a pair of beige dress slacks and a white blouse, certainly nothing suitable for a funeral. Nothing else fit properly. But she refused to take *all* the blame for an ill-fitting wardrobe. She also blamed Marilyn and the stupid Sweet Tooth. She needed to stay far away from the bakery evidently or else replace her entire closet, for which she really didn't have the funds.

Sammy resigned herself to wearing the heels and stood on two uncooperative feet as she searched her jewelry box for something simple to finish the look. As she was digging deep, her doorbell rang. She pitched out of the heels, moved to the nearby window, and flung it open. After jutting her head outside into the misty fog, she saw Heidi standing on the front concrete slab.

She rounded her hands and then hollered. "Grab the key from under the fake rock."

Heidi looked up to the second-floor window. "I thought you were ready?" She lifted her arms in disgust and then threw them on her hips. "By the way . . . why don't you announce free entrance to your house to the entire neighborhood!"

"Just grab the key, will ya please?" Sammy slammed the damp window shut and returned to the jewelry hunt. In no time at all, she heard the jiggle of the lock and Heidi bounding up the stairs. Bara must have heard too as she heard Heidi calming the dog. "It's just me, pup."

Bara galloped into the bedroom first with a flustered Heidi trailing behind. "We're going to be late. Where's Ellie?"

Sammy waved her off. "She's minding the store for me. Carter's going to the service to support Coach, so I had no one else to cover the store. Believe me, Ellie was more than happy to skip the funeral. She didn't really know Ingrid anyway."

"Nor did I. But here I am." She flung out her famous jazz hands.

"Yes, and you look amazing as always." Sammy eyed Heidi in a dark fitted dress that gave her a figure like she had just stepped off the runway. "Look at me, I feel like a stuffed sausage in this dress. I'm bursting at the seams. Literally!" Sammy sucked in a breath to have more room, but less than a moment later, as she exhaled, she felt restricted yet again.

"Here," Heidi removed the set of pearls that hung from Sammy's hand. "Lose these. You need something with sparkle."

"Heidi. It's a funeral. Seriously? Who cares?"

Her cousin instantly plucked a beaded necklace from the jewelry box and placed it around Sammy's neck and clasped it. "That's better," Heidi said as she adjusted the round pendant to sit correctly on Sammy's neck.

"What about earrings?"

"Here, these hoops should do it." Heidi handed her a pair of large silver earrings.

"Hoops?"

"Yes. I think Liam Nash is going to be there. I want you to look your best." Heidi batted her eyelashes. "I can't wait to see you two together." She puckered her lips as if she was going to kiss the air.

"Really? What makes you think he'd go to Ingrid's funeral?"

"I can't believe you would ask me that. With all your amateur investigative skills," Heidi said in jest. "The police *always* go to the funerals of their victims."

Sammy reached into her closet and tossed her cousin a navy blue baseball hat, which Heidi caught at the last possible second before it hit the wood floor.

"Speaking of amateur investigative skills . . ."

"What are you doing? I can't wear a hat."

"Flip it over."

Heidi turned the hat so the brim was facing her. The

letters S.H.E. embroidered in white stood out and her rosy painted lips curled upward in a smile. "OMG . . . You kept this? After all these years??" She laughed heartily with one hand on her stomach to ease the pain from the hilarity. Heidi tossed the hat back to her cousin to be rehung in the closet.

"What? You don't still have yours? I'm offended." Sammy laughed.

"I can't believe *you* still have it!" Heidi turned on her heel toward the door, "Come on, you goof. We're already late." She gestured her head toward the door.

Sammy clumsily made her way across the bedroom, wincing with each step after placing the heels back on her feet.

Heidi turned as she heard the complaining sounds reverberating from her cousin. "We need to get you out more often. No offense, but you're starting to act like an old lady."

*　*　*

The memorial was being held at an intimate Congregational church on the edge of town. Aside a long manure-covered field, a small white building with a golden cross jutted out unexpectantly. The smell of the field permeated Heidi's car despite the closed windows. Sammy fanned a hand in front of her face to rid the air of the scent.

"I hope it doesn't smell this bad in the church. It's revolting."

Heidi laughed. "The smell doesn't bother me. As a matter of fact, I sort of like it . . . It reminds me of home."

Heidi's parents had raised her on a nearby farm where they cultivated mostly corn and soy beans. Although they did have a few animals, the eggs and meat were mostly for family consumption or the farmers market. Most of the girls' S.H.E. games had taken place on the farm. The nearby chicken coop and barns scattered throughout the property had given them ample places for hide and seek when Ellie and Sammy had come to visit. Sammy had especially loved when her aunt would have the three collect boundless amounts of cherries from the trees for the gobs of cherry pies, cobblers, and jams she would make in the summer months for the state fair. Heidi, in her younger years, had won several ribbons with her mother's prize-winning recipes. Sammy held these memories of a treasured childhood with her sister and cousin close to her heart. Five years ago, Heidi's parents had sold the farm and now spent most of their retirement time living as snowbirds in Arizona, just a few miles from Sammy's parents.

As they pulled into the parking lot, Sammy noticed the tiny lot was nearing capacity and, rather than squeeze in, Heidi decided to retreat and park alongside the road. At that moment, Sammy committed to buying a new pair of shoes for future occasions such as these. The long walk in heels would certainly not be fun. She stepped out of the car, narrowly escaping the large puddles that sat stagnant on the blacktop. The church's parking lot was gravel filled. To cross it, the cousins had to tiptoe to the front entrance without digging their heels in the moist stones. Heidi moved more spryly than Sammy and made it to the door in record time.

"Come on," she waved Sammy forward. "I think I hear the organist playing."

The two entered the hushed space and squeezed into the

last pew. Heidi leaned in and whispered in her ear, "I'm really surprised how many people came today. Is it out of guilt or what?" Heidi elbowed Sammy by accident as the two were practically sitting on each other's laps, the bench seat was so tight.

Sammy agreed. Despite the chatter around Heartsford that people didn't get along with Ingrid, her death had sure drawn a crowd. The room was dim due to the overcast skies darkening the tinted stained glass windows. Coach was sitting in the front row, crutches leaning against the outside pew while the rest of Ingrid's extended family filled the rest of the row. Sammy began eyeing the crowd for her list of suspects. Harold and his wife were in attendance. Sammy found this interesting since Lynn had mentioned he hadn't gotten along with Ingrid and had been vying for her storefront space. What did the Heartsford police think of that little nugget? Why were they there? She did recall Harold's wife attending a few crocheting classes at Community Craft. Maybe his wife had smoothed things over for him and Ingrid due to her exorbitant yarn habit? She would have to try to speak to them after the service, but for now, she set them aside on her suspect list. The assistant coach and his wife were sitting a few rows back behind Coach, along with Carter, Mayor Allen, and Connie. In her opinion, Assistant Coach Dave had a potential motive for the attack on Coach. Big Ten colleges cost big bucks. But then why kill Ingrid? Something didn't fit. She'd have to dig deeper to find a connection to Ingrid.

The minister moved to the pulpit and interrupted her thoughtful exploration by beginning the service. After he welcomed them and spoke of the tragedy that had taken the life of Ingrid Wilson, Sammy's eyes darted around the crowd, observing everyone's reactions. Instead of finding someone squirming in their seat, she noticed Detective Liam Nash standing in the back of the church, arms folded over his chest, his eyes scanning the crowd, conceivably for the same reason she was. Even though the police department *supposedly* had their guy. Their eyes met for a moment before he continued his scrutiny. Sammy's eyes returned to the minister, who was gesturing to the large copper urn and photo of Ingrid standing in front of The Yarn Barn that stood front and center of the church. Sammy was glad it wasn't an open-casket funeral. After what she had witnessed, it might not have been a good thing for people to view Ingrid's body. It was then that she noticed the members of the knitting group huddled together on one extended row. They seemed to be the gloomiest of the mourners. Sammy suspected they had spent a great deal of time in The Yarn Barn seeking merino wool, mohair, and even local alpaca for their hand knit creations. Without The Yarn Barn, they would have to travel many long miles to find supplies for their craft. Sammy wondered if the store would find another owner and somehow remain open for business.

Greta and Gary Dixon were sitting together toward the back of the church. How did they fit with Ingrid? Greta did visit The Yarn Barn for her supplies. She wasn't as much of a knitter as she was a seamstress and quilter. But Gary? Did Gary come only in support of his sister?

Heidi stirred to find a more comfortable position in the tight seat and disrupted Sammy's thoughts again. "Hey, watch it," Sammy whispered to her cousin who rolled her eyes in defeat of claiming a larger portion of the bench.

Sammy searched for Miles Danbury, but he was noticeably absent. She leaned in and whispered in Heidi's ear. "Did they make an arrest yet? I thought today was the day?"

Heidi reached into her purse and pulled out a pen and paper. She scratched "After funeral" on the note and passed it to her like they were back in grade school. She then plucked the paper back and began to doodle like she was uninterested in the whole service. Sketches of goofy faces began to fill the page. Sammy elbowed her and gave her the cut-it-out dagger eyes. Sometimes they still acted like children in each other's company. Heidi began to get the nervous giggles which she was having a tough time containing. This led to Sammy holding her breath to keep from joining in. Funerals brought out the worst in people.

Sammy spent so much of her time scoping out her suspects and acting childish with Heidi that when people stood to exit the church, she couldn't believe the service was already over. She looked up at Heidi who was now standing and adjusting her dress.

"Good to see Coach could make it. When was he discharged?"

"This morning . . . but he's still going to need additional surgery, poor guy." Heidi winced.

The mourners were being led to a community room in the basement of the church for brunch along with the family. Heidi didn't want to stay, but Sammy convinced her.

"Just a few minutes. Please?" The crowd was pushing them

in that direction anyway. Sammy didn't see how they could go against the packed mob unless they had someone large to quite literally part the Red Sea.

"Fine." Heidi turned toward the wide dark carpeted basement stairs and began the descent.

The two maneuvered sideways down the stairs in their heels until reaching the wide opening of the basement space. Long tables covered in ivory linen lined the back wall. The tables were filled to the brim with community baked egg dishes, generational secret recipe casseroles (made only for dedicated events such as these), and lavish fruit displays. Of course, it wouldn't be Wisconsin without a large cheese and sausage platter. Marilyn had not attended the memorial but had donated a full table dedicated to a four-tiered cupcake display holding cupcakes of various flavors from the Sweet Tooth. Sammy's mouth was instantly watering.

Heidi rushed toward a familiar face from the hospital staff, leaving Sammy to stand alone for a moment. As she stood pondering whether to indeed take a plate or skip breakfast after her tight dress predicament, the detective tapped her shoulder, and she spun in his direction.

"Good morning, Detective Nash. Nice to see you joined us for Ingrid's memorial."

His eyes traveled from her two-inch heels to her eyes. "You clean up very well, Ms. Kane."

Sammy sucked in a breath, hoping to even out the creases in the dress, and smiled. She refused to tell him how amazing he looked in his sharp dark suit and light tan shirt which caused his eyes to pop like dark chocolate. Nope. Wouldn't give him that satisfaction. This was a funeral for crying out loud.

Sammy shook her head to refocus. This was not about her attraction to the detective, it was about aiding Miles Danbury. "I need to talk to you privately." She led him by the elbow to a corner of the room which was currently vacant. As soon as they were out of earshot of the rest of the mourners, she said, "I've thought a lot about our conversation the other night, and you took me completely off guard, and I needed time to process. The more I think about it, the more I realize, you can't arrest Miles Danbury."

The detective threw his head back and laughed. "What do you mean I can't? Last time I checked you were not a part of the Heartsford Police Department." He opened his suit jacket to reveal a badge. "Nor did I ask your approval."

"I'm telling you. Miles. Did. Not. Do. It." Sammy said, emphasizing each word.

"See that's your problem." Detective Nash's lips came together in a grim line.

"What's that exactly? What *is* my problem?" Sammy knew what her real problem was. Her problem was that she wanted to know what it would feel like if he kissed her . . . *that* was her problem. She hoped to God she wasn't that transparent, and he couldn't see right through her. Sammy placed her hands squarely on her hips to contain herself.

"You think you know everyone because you live in a small town . . . But you don't. You let your emotions make your decisions." Liam pointed a finger in her direction and then shook it. "That's not the way things work. Good people do horrible things in the heat of a moment. Trust me, I've seen it. Just because you think you know someone, you don't see them as capable of committing a heinous crime. The department's investigation is based on a conclusion drawn from verifiable facts and evidence. Your emotional involvement with Miles, *who is the murderer by the way*, is skewing your approach to this investigation."

"You're telling me that, because I'm an emotional woman, I can't make sound judgments?" Oh boy, that really hit a nerve. He didn't know that after their pizza dinner she felt an emotional connection to *him*. As much as she hated to admit, she liked him. He obviously didn't feel the same.

"That's not what I'm saying. Don't put words in my mouth."

Sammy took a deep breath and a pause before defending her case. "You were at the basketball game. Assistant Coach Dave wants his son to get a full scholarship to a Big Ten college. And you know what? He'll probably be successful at it now, with the way things went down, don't you think? What about that for potential motive? But killing the coach's aunt wasn't enough to keep Coach away from the basketball court. Assistant Dave had no other choice than to run him down too! My real point is, I'm sure there are other suspects, besides Miles Danbury, who have a much stronger motive for murder. Miles just isn't your guy."

"I'm shocked I have to defend myself to you." The detective threw his hands in the air, flustered. "Please, show me the DNA. Show me the evidence that the assistant coach was at The Yarn Barn." He ran his hands through his hair in frustration. "You can't, can you?" His eyes bore into hers. "Miles was there. His fingerprints were found on the coffee cup. What makes you think you're somehow privy to all the details regarding this investigation anyhow? I assure you, as a private citizen, you're not. If I need your help, I most certainly know where to find you."

"Listen. I know you want to get this crime off the books, finished, lock the guy up, throw away the key, and move on. Bring the town some normalcy." Sammy brushed her hands together as if to wipe them clean. "Trust me. We want the same things." She pointed a finger at him. "But you are going about it all *wrong*!" She stomped off as best she could in the two-inch heels in search of Heidi, her blood pressure reaching a boiling point and her heart beating in her chest like a kettle drum.

Sammy looped her arm through her cousin's and released her from a conversation, leading Heidi away from the circle she was speaking in.

"Um . . . a little rude?" Heidi tried to keep up with her cousin's fast pace as they were still linked together arm-in-arm. "Aren't you going to say hi to the mayor? Connie? What about Carter?"

Sammy spun Heidi around to face her. "We're leaving. Right. Bloody. Now."

The two removed their heeled shoes before running up the church basement stairs and heading straight out the front door. The sun had made a break in the clouds, sending blinding streams of light into their vision. The two shielded their eyes from the sun with their hands, the light so elusive of late that they were ill prepared without sunglasses.

As Heidi was placing her shoes back on her feet, she asked, "You mind telling me what's going on?"

"That stupid detective," Sammy muttered under her breath as she slipped into her shoes and began the torturous trudge across the stone-filled lot toward Heidi's car.

"Ahh . . . I see. Lover's quarrel?"

"Drop it."

Heidi must have taken the hint as she remained silent on their drive back to town.

Chapter Sixteen

After the very quiet car ride, Heidi dropped Sammy back home to change clothes and pick up Bara before releasing Ellie from her shift at Community Craft. Sammy didn't feel guilty taking extra time getting back to work; Ellie could use the extra hours. She kicked off the dreaded heels and shed the black dress upon entering. Bara came willingly to greet her, and she dropped to the floor to cuddle with her puppy. He always made her feel better. She padded to the kitchen in her underwear and bra, opened an upper cabinet, and uncapped the Tupperware full of dog treats. When Bara sat back on his hind legs in anticipation, she gave her dog his treat and patted his head. "You are the best part of my day," she said to him. She swore she could hear him say *I know* with his eyes.

Sammy scooped her dress up off the bottom stair and continued climbing. As she was moving up to the second floor to find suitable attire for work, she called her mother from her cell phone. Bara shadowed her into the master bedroom, jumped on the bed, and curled up comfortably. Sammy tried to coax him off, but he resisted and dug his nose under the blanket as if he was hiding. Or purposefully ignoring her.

Sammy, alerted to the sound of a voice, turned her attention to her phone. "Hello, sweetheart, is that you? Are you there?"

"Hi, Mom."

"What's wrong? Is everything okay? You didn't catch Tyler's sickness, did you?"

"No, Mom. I'm not sick. I'm fine." She sat on the edge of the bed and ripped her nylons off, creating a hole in the process. She flung them onto the floor to deal with later. Hopefully much later, as she hated wearing those darn uncomfortable things.

"You don't sound fine," her mother interjected.

Sammy smiled. "You sound like Ellie. Is my voice that obvious?"

"Ellie did mention you've been having a tough time. I was giving you space, dear. And waiting for you to call me and tell me what's going on. Truthfully . . . Ellie has been filling me in with every detail. I was just waiting to hear it from you. I'm interested in your perspective."

"I'm sure she has." Sammy tossed her dress into the dirty clothes basket along the bedroom wall as if she was shooting a basketball into a hoop, then eased off the bed. She then rustled through the wide white-painted antique dresser with glass knobs for her faithful old denim jeans.

"What are you doing? I hear a lot of noise?"

"Sorry, I put you on speaker phone. I just came from

Ingrid Wilson's funeral. I'm getting ready to relieve Ellie at the store." Sammy slithered into her dark-rinse jeans and fastened them before slipping on a white T-shirt and covering it with a pale blue plaid blouse. "So, I don't have much time."

"That's fine, honey. I'm just glad to hear your voice. I know you're a busy girl."

Busy girl. Did her mother know how old she was? Would she always treat her like she was a clueless child? Seriously? Wasn't her mother aware she was old enough to live on her own and run her own business? She guessed she would always be the baby of the family. "I called to ask you something. Do you remember the Dixon kids? Greta and Gary?" Sammy brushed her hair with her fingers to remove the tangles.

"Yes, dear. I remember them. Why do you ask?"

Sammy stood in the middle of the bedroom while she explained. "There was an older woman who came into my store, and I can't place her from town. And then she had coffee with Gary at Liquid Joy. I'm just wondering who she is and why she was with Gary? Does he have a grandmother close to town?"

She heard laughter across the line. "Back to your old ways, Samantha?"

"Mom. Please. Can you just answer the question?"

"Well, you know that Gary and Greta were adopted . . . right?"

"No. I actually didn't know that." Sammy tapped her chin with her finger.

"Oh, well, in answer to your question, to my knowledge, Mrs. Dixon's mother had passed when we were still living there. I think your father would know for sure. I can ask him. Hold on. No. You know what? She *did* die because I remember I was going to go to the funeral, but one of you girls, it may have been Ellie, had just come down with the chicken pox. That's right!" She was suddenly excited that she remembered something.

"So, to your knowledge no grandparents live close by?"

"Yes. Mr. Dixon's mother passed when he was a child. So that's correct," Her mother confirmed.

"And do you know how old Gary and Greta were when they were adopted?"

"They were babies, dear. They're not blood-related if that's what you are asking."

"Just clarifying a few things."

"Oh, Samantha. I do wish you would stay out of it," her mother huffed.

Sammy could almost picture her mother's face cringing. "How am I supposed to stay out of it when the police are arresting Miles Danbury today? I have to find a way to stop them."

"Miles Danbury?" Her mother's shocked voice was as surprised as her own.

"Now do you understand why I'm getting involved?"

"That's awful. He didn't kill her? Did he?"

"No, Mom." Sammy shook her head even though her mother couldn't see her action over the phone.

"Do you know that for sure, honey? If they're going to make an arrest, it must be for a good reason? I mean, he was always very nice to me . . . but . . ."

"I just can't imagine him doing anything violent. I work with the man all the time; murder doesn't seem part of his character. Maybe I just don't want to believe it."

"That must have been awful for you, dear." She could almost picture her mother clutching her chest like she often did when hearing unwelcome news.

Sammy shuddered at the remembrance. "It wasn't good. That I'll admit. It's seared in my memory, to be honest."

"Just be careful, honey. Okay? Do you need us to come home?" The worry was now palpable across the miles.

"No, Mom. I'm fine. Really. Don't you worry about it. Now you understand why I haven't called until now. I didn't want you or Daddy worried or concerned. I'm fine. Please just enjoy sunny Arizona. We don't have much sun here. The weather's been pretty crappy," she reiterated as her eyes darted to the clock on the nightstand beside the bed. "But I really have to get to work. Ellie needs to get home to her family. Love to you and Daddy."

"Love you too, dear."

Sammy clicked off the phone. Gary and Greta were adopted. That added a whole new interesting piece to the puzzle. The woman was too old to be his birth mother? Or was she?

Sammy's stomach began to roll, interrupting her thoughts. It was then she realized she hadn't had anything to eat. She rushed down the stairs and made a mad dash directly into the kitchen. She rustled through the cabinets to prepare a lunch to bring along to the store. With just the bare minimum in the cabinets, she settled on a peanut butter sandwich.

Not her favorite, but it would have to do. She chastised herself for arguing with the detective before snagging something delicious from the brunch. There were so many tasty things she could have chosen to eat. Boy, he made her blood boil. What was it about that guy that pumped her blood pressure? After tossing an apple into a quilted lunch bag along with the sandwich, she slipped on her comfortable sneakers. Her feet were sore from the heels she had worn earlier. The back of one heel was ready to blister, so the Sketchers were a more than welcomed change. She peeked out the window to check the weather before deciding that both she and Bara would make the quick trip to the store by car so Ellie could get home faster.

As she drove, Sammy called Deborah from her Bluetooth to see if she could work the full day of Spring Fling. With Carter in charge of the fundraiser brat-fry for Coach, she could use the extra hands indoors. Plus, it would give Deborah a chance to have a full trial run working at the store. When Deborah agreed, a sense of relief washed over her. This was a wonderful way to ease her in and begin working alongside Carter. She understood Carter's struggle with leaving the store, especially about losing Kate. He wouldn't feel pushed out if they were all there working together. In fact, as busy as it would be that day, Sammy thought about asking Ellie to work too. She wolfed down half the sandwich in the parking lot at Community Craft and then stuffed the uneaten half back inside the bag. After finding a loose water bottle on the front passenger seat, she took a swig of the tepid water and rinsed her teeth of peanut butter.

When she walked into the store, Bara in tow, Ellie was standing at the register ringing up items for a customer.

"Good to see you, Margie," Sammy greeted one of the members of the painting group as she stepped behind the polished wooden counter.

"Hi, Samantha. How are you today? I just found the perfect shelf for my mud room." She gestured to the bag, which Ellie had tied with a green ribbon. "Hello, pup," she said as Bara greeted her as well.

"I'm glad you found something today," Sammy smiled.

"There's always something new in here to find. It's like a treasure hunt. I just love it. I never really shop when I'm here for my painting group. It was fun to take the time today." She removed the sealed bag from the counter. "Must run. You gals have a wonderful day. And you as well puppy." She patted Bara on the head.

"You too," the Kane girls said in unison. And then they laughed.

"Having fun?" Sammy turned her attention to her sister.

"Actually, I am! A morning to spend time with adults? I love it. Although I wouldn't do it full time, I'd miss my Ty-baby too much," Ellie admitted easily. "I'm sure my morning beat yours hands down." She raised her eyebrows. "How was it? Did many people from town show up?"

"I really don't want to relive it, to be honest." Sammy breathed deep and slowly exhaled. She was thinking more of her run-in with Detective Liam Nash than she was poor deceased Ingrid.

"Totally understand." Ellie rested her hand on top of her sisters for comfort and then gave a soft pat before removing it.

"I talked to Mom."

"Oh good. Now she'll stop pumping me for information."

"Filling her in on *every detail*, I heard?" Sammy crossed her arms over her chest and raised one thin eyebrow.

"Give me a break!" Ellie threw her hands in the air in defeat. "If you called her yourself, I wouldn't have to be consistently interrogated!"

Her sister did make a valid point. Sammy backed off. As she stepped toward the office to stash what was leftover from her lunch and remove her jacket, she almost tripped on something poking out from underneath the counter. "What's this pile of stuff?"

"My wish list?" Ellie said timidly. "Can you put those items aside for me so when I have the money I can buy them?"

"Ellie!" Sammy scolded. "Randy isn't going to let you work here if all you do is reinvest in the merchandise!"

"I know." Ellie bit her lower lip. "I can't help myself. There are so many cool, unique finds in this store. We really live in a very creative and talented community. Besides, once the living room is done, I'm thinking of redoing the master bedroom. I just can't help myself," she shrugged her shoulders in defeat.

"Well you better learn, or you won't be able to work here. And I need you." Sammy said before entering the office and dropping her lunch bag on the desk and flinging her coat to the chair.

Ellie trailed behind. "I have to tell you something." She ducked her head inside the office.

"Please don't tell me you can't work here anymore." Sammy held up one hand to stop her. "I can't handle that kind of news today."

"No." Ellie waved her off as if displacing an annoying insect. "That's not what I was going to say." She redirected, "I wanted to tell you that everyone coming in this morning has been buying up Miles's display. Word must be out that he won't be around much longer to woodwork if you catch my drift."

"Wow." Sammy held her hand to her heart. "That really just hit me."

"I know, right?" Ellie's face was crestfallen. "In a way, it's kind of nice. Hopefully, it'll help with his legal costs and stuff. That can really take a person out. Of course, that's an assumption on my part. Thank God I've never had to worry about legal costs. But I can only imagine how costly that can be."

"It seems impossible that he could be capable of this type of heinous crime. I just can't wrap my head around it. I've been working with him ever since I took over the store. You think you know a person, and then they're accused of something like this? People seem so quick to crucify the guy."

"What people?" Ellie stepped over the threshold into the office, took her sister's hand, and gave it a squeeze. "Do you know something you're not telling me?"

"No . . . it's just . . . the police. It seems my account means nothing to them. Apparently, my input is too emotional." Sammy threw her hands up in frustration, releasing Ellie's grip.

"Did you have a run-in with the law? You have to respect their job. It's not an easy one." Ellie patted her sister on the shoulder. "Was it Tim or the new guy?" she asked, pressing closer to find out which officer her sister was referencing.

"I know it's not easy for them. They deal with the stuff none of us wants to even believe people are capable of. The ugliness of humanity." Sammy bit into one of her fingernails. "I may have been a little harsh on the new detective today."

"You didn't."

"I did."

"Samantha Kane!" Ellie scolded.

Sammy looked at her sister in agony. "But he's not listening to me . . ." she whined.

"You sound like Tyler. I was enjoying my adult time until you came back to the store to act like my two-year-old." Suddenly, Ellie became distracted by a noise, and she ducked her head out of the office. "We have company," she said over her shoulder as she retreated behind the cash register.

Sammy could hear a great deal of commotion filling the store, and so she followed her sister to greet the customers. Kendra, the leader of the Beautification of Heartsford volunteers, was standing with a clipboard in one hand and a pen in the other like a director for an orchestra. Ladies from the Master Gardners club gathered behind her.

"We are placing the hanging baskets today and came to use your room to organize a quick meeting. We are going for efficiency this year. We'll see if we can make this happen in one afternoon." Kendra chuckled as she looked down at the clipboard and eyed the list in front of her.

"My favorite time of year!" Sammy exclaimed as she clasped her hands together in delight. "I love when you gals decorate the downtown for Spring Fling. The town comes alive with pops of color! It's like the Wizard of Oz when the movie turns from black and white to color!" Sammy gestured to the craft room. "Go ahead and get settled. I'll be just a moment."

The group moved like a school of fish into the craft room, talking and laughing as they filed in. Kendra closed the door, and you could still hear the chit-chatting reverberating from the glass space.

Ellie turned to her sister. "I guess that's my cue to go." She leaned into Sammy for a quick hug. "Can I put that merchandise in the storeroom on layaway?" she hinted. "Otherwise I'll have to put everything back." Her lip protruded with a pout. "I did come in to work for you today."

"Yeah, but don't tell anyone else I allowed you that service. Consider it a work-here perk." Sammy leaned under the counter to see how many ribbons she needed to cut later to prepare for Spring Fling purchases. She pulled out the basket of ribbon and was pleasantly surprised. Ellie must have added to the pile while she was away. "By the way . . . Any interest in working off the bill? How about during Spring Fling? You know how busy we get in here and Carter will be working the fundraiser brat-fry to help with Coach's medical bills out in front of the store. And I was hoping Randy could bring the grill over in his truck. Hopefully tomorrow?" Sammy's mind was working overtime.

"What a wonderful thing to do for Coach!" Ellie said.

"Sure, I'll talk to Randy. I better work this off, or he'll be ready to cut up my credit cards," she said under her breath.

Ellie heaved the items that she had stockpiled into her arms and headed quickly to the storeroom before she dropped something or Sammy changed her mind. Ellie wasn't successful though. Sammy laughed as her sister dropped a trail of quilted pillows behind her like breadcrumbs.

After watching the antics, Sammy stepped back into the office and removed a basket from a locked drawer. With the basket in hand, she walked with purpose into the craft room and, as she entered, a hushed silence ensued. "I just want to take a quick minute of your time to thank you for the work that you're doing in our community. I had the privilege to walk the river walk the other day, and the perennial flowers from last year's plantings are flourishing beautifully. To those of you who took part, thank you for working hard on last year's project. Please allow us here at Community Craft to honor you by giving each of you a gift card for fifty dollars to use toward any item in the store on behalf of our craftsmen and craftswoman who appreciate all you do. Please let this small token of gratitude show we acknowledge your volunteer spirit and appreciate you."

As soon as she stopped the speech, the room erupted in applause. Sammy placed the gift card basket on the table for each of them to take one. "Now, then. Go beautify our town for our upcoming event!" she shot a fist into the air. And the room cheered.

Kendra moved toward Sammy and shook her hand, and

then leaned in for a quick hug. "Ladies, let's give this fine lady our appreciation for all she does for our community too!"

The ladies stood and clapped. Sammy's face flushed red. She held her hand to her heart and suddenly felt Kate's spirit hovering over them. When her eyes felt they could fill with tears at any minute, she waved to the women and backed out of the room. When Ellie saw on her way out that her sister was overcome with emotion, she instead rushed to her side.

"Are you okay?" Ellie placed her hand on Sammy's shoulder as they walked back toward the cash register.

"Yeah. I'll be fine." Sammy wiped a tear from her cheek and moved toward the other who brought her enormous comfort, Bara.

"Sometimes, I just really wish Kate were still with us. She would know exactly what to do. Especially now, with the town of Heartsford in complete chaos. If only the accident never happened, we'd have Kate here to show us the way.

Chapter Seventeen

Sammy admired the colorful hayrack hanging baskets filled with deep-purple, sunshine-yellow, and blaze-red blossoms on her way to work as she walked with Bara along Main Street the next day. Long strings of variegated ivy spilled over the sides of the pots. The hanging baskets were so full, it looked as if they had already been in place for a full season and not just planted the day before. Kendra must have kept the ladies in line as the volunteers carried out their goal in what must have been one very long day. The large banner strung across Main Street from the Heartsford Credit Union to Bob's Bike Shop said: *Swing into Spring . . . Downtown at Spring Fling*. Painted butterfly flags were firmly attached to each garbage receptacle to magnify their location. Several more barrels, Sammy noted, peppered Main Street.

As she walked, Sammy noticed Lynn out in full workout gear getting her morning exercise in before her start at the bank.

"Mornin'."

Lynn stopped only long enough to give Bara a quick pat

on the head before starting off again at a rapid pace. After a quick turn, walking backward she added, "I'm sure I'll see you tomorrow for Spring Fling! I'll be one of the ladies in the pink sparkle shirts for the parade. I'm dancing in it with the Jazzercise club! Can you believe it?"

"I'll look for your dancing club, Lynn! Keep it up! You're doing great." Sammy shared a quick wave.

Before Lynn spun back in the direction of her workout she whispered, "Doesn't seem like the police have anything on Harold. Just letting you know . . . I saw him at the supermarket the other night. I'm guessing if he was guilty the police would have him in custody."

Sammy gave a thumbs-up and appreciative smile. "At least you don't have to concern yourself over that thought anymore. Right?"

Lynn nodded and then was quickly on her way.

Sammy spotted Douglas in front of Liquid Joy waving his hands above his head to gain her attention. He had stopped writing the deals of the day on his outdoor chalkboard and whistled and waved for her to join him across the street. Sammy looked both ways and then she and Bara crossed Main Street to visit with the coffee shop owner.

"What's up? All set for the big event?" Sammy smiled at Douglas who was looking over his shoulder conspicuously.

"I don't want anyone to hear what I'm about to tell you."

"Oh?" Sammy's interest was instantly peaked.

"Cara said you were wondering who was having coffee with Gary Dixon? I checked the older woman's credit card the last time she was in. Her name is Charlotte Dunn. Does that name mean anything to you?"

"No." Sammy shook her head. "It doesn't. But I appreciate you telling me. She had come into Community Craft, but I don't know her from around town. I was just curious how her necklace ended up in my store? She doesn't seem to have any connection to any of my craft groups. It's a bit perplexing, to be honest."

"Also, Larry's wife was here recently with a friend. I swear I overheard her say she was relieved Ingrid had died!"

"Relieved? What? Why?" Sammy couldn't believe what she'd just heard.

Douglas looked back over his shoulder before continuing, "She told her friend that Ingrid wasn't only going to try and get Larry kicked off the school board, she was also going to press charges against him. Apparently, Larry was drunk one night and groped Ingrid at a bar! She threatened that if he didn't resign from the board she would file a report. It didn't have anything to do with Ingrid wanting to take over his position on the school board at all."

Sammy took the information in. "Wow. I didn't see that coming."

"Well, friend to friend I just had to share these tidbits. You know I'm not much of a gossip, but I know this has been difficult for you with this cloud of suspicion hanging over our town. I don't know if it helps at all, but I've been keeping my ears open." He patted Bara on the head and smiled at her puppy.

"Thanks, and keep it up, will you? We really need to get

to the bottom of this; until we find who killed Ingrid it seems the whole town is on edge." Sammy added sincerely and then jutted a thumb back toward Community Craft. "I better get back to it, I still have lots to do. Have fun with Spring Fling."

"Yeah, you too. Been looking forward to it all winter. It will be nice to see folks out on Main Street again. Instead of rushing to the next destination and not stopping to chat because of the cold."

Douglas turned back to writing on his chalkboard as Sammy and Bara made their way across the street. Her mind swirling in possibilities as she went. But she didn't have much time to think. Not with the preparation of events getting underway.

Kendra passed Lynn, almost bumping her off the sidewalk before calling "excuse me" and rushing toward Sammy. "It's all coming together!" Kendra readjusted a red and white Heartsford ball cap on her head. Her dark hair poked out of both sides as if it had to escape. It was clear by Kendra's appearance she hadn't gotten much sleep before returning to prepare the town for the big day. But what she lacked in appearance she must have gained in caffeine from Liquid Joy because she was practically bopping in the street already. That upcoming caffeine crash was sure to hurt.

Sammy smiled wide. "I've been admiring the decorations. It looks great. You guys did an amazing job, as always."

"I have a few things left to do," Kendra said excitedly as she ticked off the list on each of her fingers. "I have to find the parade line and mark it, so we know where to start. I must check to see if we have enough garbage bags. I need to call on a couple of our volunteers to help with clean up. I really must get everyone's cars off Main Street soon." Kendra waved her hand in one big circle. "This road has to be blocked off for tomorrow." She stopped and sucked in a much-needed breath.

"Well, you don't have to worry about me. No car today, just us." Sammy chuckled as she looked down at Bara sitting obediently by her feet. "Thanks for the reminder. Now that you mention it, I'd better get Randy on the phone and get that grill moved over here before you close the road."

"Yes, do that," Kendra said and then ran off to catch Marilyn by waving a hand frantically to get her attention as the baker had just stepped from her car.

Sammy unlocked Community Craft and flipped the sign to Open while Bara sauntered inside and found his bed by the cash register. Evidently, his walk to work had just been too strenuous. Sammy snorted. He was going to have to get his spring step back in gear. Coming out of hibernation was a slow process. Even for her dog.

Immediately she called Ellie, who didn't answer her phone. She left a message to please convince Randy to bring the grill to the store as soon as humanly possible before the road closed. Or they would have to take the chance and park out back and then haul it through the back door, through the merchandise, which would be problematic. Hopefully, she would catch him before he left for work. Randy was a loan agent for a mortgage company on the other side of town so it wouldn't be too much of an imposition, she hoped.

As Sammy moved into her office, her phone was beeping a return call from Ellie, but she was already on the phone with the local grocer: "Yes, we need a few cases of your best home-made brats. Do you have any of the jalapenos? The cinnamon apple spice is always a hit. What about the green pepper and cheddar ones? I think we'll buy out whatever you have in stock. I should have called ahead of time to order. My apologies." Sammy hoped they would have enough. With everything on her mind, she had dropped the ball on ordering the food for the coach's fundraiser. She would have to double check the refrigerator in the office to see if they had enough condiments from the last fundraiser they'd held. And hope to God the ketchup and mustard weren't expired. "Yes, I'll hold."

While the grocer was checking the inventory of meat, Sammy walked purposefully to the back door to unlock and set the sign to OPEN. When the grocer came back on the line, she said, "Yes, I'll take whatever you've got. Can I get a delivery? I'll need to add buns to that order. And chips. Oh boy, if I forgot anything I'll call you back. If you don't hear from me, that's all I need!"

Why didn't she plan this better? She felt suddenly over-whelmed. She looked at Bara who closed his eyes. *So not fair. I'd certainly love to curl up and sleep right about now! Enjoy yourself, puppy!* If reincarnation existed, she decided she was coming back as a golden retriever.

Sammy was getting ready to work on the next task on her mental to-do list when she heard the jingle and the front door swung open. Greta Dixon stepped into Community Craft and made her way directly into the craft room. Sammy quickly followed her into the room to take the opportunity to pump her for information about her brother and the unidentified older woman who she now knew as Charlotte Dunn.

"Hey there, Greta! Something I can help you with?" Greta jumped with surprise, and her startled reaction was clear. She was on her hands and knees and bumped her head against the side of the craft table as her eyes met Sammy's. "No. I thought I lost something. But I don't think it's here." She rubbed her head, grimacing in pain.

"Do you need an ice pack? You may end up with a doozy of a bump." Sammy offered as her face mirrored Greta's grimace. "I'm pretty sure I have one in the medical kit in my office if you need it."

"No, it's really nothing. Don't worry about it." Greta stood and wiped a couple of random threads off her knees. Reminding Sammy it was time to run the vacuum again.

"Are you missing something? Did something fall from your purse the last time you were in? I think the lost and found box is empty, but I could double check?" Sammy gestured a thumb toward the front counter.

"No. It's not here."

"You know a funny thing happened recently." Sammy chuckled. "An older lady came in and claimed a piece of jewelry from the lost and found, but I don't think she's even taken craft classes before and thought for sure she'd only come into the store a few times." She eyed Greta carefully and was cautious in her tone when she uttered her next thought. "But then I saw her again with your brother at Liquid Joy . . ."

Greta held a stern hand out to stop her. "You're just like everyone else in this town. Anything goes wrong, and it's my brother's fault. I'm so sick of it," she spat. "My brother did not steal the locket."

The locket.

Sammy caught the word. She'd never said it was a necklace, let alone a locket. She'd only said *jewelry*. "Is that what you were looking for? How do you know Charlotte? The woman who lost it? And why did *you* have it?"

"I wish you could just stay out of it!" Greta snapped. "Why don't you mind your own business?" Greta pointed a warning finger in Sammy's face. "Leave me and my family alone."

Sammy opened her mouth to respond, but then quietly closed it again.

Greta stepped past her, over the threshold, and bolted out the front door, leaving Sammy stunned and even more curious about the woman with the locket. She wished she had more time to ponder all of this, but so much work lay ahead before the big event. If she didn't sideline this train of thought now, she wouldn't accomplish anything. Desperately trying to refocus on her mental to-do list, she stood in limbo, unable to move forward, feeling completely dazed by what had just occurred.

Just as she was feeling sorry for herself and completely overwhelmed, Heidi came bounding through the back door wearing black yoga pants and a lime green sweatshirt. Her newly colored hair hung in two low ponytails framing her face. She looked like she'd just stepped out of a Jillian Michaels workout video.

"Guess who has the next three days off with no shift at the hospital?" Heidi said as she displayed her famous jazz hands.

"*You*! I guess," Sammy mirrored her enthusiastic pose.

Heidi slung an arm around her cousin's shoulder. "I know I don't often offer, but I'm here to work. I can help tomorrow too if you want."

In response, Sammy practically jumped into her cousin's arms to tackle her with a hug. "Thank you so much! Your timing is absolutely perfect. I'm ready to rip my hair out!"

Bara jumped from his slumber in all the excitement, and Sammy regarded her dog. "Yeah, he's not much help at all."

Heidi laughed as she leaned down and stroked Bara along his back. "But he's really cute! Isn't he a good doggie?" Her cousin hugged the puppy closer.

"That's really great, Heidi. Right now, I can use all the help I can get." Sammy blew her bangs away from her face with a large puff. "We'll be ready," she told herself, but didn't honestly believe it. "We. Will. Be. Ready." She said it again, hoping the words would stick.

Sammy didn't know why she worried about getting everything done, as Ellie appeared in record time along with her husband to deliver the grill. Tyler rushed through the front door and beelined through the merchandise to tackle his aunt with a squeeze. Ellie trailed behind her son and jerked a thumb back to the front door. "I'm going to go help Randy unload if you can watch Ty-baby for a second?" Ellie started to walk toward the front door and then turned, a sharp finger pointed in her sister's direction. "Do *not* give him candy. He's on his way to preschool," she added firmly before heading out the door.

Heidi laughed and then turned to the little boy. "You're

growing fast, huh?" she ruffled the top of his head, and he looked up at her before glancing at Bara.

"I'm going to help them unload the grill so they can get going." Heidi walked to the front of the store and left Sammy with her nephew.

"Can you make sure they put it on the left side of the window?" Sammy hollered after her.

Heidi turned before stepping out the door. "You bet."

Sammy refocused on her nephew. "Are you going to have fun at school today?" She noticed Tyler's bright round eyes were wide with wonder. He nodded his head vigorously, sending the soft curls on his head bouncing as he said, "Yep. Yep! Lol-ee?" The toddler pulled his aunt's hand toward the office.

"Not today, sweetheart. But if you come tomorrow for Spring Fling, I'll be sure to have one with your name on it." She popped him on the nose with one finger and then pulled him in close in an embrace. "Alright, kiddo."

Sammy noticed Ellie at the front of the store motioning to her son. "Come quickly, Tyler. We're running late."

Sammy took Tyler by the hand and led him toward the front of the store where Ellie took over. "I'll be back after I drop him at preschool. I have a few errands to run but can help later."

"Have I told you lately how much I love you?"

Ellie huffed. "Not often enough," she chuckled as she manipulated her son out the front door.

Sammy followed them into the morning sunshine and waved to Randy, who was already seated behind the wheel in the extended truck. Ellie opened the back door and helped Tyler into the safety seat while Randy rolled his window down.

"Thanks, guys." Sammy tapped Tyler's window as Ellie quickly jumped into the front passenger seat and they sped away. Tyler's little hand fluttered out the window.

Heidi, who was across the street with Douglas, yelled across Main between traffic. "Coffee?"

Sammy held her hand to the side of her mouth and yelled back, "Sure." She gave a thumbs-up before retreating into the store, where she stepped into the window display to rearrange the items yet again. The carved bear mailbox that Miles had crafted had been sold and removed, leaving a hole in the display. She tapped her finger on her lips as she decided what to put in as a replacement piece. After a few minutes contemplating, she finally settled on a white- washed farm side table with a small wooden drawer and a large pottery vase. A trip to Blooming Petal, the flower shop next to the bank, would be next on the agenda. She could send Heidi on that errand. Fresh flowers in the pottery vase would sure finish off the look beautifully for the event.

As she stood in the display rearranging the small pieces of furniture, she gazed out the window and noticed Heidi talking with Tim in front of Liquid Joy. She held two coffee cups, one in each hand. He must have caught her on the way out. Tim kissed her on the cheek and then Heidi headed across the street. With her cousin's hands full, Sammy opened the door wide for Heidi to step back inside.

"How did the display window look from outside? I'm wondering if you wouldn't mind running to Blooming Petal for a spring bouquet?" Sammy pointed to the vase. "What do you think?"

Heidi handed her the coffee from Liquid Joy. "Sure. But I have something to tell you first. You're not going to believe it."

Sammy paused at Heidi's tone of voice. "What's that?"

"The police let Miles Danbury go. For now . . ."

"What?" Sammy couldn't hide her surprise. "Why? I mean, it's great news. But why?" She secretly wondered if her conversation with the detective had anything to do with it.

"Let's just say an alibi came forward." Heidi gave an exaggerated wink.

"What do you mean came forward? Why didn't Miles tell them right away when the police questioned him? *Before* he was arrested?"

"It's a little bit complicated." Heidi's eyes darted around the store to verify if there were any lingering customers.

"No one's in here yet. It's early." Sammy encouraged her to keep talking.

"Annabelle Larson is the alibi."

"What was he doing with Annabelle Larson that he didn't want anyone . . . Ohhh."

Heidi nodded her head. "Apparently, he didn't want to expose the affair. Annabelle's husband isn't very happy I hear." She cringed.

"Ohhh."

"I think at this point, Miles is wondering if prison might have been a better option. Have you ever seen the size of Annabelle's husband? It's strange to think of Miles and Annabelle together? I mean, it certainly goes to show you affairs are not about looks. Annabelle's husband is a much better-looking guy than Miles, don't you think? Anyhow, the police department has enough reasonable doubt to hold the arrest . . . For now."

"Ohhh," was all Sammy could say.

"Your wheels are moving, but your lips are not. Spill it. I thought this news would make you happy. You have been all Team Miles all the way! Haven't You? Why the sudden change?"

"No. I mean, I don't know. Honestly, I'm not sure if it is good news. I have reasonable doubt, but if he can hide an affair from everyone, maybe he is capable of hiding a murder? I think I feel worse about the situation now."

"What do you mean? Now you think he *did* do it? Girl, you really have me totally confused."

"I don't know now. What about the coffee cup that places him at the scene of the crime? It had his fingerprints on it. And it was fresh, because it was still steaming. Obviously, the murder wasn't premeditated. What if Ingrid was going to expose their affair? In my opinion, it makes him look even more guilty." Sammy's wheels were turning fast.

"Wow. I thought you'd be happy to hear this news. Especially after you chewed out the new detective."

"How did you hear about that?" They hadn't spoken about it at Ingrid's memorial, or the ride home for that matter.

"Um, hellooo . . . Who's my boyfriend? He talked to Tim about it. I guess you upset the guy pretty bad. He's still reeling."

Sammy found this mildly interesting. She didn't think her

little outburst would have had any effect on Detective Liam Nash.

"That surprises me," Sammy said and then took a sip of her coffee.

"I don't know what I was thinking sharing this information with you. I bet now you'll be smack-dab back to investigative mode." Heidi threw up one hand in defeat and then drank some of her coffee. "I think I'll go buy those flowers now. I'll take my coffee with me."

"Just tell Fran to add it to my tab. Oh, and can you tell her the flowers at the memorial were absolutely stunning. She did an amazing job, didn't she?" Fran was the owner of Blooming Petal and often came to various craft events and fundraisers held at the store. Sammy wondered if she too felt completely overwhelmed by preparations for Spring Fling.

"Better yet, why don't you go and tell her? I can mind the shop. Go ahead. Then you guys can catch up. I know you don't get the opportunity to leave the store too often. Sometimes I forget that. You go."

"Are you sure?"

Heidi gave her a light one-handed shove in the direction of the door. "Go."

Sammy welcomed the opportunity to stroll along Main Street in the sunshine. Feeling the warmth of the rays hitting her face, she felt encouraged that winter might finally take a hike for good. She sipped her coffee along the way and didn't rush the journey. With all she had to finish to prepare for the event, she realized she needed to calm down. It would all come together in the end, and if she missed something, oh well . . . Life goes on. As she became fully present and was thoroughly enjoying the stroll down Main Street, she caught sight of the unfamiliar, tall, thin-haired man she'd seen that day outside the credit union. Her memory jolted to Coach lying in the road after the incident. This stranger had been there. Watching. Her eyes followed as he quickened his pace and turned down a side street. Something in her gut prompted Sammy to trail him. Her stride quickened to not lose sight of him as he turned onto Second Avenue. He was moving at such a rapid pace that she almost lost him. Sammy's pulse quickened, and her breath caught in her throat. In the distance, she watched as he pulled away from the curb in a familiar dark blue car.

Chapter Eighteen

The mood was electric, and a palpable feeling of jubilation filled the air. Finally, the town of Heartsford was coming out of the winter blahs. So far, the weather looked as if it would cooperate and give them a full cloudless day to celebrate Spring Fling. That alone was something to celebrate. Sammy had risen early in the morning, and she and Bara were at Community Craft by seven AM. The aid from Heidi and Ellie the previous afternoon made Sammy feel well prepared for the day's events. Community Craft was restocked with loads of fresh spring merchandise. Out with the winter scarfs and hats, and in with the handmade purses crafted by the quilting group in vibrant spring colors. New smocks, aprons, and dresses were ready for the spring fashion season, created by talented seamstresses. The store had a renewed appearance, and a new line of fragrant spring and summer soaps filled the air with a lovely fresh scent.

Sammy stepped into the office and narrowly avoided bumping into Carter. He was loading packages of bratwurst that the grocer had delivered into the refrigerator. As he heard

Sammy ruffling through papers on the desk, he spun in her direction.

"You got a minute?"

Sammy stacked the papers and then gave the teen her full attention.

"Coach asked why you left the memorial brunch so fast. He wanted to speak with you. I told him we were holding a fundraiser today on his behalf. He really wanted to thank you for helping him. What happened? You didn't say hi to Mom or Dad either. Did we do something?"

When Sammy noticed the look of disappointment that spread across his face, she reached out and touched his arm with one hand. "Oh, Carter, I'm really sorry about that. Please give my regards to your folks. I had to get back to the store to relieve Ellie, and Heidi was my ride. I have no excuse for not saying hello, and I should have paid my respects to Coach . . . I'm sorry. I was rushing as usual."

"Okay. I just wanted to make sure it wasn't something I said the other day when you mentioned Deborah working here."

"Oh, my goodness, honey! No." She forgot how sensitive Carter could be. She reached for his shoulder, gave it a light squeeze, and then instantly let go. "Carter. You are my little brother. I could never be mad at you and not speak to you, I hope you know that. I was in my own head that day. It had absolutely nothing to do with you or anyone else. I'm really sorry I didn't say hello, and if I offended you. I really need to pay more attention to my behavior." Sammy held a hand to her heart. "You are the last person in the world I'd want to hurt or offend."

"I'm just glad we're okay."

"We're *always* okay. And I'm so glad you came to talk to me. We can talk about anything. Okay? Please don't hold this stuff inside. You can always talk to me anytime."

"Okay," the relief on his face was noticeable.

"I'll make a point of finding Coach today to talk with him and pay my respects properly. And I'll work on getting out of my own head and pay more attention to my behavior. I'm really sorry."

Carter nodded.

She never should have let her altercation with the detective lead her so off course. Why did it? Was she trying to prove her worth to him? That was something she needed to ponder later. For now, they had a full day ahead.

"Do you need help with the brats? I think we should wait until after the parade to start the grill. If we start it before, the parade watchers might veer off course following the delicious scent to buy one! Boy, then we'd be in trouble. I'd have the mayor complaining." She grinned at him. "You know I'm only kidding about your dad." Sammy poked him in the side with one finger.

"Yeah, I know," he chuckled. "Good idea, though. I could totally see that happening. I have some of the team coming to help sell brats too. That should work out great. Some of the guys wanted to know if I could join the basketball team on the back of a pickup float, but I said no. Should I run home and get my uniform?"

"Yes, of course! You should be with the team in the parade! Go . . . go . . . go!"

"But I thought you needed me?"

"I do! After the parade, you can come back to work the grill. Heidi and Ellie are on their way in, and Deborah is going to help for the day too. Seriously, enjoy this moment. It's your senior year! Before you know it, you'll be graduating." Sammy gave him a shove with her shoulder in the direction of the office door.

"Awesome! Thanks. I'll be back!" He waved goodbye and took long strides out the back door.

Sammy reprimanded herself. Seems like she owed everyone an apology. The Allens, Coach, and even Detective Liam Nash. *Kate, I need your help here. Why can't I be less impulsive and more patient and loving like you were? I need you, Kate.* She missed her best friend enormously. Kate loved community events such as Spring Fling. God, how she wished things were different and Kate was still alive to join in the celebration.

In his haste to go home to retrieve his basketball uniform, Carter had left the remaining brats on the side table. Sammy stacked the rest of the packages into the refrigerator.

A nagging feeling of remorse for her impulsive behavior dogged her. But if she continued to carry it around, she would be ignoring the very advice she had just given to Carter. She decided to make an apology and try harder next time. Her eyes darted to the clock as she lifted the phone to call Liam Nash. When he answered he said they must be on the same wavelength because he had planned to stop in after he made it through the coffee line at Liquid Joy.

While Sammy was waiting for the detective to enter the store, she decided to fill helium balloons. Yesterday afternoon, she had rented the machine from the hardware store and decided there was no better time than the present, especially since it was still quiet in the store. Each of the children who came into Community Craft would get a balloon tied to their wrist. Sammy would also bring the balloons outside during the parade to hand out to the children along the sidewalk. She loved the fact that during the entire day she would see these waves of colorful bopping balloons as the children walked throughout the town. It became a yearly tradition. So much so, the children this year would be seeking her out for a balloon. She hoped she had enough. By the time the detective arrived, Sammy had already filled well over twenty balloons. They hovered along the ceiling, their multicolored ribbon strings hanging in wait.

As she noticed Liam move closer, she turned, secretly took a filled yellow balloon in her hand, and sucked in a little helium. In a high pitched squeaky voice, she said, "I'm very sorry for my behavior the other day. I'm an ass."

The detective laughed heartily. "How can I take your apology seriously when you say it like that?"

"You want some?" Sammy tried giving him the untied balloon. She wanted to hear his helium voice, but he refused and put a hand up to stop her.

"No, thanks. I'm on duty." He jutted his hip to show his ever-important badge.

Sammy was going to have to change her attitude. She presumed he was here so they could clear the air. Not so she could judge his ego.

He handed her a coffee. "Truce?"

"Truce." She nodded and took the coffee from his hand. "You didn't have to do that."

"Do what?"

"Bring me coffee. But thanks." She lifted the yellow smiley cup in cheers.

"The barista said she knows what you like so you can blame her if she didn't get the order right." He grinned.

It was then Sammy noticed he had one tooth on the bottom that jutted out in front of the rest. *Why was she looking for his imperfections?* This had to stop. Immediately. She was having trouble finding any flaws in his good-looking appearance. He wasn't gorgeous, but there was just something about him that drew her in with a magnetic pull. She wished she could put her finger on it. At that very moment though, it eluded her.

"Please let me apologize again, without helium, for my behavior at Ingrid's memorial. In no way did I mean to get in the way or undermine your investigation. I'm sorry."

"Apology accepted." Liam nodded.

"Now that I've made that clear, there is something I need to tell you." Sammy took a deep breath before continuing. "Yesterday, on my way to the floral shop, I saw a man who was on the scene when the coach was hit. I'd never seen him in town before. Something prompted me. Call it woman's intuition maybe? Anyhow, I followed him down Second Avenue. Do you want me to help a sketch artist do a markup?"

"I accept your apology. However, now I'm beginning to think that was just a ploy to get my attention and badger me further." He placed his coffee on top of the wooden countertop and then placed his hands firmly on his hips. "Do you watch a lot of television? Prime time crime dramas perhaps? Although I appreciate your enthusiasm, just because someone was standing and watching an event unfold, that's not exactly recognized as a crime. He could have said the same of you," he said pointing directly at her.

Badger me? I thought he liked being around me? Obviously, my radar is way off if this is how he sees me. "Look, I'm not trying to pester you. But the guy drove a dark blue car, and I think it might be the one I saw screech out of the parking lot the day Ingrid was murdered."

"You think? Or you know?"

"I think."

"What's the make and model of the car?"

"I don't know."

"License plate?"

"No, I was too far away. That's why I can't confirm the make and model."

"If you're trying to help, you're not. Although I appreciate your concern for the community, you're going to have to do better than a dark blue car and an unfamiliar guy."

"Sketch?"

"No. There isn't nearly enough information for a sketch. If you don't know the make and model of the car, we could be sketching the wrong person. Have you ever been wrongfully convicted of a crime? Or even accused? It doesn't end well. Besides, if he was the one who hit the coach with his car, how could he be standing there watching the event unfold?"

"He wasn't," Sammy corrected. "He showed up at the end.

And besides, I know perps like to watch after they commit a crime. It's a creepy thing they do. I know. I watch *Dateline*."

The detective forced a smile. "Listen. Why don't you concentrate on your Spring Thing? And leave the investigation to the police department. I think we've got it covered." Liam tapped his chest with his finger, letting her know he was in charge.

"It's Spring *Fling*," Sammy corrected *again*.

Why couldn't he get that right? Maybe it really wasn't a date the other night. She doubted if they could even still be friends at this point. She thought apologizing would make her feel better. Instead, she felt as if she was a child who just gotten her hand slapped for stealing a cookie from the cookie jar.

"I guess I'd better get back to it then." Sammy placed an unfulfilled balloon onto the helium machine and gave it a go. The noise was an obvious *I'm done with you* signal, but the detective didn't pick up her cue. He just stood there watching her. Sammy continued to fill balloons and tried to ignore his presence, but his stare was unnerving. After filling three more balloons and attaching the ribbons, she said, "Either tie a ribbon or you can fill these." She shook an unfilled balloon in her fingers and dropped it on the counter. "Or, you certainly can go. I don't want to keep you from your important *detective* work." She emphasized the word in a sarcastic tone and added air quotes to drive the point home.

"I don't know what to make of you, Samantha Kane." He stared at her. It was obvious he was waiting for her to stop what she was doing to give him her full attention, but the stubborn child in her refused.

"Ditto."

He leaned an elbow on the counter casually. "It certainly seems that I irritate you. I guess I'm trying to figure out . . . why?"

Sammy opened her mouth to respond and then changed her mind and closed it. She wanted to say, *Because I'm wildly attracted to you. And it scares the piss out of me because just when I think you're interested in me too you either want cake or you find me mildly annoying.*

Detective Liam Nash tapped the counter twice with an open palm. "Have a good day. Enjoy your spring *thing*."

Did he just say that to irritate her? She thought so. "Spring. F-L-I-N-G. With an F." She spelled out each letter for the last time. And then shooed him from her counter.

As she watched the detective saunter out the back of her shop, she grumbled to herself and returned to the task at hand.

Heidi and Tim stepped into the back door of Community Craft directly into the path of Liam Nash's exit. As Heidi rushed past the detective to greet Sammy, Tim stepped backward half inside and half outside the door to talk to the other investigator.

"Good morning! Looks like we're going to have the perfect day for Spring Fling!" Heidi gushed.

Sammy smiled. "We certainly lucked out this year, that's for sure. I think it will warm up nicely too."

Heidi eyed her cousin carefully as she approached. "You seem a little flushed. Maybe I should go grab my blood pressure cuff." She moved closer to Sammy to more thoroughly look her over. "You okay?"

Sammy breathed deep and then let it out slowly. "Yes. I'm fine." Then she huffed audibly as she blew the hair away from her face.

"This doesn't have anything to do with *that guy*." Heidi pointed toward the back door where Tim stood halfway, blocking the visual of the detective as they stood and talked.

"You know how my mom says if you can't say something good, don't say anything at all." Sammy zipped her lips with her fingers, mirroring what Heidi always did when she wanted to shut something down.

"Oh, no. What happened this time? Whatever it is, I think your blood pressure is climbing to an unsafe level. Liam Nash sure knows how to get underneath your skin."

"Or, it could be from sucking too much helium." Sammy brushed the comment off as she tied a ribbon and let a green balloon bop up to the ceiling.

"Am I wrong to assume you had another argument with our new detective?" Heidi flung a hand to one hip.

"Do you really want to hear how I'm butting into the investigation? That I'm still playing S.H.E.? I'm assuming you don't want to hear that." Sammy placed her hand over her ears like she was putting on ear muffs to make a point.

"You're right. Let's talk about something else." Heidi looked at the ceiling and noticed the large collection of balloons, the ribbons swaying lightly. "I think you can probably stop soon. Don't you think that's plenty?"

Sammy looked up and smiled when she saw how many she had filled. "I guess you're right."

Tim approached and made a path with his hands through

the hanging ribbons, sending the balloons bouncing along the ceiling and knocking into the hanging umbrellas.

"Really? Did you have to go that way? Did you have to make my balloons go flying everywhere?" Sammy asked sarcastically.

"I heard you were a little prickly today," Tim retorted.

Heidi shook her boyfriend's arm. "Don't go there," she warned.

Tim leaned his full weight on the wooden counter. "I gotta get home and suit up for work. For you gals, this is all fun and games." He waved his hands up to the scattered balloons. "For me, it's extra duty."

Sammy rolled her eyes. "I think it will be okay, big guy. No big crimes today. It's too festive a day. The whole town looks forward to Spring Fling!" Sammy said aloud, then added under her breath, "at least those who know it's not just a *thing*."

"Oh, to live in your world." Tim pushed himself off the counter and scooped Heidi off her feet easily and kissed her goodbye.

"Gross. You two can swap your germy spit somewhere else," Sammy said.

Tim winked at Sammy. "You're just jealous." He turned and moseyed toward the back door. He turned one last time to gain Heidi's attention. "Save a dance for me on the street later," he said, wiggling his hips and jutting his backside along the way. A very sad attempt at dancing out the door. Very sad indeed.

"What a weirdo." Sammy hollered after him.

Heidi waved goodbye to her dancing boyfriend and then gathered the hanging ribbons to relocate the balloons that he had displaced into one large grouping. "You know he might be on to something. Maybe Tim is right."

"About what?"

"Maybe you are jealous? Not of Tim and I per se . . . But of the idea of a relationship. You think?"

Sammy huffed, "I'm actually enjoying the single life. And besides, I have Bara." Her dog lifted his head to acknowledge his name and then set it back between his two paws, covering his eyes.

"I disagree. I think you're starting to like Detective Nash, but you've been throwing your guard up. I think you're afraid of building any close relationships for fear of losing someone else. Ever since Brian broke up with you and since we lost Kate, you've been so closed off. Just because you lost them doesn't mean you'll lose everyone you get close to.

"Well thank you, Sigmund Freud."

Heidi's words stung. But Sammy knew her cousin was only speaking from her heart. And, if she was being honest with herself, her cousin might just be exactly right.

Chapter Nineteen

The Spring Fling parade was minutes from crowding Main Street with floats, animals, and participants. Since it seemed the entire town was out on the sidewalk waiting, Sammy decided to leave the cash register unattended. Customers would know where to find her. Heidi had already left her side and was outdoors handing balloons to swarms of children. Sammy scooped up another handful to replenish Heidi's stock on her way out the front door. As she stepped outside, she felt the anticipation of the people sitting in lawn chairs along the parade route. Moms and dads, along with grandparents, relatives, and friends, sat patiently, while anxious children waited to fill empty candy bags. Heidi reached for more balloons in haste. "Where's Deborah? I thought you said she was going to help out today?"

"She is. I told her to stop in after the parade. Her kids are marching in it. I didn't want her to miss taking pictures of her own kids. I figured it would be no big deal since you, Ellie, and Carter would be here. I didn't know I would lose Carter to the parade . . . And I haven't heard from Ellie yet today. Have you?"

"No. But you better go back inside and grab some more of these. I guess I shouldn't have stopped you filling balloons. I seriously underestimated how many we'd need. I think every kid in Heartsford is after me!" A look of panic crept across Heidi's face as swarms of children began pushing and shoving in her direction.

Sammy laughed aloud at her cousin's predicament and then retreated inside the door. "I'll be right back!"

She hurried toward the hanging ribbons and just as she was going to grasp them in her hand, something grabbed ahold of her wrist and stopped her. Her eyes lifted and took in a person taller than her own five-foot height, who was wearing what appeared to be a super hero costume. Or was he dressed as a villain? His face was completely covered in dark green paint, and a bizarre purple hat with points jutting out on all sides hid any hair.

Sammy laughed aloud. "Is that you, Carter? Did the guys on the basketball team put you up to this for the parade? I didn't know Heartsford had a new mascot? You look absolutely hilarious!"

But the person didn't answer. He only grasped her wrist tighter—so tightly she wondered if it would bruise. Pain seared through her arm as he reached for her other arm. It was then Sammy realized this was no joke. Her heart hammered in her chest.

"Let me go!" She seethed as she ineffectively wriggled to remove her wrist from his clutch.

The man squeezed tighter and yanked her in close. A slight whiff of stale booze caught her nostrils and made Sammy's empty stomach turn. Still holding her wrist, he untied a string with one hand and took a hit of helium from a balloon before bringing his wet warm breath to her ear and warning her with a squeaky voice. "Back off or you'll end up like Ingrid." A cruel, hideous, high-pitched giggle followed.

Sammy tried hard to place the voice but couldn't distinguish who it might be. The helium disguise had worked in his favor. She strained to shake her hand loose and free her body which only angered the man more. He shoved her to the ground, releasing her wrists for a moment. Sammy scrambled backward on all fours, like a crab. Before she could make her escape, he grasped her leg and slid her body across the hard floor. He was now on top of her, holding her down. Panic started to set in. Sammy could hear herself taking small quick breaths, panting like a dog. Where was Bara? She knew while the parade was taking place, the store would be empty. Nobody would be in Community Craft to rescue her. His hands reached for her throat, which made Sammy gasp. Abruptly she heard Heidi's voice calling from a distance.

"Hurry up! I can't keep up with these kids coming after me looking for balloons. What's taking you so long?" The costumed man panicked. He jumped off Sammy, jerked quickly to his feet, and vanished past Heidi, out the front door. Sammy sat upright, clutched her bruised wrist to her chest and tried to catch her breath as Heidi rushed to her side.

"Oh, my God. Are you okay? Did you fall? What are you doing on the floor?" Heidi's eyes darted around the area, trying to make sense of what had happened. But not putting two and two together.

Sammy's words spurted out fast as Heidi helped her to her feet. "Did you see that guy?"

"You mean that flash of green that near knocked me off my feet?"

"Yes! Stop him!" Sammy scrambled to her feet and tripped forward. After collecting herself, she sprinted out the front door with Heidi in pursuit. The parade had begun, and swarms of people crowded the sidewalk. Sammy tried to get a visual, but the costumed man had disappeared. Gone. She squeezed her body between bystanders, cheering as the Heartsford Marching Band went by, playing a familiar fight song they often played at the high school football games. She pushed forward on the crowded sidewalk, dodging lawn chairs and bystanders. Kids sprinted in front of her to catch the candy tossed from a float following the marching band, slowing her pace. A quick sighting of the weird purple pointed hat caught her attention, sending her adrenaline into overdrive. She maneuvered through the crowd, careful not to lose him, but her short height worked to her disadvantage as her head bobbed between people and she tried to follow him with her eyes. But it was no use. The costumed man had dissolved into the crowd. He was gone.

Sammy threw up her hands in defeat. "I lost him." She bent over and rested her hands on her knees to catch her breath.

"Lost who? Why are we following that green blob anyway? You mind telling me what's going on?" Heidi squeezed next to her and spun her cousin to squarely face her.

A look of panic crossed Sammy's face. "I have to find Bara. Where's my dog?"

Sammy turned from her cousin and maneuvered back through the crowd and pushed her way back to Community Craft. She sprinted back inside the store, calling her dog in a panic, "Bara! Bara!"

When she noticed the office door closed, she ran toward it and threw it open wide. Bara stood on the other side of the door with his tongue hanging out of his mouth. Sammy sighed with relief as she fell to one knee and grasped him tightly. The dog wiggled until she released him to lick her cheek with his tongue. "Oh, Bara! You're here! Thank goodness."

"Okay. You mind telling me what the heck is going on?"

"That guy attacked me. The green blob!" Sammy pulled herself to her feet and rubbed her wrist. Now that the initial shock of the attack was over, she tried to soothe the throbbing pain in her right arm.

Heidi reached for her cousin's arm to take a closer look. "He *attacked* you?"

"Yeah."

"Whaaat?"

Sammy was afraid to tell her cousin what the costumed man had said, for fear she would again tell her to back off the investigation again. But the words tumbled out anyway. "He threatened me and told me to stay out of it or I'd end up like Ingrid."

"Nooo." Heidi's hand flew to her mouth and covered it. After the surprise had worn off, she said, "Do you know who it was? Any idea at all?"

"Nope. I haven't a clue." Sammy stroked Bara's back to help relax her breathing and calm her nerves. "He used helium to disguise his voice. But he did smell of alcohol. Maybe it was Larry? Who else do you know that drinks this early in the day?"

"Well, whoever it was, we have to find this guy and bring him to his knees." Heidi's nostrils flared, and her eyes were blazing. Sammy couldn't remember ever seeing her cousin this angry. "This is downright ridiculous," Heidi added.

"I thought you'd be mad at me and tell me to stop with my nonsense sleuthing?" Sammy rubbed her hip, which now was beginning to throb. She must have hit it hard when he dropped her to the floor. Her body would ache after the adrenaline wore off, of that she was certain.

Heidi put her arm around Sammy's shoulder and gave a light squeeze. "No, cuz. I think it's time we all put on our S.H.E. hats. This is getting out of hand. I'm tired of looking over our shoulders wondering who's involved in Ingrid's murder and who's making threats at you. And if the police can't do it, then we will."

"Really?" Sammy smiled weakly at her cousin.

"Really. No one does this to my family and gets away with it." Heidi reached for the ice pack in the freezer and handed it to Sammy after wrapping it in a nearby paper towel. "Here, you're starting to swell."

It made Sammy chuckle as the nurse in her cousin couldn't help but do her job by fixing the hurt.

"What about Ellie? Do you think she's willing to help? We need all three of us to bring back our childhood club. Three brains are better than one. If I remember correctly, we were a pretty good team."

"When she finds out what happened to you, I'm sure she'll join in. This. Has. Got. To. Stop. And I guess us three chicks are the ones who are going to have to make that happen." Heidi rubbed her jaw hard.

"What about Tim? Won't he be upset if you start meddling along with me?"

"Never mind him." Heidi waved a hand, brushing the thought aside. "He doesn't have to know everything I'm doing all the time." She winked. "Besides, it doesn't look like they're getting any closer to solving this thing. We've got to stop this guy. I definitely think it's a man who committed the crime. Don't you?"

Ellie rushed into the office. "There you are! I've been wondering where you two were hiding! You're missing the parade. What is so important that it can't wait? We've waited all winter for this! *You guys*! It's time for Spring Fling!"

"You're right! I for one am not going to miss another minute." Sammy dropped the ice pack to the desk. "Let's get out of this office." She leashed Bara to bring her dog outside with them for protection and comfort.

Ellie's eyes darted from Sammy to the ice pack to Heidi. "Is somebody going to tell me what's going on here?"

"Later." Heidi gave Ellie a light shove toward the door. "Trust me, we'll talk about it later. But for now, let's go." She gave Ellie an encouraging smile. "You're right . . . we waited a long winter for this. Everything else can wait for now."

The three stepped out onto the mobbed sidewalk. Sammy made a conscious effort to not let the attack ruin her day. She'd waited too long to come out of hibernation. For now, she would set the episode aside and feel the warmth of the sun on her face and the jubilation of the crowd. She would report the incident later, but right now she was going to enjoy the long-awaited parade. The Jazzercise club was now dancing their way down the parade route. Sammy searched Lynn in the lineup and waved, as her friend in black biker shorts and a bright pink sequin top danced her way past them. Lynn's smile widened as she caught Sammy's eye.

The Heartsford basketball team was next in line, in full red and white uniform. Sammy was so glad she hadn't missed this part of the parade. The coach sat in a lawn chair on the back of the red pickup truck, surrounded by a few team members, driven by Assistant Coach Dave. Other players walked alongside the truck with the cheerleaders, shaking their red and white pompoms. Carter sprinted toward the three of them and gave them all a high five and then handed candy to the nearby kids. His face was flushed with excitement. The sight of him happy and enjoying the day made Sammy's heart swell.

Next the horses, along with their owners, decorated in full parade dress, strolled in a unified pattern. Strings of live flowers adorned the horses' necks, and the riders wore large matching straw hats ornamented with large silk daisies. Two of the riders tossed candy from their satchels as they rode by. Heidi leaned in close to Sammy and pointed out the two alpacas that followed along with the knitting group. The ladies of the group were tossing pairs of hand knit alpaca socks, and folks in the crowd were fighting to catch a pair. Annabelle Larson didn't miss a beat, despite the new gossip of her affair with Miles Danbury. She waved to Sammy and tossed a pair of socks to someone standing nearby. In the commotion, Sammy turned her head to see who had won the prized possession, and it was Harold. Until that moment, Sammy hadn't realized he was standing within a few feet of them. Harold handed the pair of socks to his wife who seemed riddled with excitement over the catch. Sammy handed Bara's leash over to Ellie and then moved over to the couple and took the opportunity to make a connection.

"Lucky you. It looks like you won the prize," Sammy said to the older man. His wiry gray hair jutted out from his head in a random way, completely absent of style.

Harold smiled and folded his arms across his chest. "I guess I am pretty lucky. You'd sure think so, the way the crowd is fighting to catch a pair, eh?"

"Hey, I heard you were going to open a new hardware store in town? I sure could use an update on the tools in my kit here at the store. I never have the right screwdriver and whatnot." Sammy tried to sound nonchalant but, even to her own ears, she sounded ridiculously sneaky.

The older man's gray brows came together in a frown. "Now where would you hear the likes of that? I'm too old to be opening a new store." His attention left her, and his eyes returned to the parade as if to say *We're done here.*

Sammy could see she wasn't going to get very far, but she pushed anyway. "I'm glad you caught the socks. The knitting girls are sure going to miss Ingrid's shop. They won't be able to make those anymore without The Yarn Barn selling that local alpaca fiber. And your wife won't get to crochet either, not without driving for miles to pick up a natural skein."

She thought she saw the old man flinch before she moved back to stand with her cousin and sister, both of whom looked at Sammy with their mouths agape.

Heidi leaned into Sammy and spoke privately in her ear. "Did you find anything out?"

"No, but at least I know he wasn't wearing green paint on his face today. Lynn mentioned the police already questioned him. If he was a viable suspect, I guess he wouldn't be standing here watching the parade with us anyway. You know me, though . . . I still had to poke the dragon."

The crowd cheered as Mayor Allen and Connie drove slowly down the parade route in a canary yellow Mustang convertible. Connie was tossing full-sized candy bars, which made the kids go absolutely ballistic. Sammy noticed Randy snag one for Tyler nearby. He held it over his head like a trophy, making the two cousins laugh and Ellie scowl. Sammy's sister was convinced giving Tyler candy made him hyperactive, which it did. However, her reaction always made people want to give it to Tyler even more. Heidi leaned into Sammy as she pointed inconspicuously across the street. "Isn't that Larry's wife?"

Sammy turned her head in the direction of her cousin's finger. "Yeah. So?"

"I can't help but notice her husband isn't with her."

Heidi was right. Upstanding Larry. President of the school board. Was noticeably absent.

Chapter Twenty

The aroma of cooked sausage wafted through the entrance of Community Craft as Sammy opened the door and stepped outside in search of Carter, who was manning the grill in front of the store. Ellie was teaching Deborah how to run the cash register, and Heidi was aiding customers on the display floor. With the store coverage in decent shape, Sammy had a moment to check on the progress with the fundraiser. A few other basketball team members along with Carter had the lid of the grill open and were rolling the sausages to keep the meat from charring as it cooked.

"Looks like you guys are experts!" Sammy leaned over the grill and breathed in the scent. Her stomach rumbled in agreement. "I'm going to have to try one."

Carter handed her a bun, while a basketball team member plucked a sausage from the grill with a set of tongs and centered it on the bread. Sammy blew on the food and then took a bite without adding any condiments. With a full mouth, she said, "Fantastic job, guys!" She showed approval with a double thumbs-up.

"Actually, looks like we may sell out." Carter pointed to the white Styrofoam cooler.

Sammy flipped the lid with her empty hand and noticed only a few packages left. "I can't get any more. We literally bought them out."

Carter shrugged. "That's okay. We're doing really well." He reached down and picked up a coffee can and flipped the plastic lid in front of her to reveal the contents stuffed with cash. "People are so generous in our town. Knowing this money is going to help the coach, they aren't paying our cost. Instead, they've been handing us tens and twenties. Isn't that nice?"

"That's great news. I think I'll take the can inside for you and empty the cash into the office drawer, so it's safe and then bring it back." Just as Sammy was about to retreat inside, she noticed the coach slowly approaching on crutches. She set the can of cash in a safe place, inconspicuously back behind the grill.

The coach gradually made his way closer to his team. Carter plucked a nearby empty lawn chair and set it down for him to take a seat. "Here, Coach."

The coach nodded his head at Carter. "Thanks, Allen." Then he turned his attention to Sammy. "I can't thank you enough, Samantha, for what you're doing for me." The coach placed his crutches against the lawn chair as he carefully maneuvered into the seat. He then shifted the crutches to rest in his lap.

"We are so sorry for your pain. But, honestly, your appreciation should be directed to Carter. He's done all the hard work and preparation for today." Sammy lightly touched her adopted brother on the arm.

Carter's face flushed with embarrassment. "Not true." He shook his head in disagreement. "It's all Sammy." The teen retreated closer to the grill and returned to helping the rest of the basketball team as they served customers and flipped meat on the grill, leaving Sammy and Coach a bit of private time.

Sammy took a seat on the sidewalk next to the coach's lawn chair and rested her arms on her legs. "I'm so sorry for the loss of your aunt. I didn't properly pay my respects to you at her funeral. I had to get back here." She raised her hand and gestured backward toward Community Craft. She wouldn't dare mention that the new detective in town had her hot under the collar during the memorial. And it was driving her crazy not to know every detail of the investigation.

"It's okay, Samantha. I appreciate that you came. And everything else you've done for me. It's incredible. Really. The generosity . . . it's overwhelming."

Carter interrupted them by handing the coach a bratwurst. "This is the jalapeno and cheese one. It's good. Do you want ketchup?"

"I'll take a little sauerkraut. If you don't mind?" He held up the bun and Carter returned with the condiment and spread it on top with a plastic spoon. Coach took a bite and nodded as he chewed. "Wow. I can see why you've drawn a crowd over here. You kids are not only great on the basketball court, but you can also cook a mean brat." He took another large bite, and Carter grinned before returning to the grill.

As the coach sat and relished his bratwurst, Sammy said,

"If there is anything else we can do for you here at Community Craft, please don't hesitate to ask. You have been incredibly instrumental in Carter's life. I'm sure you already know that. He's been through so much in his young life. You've done a great deal to lift his spirits. He talks very highly of you."

The coach devoured the last of his bratwurst and brushed her compliment aside along with the crumbs. "He's a great kid. One of the best I've had over the years." The coach breathed deep and took a slight pause before saying, "You know what, Samantha? There is something you can help me with. I hate to even ask with all you've done for me already. But I know how connected you are in this community, and maybe you can suggest someone who would be willing to help me with this type of thing . . ."

"What is it that you need?" Sammy redirected her attention from watching the boys cook to focusing squarely at the coach.

"I'm going to have surgery in two days. And I need some help with Ingrid's things. I didn't have a close relationship with my aunt, and truly I'm not sure why her family is leaving me in charge of her stuff. Especially in my condition. Not very empathetic I'm afraid." He looked down at his leg for a moment and then returned his eyes to Sammy. "My aunt was estranged from most of our relatives at the time of her death. She was pretty good at alienating people, God rest her soul. I think it had something to do with the way the old family money was distributed—with her at the top of the heap. It ticked off a lot of family members. I don't know. I try not to involve myself in all that family drama. It's too exhausting."

He adjusted his arm in the chair and winced. "I honestly don't know what made her move back here to Heartsford to set up shop. It baffles me to this day. She mentioned she had to right a wrong but never really explained what that meant. It certainly wasn't with me; I didn't have any beef with her. And now she's gone so . . . Guess I'll never know."

Sammy wasn't sure how to respond. She didn't want to agree with him and risk offending, but she certainly didn't disagree that his aunt was hard to get along with. Instead, she suggested, "Don't worry about finding someone, I'll do it. My sister and cousin can help too. You tell me specifically what you're looking to do and we'll handle it for you."

"Really? Are you sure?" The coach reached for a crutch that was about to fall from its perch.

"Absolutely. No problem. What exactly can I do for you?"

"I can't believe I'm asking you for more help. You don't know how much I appreciate the fundraiser right now. I owe the funeral home money. I was the one who had to front the deposit for her memorial and cremation. The rest of the family refused to help. Can you imagine? Yet they had no problem traveling out here to attend," he grunted. "Sometimes true family are the ones in the community who you live and work with. The ones who really care, such as yourself. My blood relatives leave a lot to be desired."

"Didn't your aunt have a Will? I imagine, with The Yarn Barn, there's money in her bank account . . . If only from her shop? I know firsthand the knitting group sure loved to spend their money over there."

"I haven't found a will yet. But right now, that's not

important. The family would probably contest it anyway; they're always fighting over money. Why would they stop now? But they have no interest in her personal belongings. My extended family is only interested in the money. The funeral home is being lenient, they know there's money in her estate and the bills will eventually get paid. I was hoping you would know who in the community might need some clothes? She has a closet filled to the brim with designer clothing. Even though she was an older woman, she sure had nice taste. I'd like you to donate her clothes, purses, shoes, and any other personal items. You know what? Any of her crafty stuff can go too. Also, if you know anyone who would need furniture? If you can handle those items, I'll figure out what's going to happen with her house and her retail store after my operation. The sale of her house should cover the funeral home bills too. Although, I have no idea how much she had in equity. Until I find the will, I might have to petition the court to sell it. For now, one thing at a time."

"I'm so sorry you're going through all of this in your condition. How are you feeling?" Sammy wasn't sure how deep she could dig into the investigation without hurting his feelings. She would have to tread lightly.

"I'm not excited about Doc wanting to put a pin in my leg," he chuckled. "I'm not looking forward to that at all." The coach grimaced.

"I can't even imagine." Sammy's face mirrored his expression. Just as she was going to prod deeper, he lifted himself from the lawn chair.

"I'm due for a pain pill. Thanks again, Samantha. For

everything." He leaned forward on the crutches and dug a key out of his khaki pants pocket and handed it to her. "This is my only key to my aunt's house, don't lose it, okay? Otherwise, we're screwed."

"No problem. I'll keep it safe."

"I was going to stop in there today to try and work on organizing some of her things, but I'm just not feeling up to it. Her place is over on Old Lannon Road; number thirty-five. Carter knows where it is if you want to bring him too. He can show you." He waved a hand toward the teen. "Whatever you can do is a tremendous help to me. Thanks again."

"Sure, Coach. Can I ask you one last thing before you go?"

"What's that?" His face twisted in pain as he put his full weight on the crutches.

Sammy took a breath and went for it. "Any idea who hit you?"

"Nope. I have to believe it was an accident. For me to think otherwise sends my mind to places I refuse to go." His eyes moved from hers to his injured leg.

Sammy nodded. She silently wondered if the coach thought Assistant Dave could be capable of such an act. "Don't worry about a thing. I'll take care of as much of Ingrid's personal belongings as I can. And thank you for your willingness to help someone else in our community who may be in need, with her clothing and other items. That's very kind and generous of you." She pushed the key deep into her jeans pocket.

The coach laid his hand on Sammy's shoulder and gave it a light pat before moving closer to the grill. "Can one of you guys give me a ride home? I can pick up my car later."

The basketball team's back-up point guard, Danny, rushed to the coach's aid. "No problem, Coach. I'm parked the closest. My car is over on First Street. Think you can you make it?"

The coach nodded, and Sammy watched as the two slowly made their way through the crowd of people who now filled the empty parade route. She dug her fingers on the outside of her jeans pocket, feeling the key. Her heart beat fast in her chest. Wait until the S.H.E. girls found out what she had in her pocket. They were about to embark on an investigation of mass proportions. Sammy could hardly wait to tell them. She just might be holding the key to everything.

Chapter
Twenty-One

The temperature Sunday afternoon remained unseasonably warm and humid. The spring day had started out scorching, feeling as if they had skipped a season, and headed directly into late summer. Typical Wisconsin. The dense wet air caused a trickle of sweat to drip from the side of Sammy's face. She wiped it with her bare forearm and looked up to the sky. No doubt a severe thunderstorm warning would come later. With the weather instability and a cold front that was approaching from the northwest, Heartsford would be getting its first tornado warnings of the season too. The conditions were certainly ripe for it. Sammy just hoped they would have enough time to make a dent in the clean out process before the severe storms hit.

After loading flattened boxes from Community Craft into the back of her car, and making sure Deborah had everything she needed to man the store, Sammy closed the trunk and headed to the home of Ingrid Wilson. The three S.H.E.s had decided to meet at the deceased woman's former home. With three cars, they might have enough space to pack up, box up, and remove the personal items in one visit.

Sammy drove out of the back parking lot behind the store and made a left turn on Sumner Street. She noted people walking their pets along the river walk, kids playing frisbee in the park, and the swing sets at full capacity. As Sammy's car passed the tennis courts, she observed they too were also occupied. The community was out in full force, attempting to log a few hours outdoors before the harsh weather would prevent it. She was glad they had lucked out this year and had perfect weather for Spring Fling. The day had turned out to be another success for the books. Community Craft had made many sales, even bringing them out of the red and back into the black; eliciting a huge sigh of relief from Sammy. Deborah seemed to be working out too. Hopefully, Sammy would be able to hire her on a permanent basis. Especially when Carter headed off to college next year.

The only nagging feeling that hung in the humid air was when she reflected on the physical attack and verbal warning. Who had done that? The disturbing costume was now seared in her memory. The questions had kept her up most of the night. She replayed over and over the features of the attacker in her mind, and yet, she continued to come up empty. Only because it had happened so fast and taken her completely off guard. Sammy yawned in response to her lack of sleep. A quick look in the rearview mirror revealed what she already knew she would see—dark circles. This time, she didn't need the detective to point them out. A honk from the car behind her warned her the light had turned green. She flicked on her blinker and headed right onto Old Lannon Road. The winding road snaked through thick pines, yellow forsythia, and blooming lilac. The residential homes were set back far into the impenetrable woods, making it difficult to view the properties from the road. Sammy searched the house markers at the end of each driveway to find number thirty-five. It was then Sammy noticed Heidi's car ahead and followed her onto a blacktop driveway deep into the woods. The smell of fresh pine permeated the car as she rolled the car window to rid the buzz of a trapped fly, and then a quiet calm ensued. As the two exited their cars, they both admired the Lannon stone Tudor in front of them. A dark-pink explosion of crabapple in full bloom flanked each side of the stately home.

"Lovely place," Heidi said.

"It's very peaceful in here. I love the trees." Sammy popped her trunk and heard a car pull in behind them. Ellie gave a honk, disturbing the quiet aura of the property. Sammy hauled a few collapsed boxes along with a roll of packing tape out of the trunk and handed a couple to Heidi who tucked them under one arm.

As Ellie stepped from the car, she looked up at the grand Tudor and nodded her approval. "Nice. Who knew Ingrid had such good taste?"

"That's what we said." Sammy agreed.

Ellie gazed the front yard of the property and added, "I wonder what year this was constructed? The house looks like it's built of pure Lannon stone. Did you guys know that rock comes from underneath the Great Lakes? It's where

Milwaukee gets the name '*Cream City.*' Most think it's from dairy farms, but it's actually named after this here brick." She pointed to the stone stacked on the face of the house. "Back in the day, settlers lifted this right off the ground and built thick stone walls with it. Today, it's just built with veneer, but this certainly looks original."

"Listen to you, little miss history buff." Heidi chuckled as she moved toward her cousin and gave her a quick half hug with one arm. She then handed Ellie a few of the boxes.

"No, I give all the credit to my sweet Randy. He learns neat stuff working at the mortgage company. Plus, he's part of the Heartsford Historical Society. Occasionally, these little tidbits leak out of him."

Sammy yawned, catching her sister's attention.

"Am I boring you?"

"No, I'm exhausted. Didn't get much sleep last night."

Ellie moved closer to Sammy and then noticed the red and bluish ring around her arm. "What happened to you?"

Heidi pipped up. "She was *warned* yesterday at the store. Remember when you came in scolding us for missing the parade?" She gestured to Sammy's arm. "That's why. See exhibit A."

"Warned? By whom?" Ellie's attention bounced between the two and finally landed on Sammy.

"Don't freak out. It's actually why you're here."

"I thought I was here to help with Ingrid's things?" Ellie's tone was that of irritated confusion.

"You are," Heidi encouraged. "But we need to do a bit of investigating too."

"Wait a minute. Let me get this straight. Sammy's now got *you* into this too?" Ellie pointed a finger toward her cousin. "I thought you were encouraging her to back off the S.H.E.? What changed your mind?" Ellie crossed her arms over her chest in a defensive stance.

Heidi reached over and lifted Sammy's wrist for show. "That changed my mind. This is getting out of hand, and we need to get to the bottom of it. Hopefully, with our three intelligent heads together, we can figure this thing out! The police are understaffed and overworked. At least that's what Tim always complains about. We've got three smart female brains here. Time to put them to good use."

Sammy dug deep into her pocket and revealed the key to the house. "Okay, girls, no time like the present."

They walked up the wide stacked brick path to the arched front door. Sammy set the key in the lock and gave a push on the inside wooden door. The stale smell of unoccupied living space greeted them.

"It smells like Grandma's attic." Heidi fanned her hand in front of her face.

"It's definitely stuffy," Ellie agreed. "Maybe we should leave the front screen door open and see if we can get some air in here."

The two dropped the flat compressed boxes to the floor to deal with later.

"Not much air outside I'm afraid, as humid as it is. But you can certainly try." Sammy removed her multi-colored Sketchers before stepping on the thin planks of the off-set hardwood floor. The arched windows inside the living room and dark crown molding gave the room a feeling of rich sophistication.

"This is a really cute house," Heidi said. "I wonder how much it'll sell for?" She flicked on a crystal light that sent an interesting pattern across the ceiling. "Hey guys, check this out."

The three stood looking at the design of light across the ceiling.

"Can we check out the rest of the house first before we start packing up her stuff?" Heidi's eyes left the ceiling, and her head craned to examine every nook and cranny of the space.

"Doesn't it kind of creep you guys out, being in a dead woman's house?" Ellie's eyes darted back to the entryway as if she was looking for the ghost of Ingrid Wilson, who might slap her hand if she touched anything.

Sammy crept behind Ellie and yelled "Boo!" Making her sister jump two feet off the ground. And causing Heidi to double over in laughter.

"Not funny," Ellie slapped her sister on the arm with the back of her hand. "Sooo *not* funny," she warned with a pointed finger.

The three stepped through the rounded arched door leading into the formal living room. Hand-knit afghans in varying hues of gray lay across the living room sofa. The formal mauve sofa looked as if it had never been touched. As if it was there merely to display the hand-knit blankets and not to provide a seat.

"This is eerie," Ellie said as she regarded a half finished

knitting project, the blue aluminum needles still attached to the yarn, waiting to be picked up at a moment's notice.

"I think this house is really charming." Heidi disregarded Ellie's comment as she moved to find the kitchen, which in her eyes was equally impressive.

The two sisters heard her gasp, "Ohhh . . . I love it!"

The kitchen was a timeless remodel with updated stainless steel appliances. The cream-colored cabinets were adorned with simple round black knobs, and an oversized, light quartz-topped island with an added sink took center stage as shiny copper pots hung above it, waiting to prepare the perfect meal.

"I'm going to put in an offer on this place. I think I've found my dream house." Heidi tapped her index finger to her lips. "Can't you see me cooking up some fine cuisine in here? Yes indeedy. I can almost smell the shrimp scampi."

"Seriously? You would consider purchasing a dead woman's house?" Ellie said flabbergasted.

"She didn't die in *here*," Heidi said. "In my line of work, I guess I'm used to disease and death. This place is like a peaceful sanctuary." She leaned over the copper farm sink to peer out the kitchen window, revealing a wooded backyard that blocked neighbors on all sides. "It's perfect. Just look at the privacy."

"Alright, you two. Let's get on with the tour. We have too much work to do and not a lot of time to do it." Sammy encouraged them to retreat to the bottom of the stately oak staircase that led to the second floor. The three made their way up the steps, like a train of cars. Up to the oriental runner at the top of the staircase, down the elongated hallway, to where Sammy assumed the master bedroom would be located. She stepped inside a deep room with a stone fireplace that held a dark, ornate canopy bed. The bed was antique, from the French Renaissance period, covered with creamy white linens and perfectly made as if it were ready to hold the queen. The wallpaper behind it was an off-white muted floral design. An attached en suite bathroom held a clawfoot tub.

"Wow. That woman certainly lived large. Look at the size of that bed!" Ellie said. "Did she sleep in it alone? Holy cow, the thing is huge! My whole family could sleep in it, and there would still be room."

"Yeah, I don't think Coach has any idea what her stuff is worth. I don't know if he really wants to donate this furniture or sell it? It's got to be worth a fortune. I think we'll just stick to her personal items for now. I'm going to have to talk to him about possibly hosting an estate sale for the big furniture." Sammy walked over to the large window and flipped the white center shade flanked by lavish creamy drapes which allowed overcast natural light to fill the room. Sammy then moved over to the closet door and shoved it open. "He was right about one thing. Her closet is absolutely stuffed to capacity. My word, she has a lot of stuff. We might be here a while, girls."

"What about her will? I find it hard to believe she didn't have one prepared with all these expensive items." Heidi leaned into the closet and pulled out a posh designer handbag. "Isn't this a Gucci? I don't think it's a knock-off."

"According to Coach, he has yet to find her will. Apparently, she wasn't very close to her relatives, there were some contentions over the family money. Maybe she just decided not to care about where her personal belongings went after leaving the planet? I'm hoping we find one though. Maybe, it'll give us a clue as to why she was murdered." Sammy began to remove padded silk hangers draped with dresses from the closet and place them on the expansive bed. "Can one of you guys go grab a few of those boxes from downstairs?"

"I'm on it." Heidi tossed the empty handbag onto the bed and then rushed out the bedroom door.

"You don't find this creepy at all? Going through Ingrid's things?" Ellie's face twisted as she fingered the clothing on the bed. "It's so morbid."

"Hey, I guess it's a reminder, we can't take it with us. We come into the world naked and leave everything behind when we die."

"Gee, that's a lovely thought." Ellie dropped the clothing from her fingers and made an unpleasant face.

"Besides, we're here to find clues. Stop thinking morbid and start thinking *why*. Why was Ingrid Wilson murdered? That's what we've been given the opportunity to hopefully discover while we're here. Yes, we're here to help Coach, we're also here to snoop. Please. Feel free to go snoop. You should have brought your S.H.E. hat!"

Ellie rolled her eyes. "Fine. I'm going to check out the other bedrooms to see what *big secrets* the old woman could have been hiding," she said as she stepped out of the master bedroom.

"That's the spirit!" Sammy grinned as she watched her sister take a right turn down the hall.

As Sammy placed clothing atop the expansive bed, a book of matches fell from a jacket pocket. She opened it, revealing it was almost full. Only two matches were missing from the matchbook. After closing the cover, she turned the matchbook over to read Knucklehead Bar and Eatery, a known biker bar that was located a few towns over from Heartsford. To Sammy's knowledge, Ingrid didn't smoke or *ride a motorcycle*. Sammy decided to think on that some more. She tucked the matchbook in the back pocket of her jeans. The idea of the older woman at a biker bar only brought more perplexing questions to her mind.

Heidi entered the room and immediately began taping up the bottom of a box. As soon as she had a box ready for clothing, she turned to Sammy.

"Should I empty these drawers over here?" Heidi moved toward a long, darkly stained chest of ornate drawers that matched the bedroom set.

Sammy set more dresses on top of the bed and turned to her cousin. "Sure. I think I'll just throw a garbage bag over these closet items instead of boxing them. We can bring them to the donation center on the hangers without wrinkling them. I have a box of trash bags in the backseat of my car. I'll run and get them in a bit."

Heidi hauled a box closer to the dresser drawers and began to fill it with miscellaneous clothing items.

Darkness began to fall through the window, evidence of the brewing storm, leaving little in the way of natural light. Sammy flicked on a nearby bedside lamp that barely helped illuminate the room. "Thanks for helping on your day off from the hospital. I really do appreciate it." Sammy said over her shoulder. She was halfway in the closet, digging out more dresses.

"It's no problem." Heidi must have noticed Ellie enter as she tossed a set of rolled socks into the box. "What else did you find? Anything interesting to share?"

Sammy popped her head out of the closet to better hear what her sister had to reveal.

"I'm going to wait to do more snooping with you two. One of the bedrooms was a craft room filled with knitting stuff. Ingrid must have kept half The Yarn Barn here. You wouldn't believe the skeins of yarn in that room, every color imaginable! The other bedroom had a creepy doll collection. It gave me the willies. Those doll eyes following me around the room? I couldn't handle it. Very disturbing."

Heidi laughed aloud and snorted through her nose, and Sammy smiled as she rolled her eyes. "When did you get to be such a scaredy cat?"

"I don't know. Doesn't being in the private space of a murder victim give you guys the creeps? I hope you don't buy this place, Heidi. I'll never come visit. Ingrid's ghost is probably going to haunt the next occupant."

Just as the words came out of Ellie's mouth, a loud crack of thunder shook the house and made the three gasp aloud. Ellie covered her mouth with her hands. A flash of lighting briefly filled the dim room, and the bedside lamp flickered.

"Oh, dear God. We're going to lose power, aren't we?" Ellie said as her eyes darted around the room. She held a hand to her heart. "I told you Ingrid's ghost would haunt us, I just didn't think it would be this soon."

"Cut it out, Ellie. We're fine." Heidi waved a hand to encourage her to come closer. "Hold the box while I stuff the rest of this junk inside." Just as Ellie was approaching the dresser, another crack of thunder blasted through, shaking the walls, gaining their attention once again.

"That storm is really close. I should have counted between thunder claps. I can't believe I'm going to say this, but I think we might have to hit the basement. What do you guys think?" Ellie rubbed her hands together nervously.

Sammy tossed the items that were in her hand on the bed and then stopped to listen. Just then, the sound of hail pounding the roof of the Lannon stone house made her take serious note of her sister's idea. Sammy moved to the window and peeked outside, "Ellie, you might be right. I think we're in for a tornado. Let's go to the basement until the storm passes."

"Fine," Heidi shrugged, as she put the last of the items from the first drawer into the box. "Let's go. In any event, I'll be able to check out the basement of my new house," she teased.

The three trudged back out of the master bedroom, down the stairs to the main level. The screen door was swinging wildly as the front door had been left ajar to air the house. Sammy rushed to close it. "Marble-sized hail. Hopefully, we won't get damage to the cars. The sky is looking awfully pea-green too. We'd better hurry."

"Where do you think the basement door is?" Ellie shadowed Heidi, saying close behind her heels like a puppy, as the crystal light that had patterned the ceiling suddenly went out.

"We just lost power," Sammy said.

Ellie made the sign of the cross across her chest. "Oh, dear God. We're going to have to go to a strange basement in the dark. I think I'm living my worst nightmare."

"Don't be so dramatic," Sammy said as the three scurried to the kitchen. Secretly, she wasn't exactly looking forward to heading below ground either. But somebody had to keep a positive attitude.

"Well, if only you had let us finish the tour before we started packing, we might know where to go." Heidi opened a door in the kitchen and then quickly shut it. "Nope. That's the pantry."

Sammy noticed a handmade mason jar candle like the ones sold at Community Craft and plucked it from a decorative shelf in the kitchen.

Ellie looked at her incredulously, "Seriously? What are you going to light that with?"

Sammy smiled. "Ingrid's matches."

Heidi piped up, "I missed something."

"I found a book of matches in a coat pocket upstairs. She must have known we'd need it today."

Ellie shivered, but not because of the air being cold. "Now *that's* creepy. Tell me you don't think that's creepy? What's wrong with you two?"

"Honestly, Ellie. I put it in my pocket to try to figure it out. What would Ingrid be doing at a biker bar in another town?"

"Good question. Why Ingrid would be at the Knuckle-head place?"

"How did you know it was the Knucklehead? I didn't say that."

"Seriously? What other biker bars are there within a sixty-mile radius?"

"Good point."

Heidi opened another door and interrupted the two sisters, "Found it. Maybe you should light that candle first and lead the way."

Sammy dug for the matches in her back pocket, set the candle on the counter, opened the matchbook, plucked one and struck it, causing the match to whoosh with flame. She touched it to the candlewick and then shook out the match, leaving a trail of smoke in her wake. Sammy led the three slowly down the open wooden staircase deep into the basement. Meanwhile, the sounds of howling wind and thunder shook the sides of the house. Sammy hoped for all their sakes the storm wasn't going to linger.

The musty smell of the home's underground greeted them as Sammy opened the doorway at the bottom of the basement stairs.

"Someone needs to get a dehumidifier down here," Ellie said. "How do you like this part of the house? Not so nice now, huh?" Ellie said to Heidi in a sarcastic tone.

The three huddled close to the candle and exchanged glances as they stayed close to the bottom of the steps.

"Sorry guys. I'm sure this isn't how you thought you'd spend your Sunday." Sammy handed the candle to Heidi to hold as she moved closer to a metal shelf along the side wall filled with Rubbermaid bins.

"You don't make the weather. Not your fault." Heidi said.

"Please bring the light over here." Sammy lifted one of the Rubbermaid containers off the shelf and opened it. Christmas ornaments in bubble wrap filled the container. She closed the lid and flipped open another. "Come on, girls. While we're here, we might as well explore. It's S.H.E. time!" Sammy encouraged them to help dig into the Rubbermaid containers.

Heidi set the candle on the top shelf, and with the meager light, the three began to sift through the large containers.

Ellie popped a box open and said, "This might be something. Looks like a lifetime of memorabilia. You want to check it out?"

Heidi plucked the candle from the shelf to bring the light closer, and the three peered into the box.

"Yeah, let's go through this." Sammy found an aged multi-colored knit afghan, probably knit with Ingrid's own two hands. Sammy plucked it from the bottom shelf and spread it out on the basement floor for them to sit. Heidi placed the candle in the middle as they removed stacks of albums and papers, placing them in their laps to examine more closely.

Ellie shared a photo with the other two. "This must be Ingrid's high school graduation picture. Wow, does she look different? I'm assuming it's her. I found it here . . . in a year-book. I'll flip through the yearbook and see if I can find her name."

"I've got a newspaper article over here. I think you guys

are going to want to see this." Heidi handed it to Sammy who read aloud:

Dodge County Community Mourns Young Mother

A tragic accident in Dodge County took the life of a young single mother Friday night. Twenty-one-year-old Olivia Dunn, who gave birth to a son less than a month ago, was pronounced dead at Memorial Hospital, shortly after arrival. The single vehicle crash on Highway MM likely was the result of avoiding contact with a deer. Rain may also have been a factor in the accident. According to County Police Officer Jay Rant, the crash is still under investigation. The driver, Ingrid Wilson, remains hospitalized in stable condition at this time. No other persons were involved in this crash.

Sammy's eyes left the article and stared at the two, wide-eyed. "Now we have a name. Olivia Dunn. *And* we know she had a son. Wow. If my memory serves me right, the woman from the store who claimed the lost necklace said her sister's name was Olivia! The name of the girl pictured inside the locket. It's got to be her! Charlotte Dunn's sister! Charlotte *was* telling the truth in my store."

"What's the date of the article?" Ellie asked. "Then you'll know how old her son would be today."

"October second, nineteen-eighty-two. That means her son would be thirty-five-years-old."

"I have another idea, flip to see if there's an Olivia Dunn in the yearbook. Maybe Ingrid and Olivia were classmates." Heidi said.

Ellie flipped the book alphabetically until she reached the graduation photo of Dunn, Olivia. She held the book closer to the candle for Sammy to get a clear view. "They weren't only classmates, they were best friends. Look what Olivia wrote across her picture." Ellie pointed to the photo: **Olivia + Ingrid = best friends for life.**

"Wow. The shape of Olivia's eyes are very similar to his. See how they squint like half-moons when she smiles? I can see the resemblance . . . it's certainly possible they come from the same gene pool." Sammy wasn't interested in the fact that Olivia and Ingrid were best friends, she was more interested in the image of the girl who looked oddly familiar.

"Who? What are you talking about?" Heidi asked.

Sammy's turned her gaze to the S.H.E. team. "Gary. I'm talking about Gary Dixon. The resemblance when they smile is uncanny. Olivia's son had to be adopted after she died. Mom told me Gary and Greta were adopted as infants, but they aren't blood-related. Which I never knew—even though he dated Kate in high school. And I think you two know his adopted sister, Greta. So . . . Gary has been having coffee with his Aunt Charlotte. Gary's biological mother has to be Olivia Dunn, the passenger who died in the car accident . . . And Ingrid Wilson was the driver who killed her."

Chapter
Twenty-Two

The wind continued to quake the Lannon stone house, but the three S.H.E.s were so engrossed in learning more about the late Ingrid Wilson, the gale hardly piqued their interest.

"If Gary Dixon is indeed Olivia's son, then that means the woman who lost the locket at Community Craft would be his biological Aunt Charlotte, because she said it was her sister in the photo. I wonder why she didn't adopt Gary herself? And why would Greta be looking for the locket? According to Mom, Greta and Gary weren't biologically brother and sister." Sammy dropped the newspaper article to the side and continued to dig through the Rubbermaid for a new pile to sift through.

"The more we uncover, the more questions we seem to have." Heidi stood and placed an enormous stack of yearbooks and photo albums on the floor and returned to cross her legs before continuing her search through the items.

"I'd like to know more about the warning you received during the parade. How come you can't identify the person?"

Ellie reached over to place a hand on her sister's, her brows coming together in deep concern.

"I can't stop thinking about it. It's why I'm so tired today." Sammy squeezed her sister's hand and then ran her fingers through her hair and stifled another yawn. "He was in costume, and he disguised his voice with helium."

"Oh."

"Ellie, did you see anyone else wearing costumes for Spring Fling? Sammy and I missed some of the parade. If we can backtrack and figure out who was wearing those types of costumes, maybe we could ask that group who it was?"

"Good point, Heidi. There were a few clowns I think. Was he dressed as a clown?" Ellie turned to face her sister for an answer.

"No." Sammy shook her head. "His face was painted with green paint, and he wore a weird pointy purple hat. And he smelled of booze."

"Maybe it *was* Larry? Everyone knows he's the town drunk!" Ellie gasped.

"Douglas recently shared with me that Ingrid was going to press charges against Larry because he groped her at a bar. Maybe he killed her to shut her up."

"Or maybe it was someone who had a drink to make you *think* it was Larry, because as you just mentioned, the whole town knows he drinks no matter the time of day." Heidi wiped dust from an album before opening it to view the photos inside.

"One thing I know for sure, it wasn't Harold. I saw him up close at the parade. And Assistant Coach Dave was driving the basketball team in the parade, so that eliminates those two . . ."

"And Larry's was noticeably missing from his wife's side with the other spectators," Heidi added.

Ellie looked at the two, "I don't suppose either of you has a cell phone down here? I wonder if Tyler and Randy are doing okay in the storm?"

"Mine's in the car," Heidi said.

"Mine too."

"Well, I left mine on Ingrid's bed. Some great investigators we all make! None of us has a phone? You two leave your cell phones in the car?" Ellie rose from her sitting position on the floor and stretched her arms to the ceiling. "I'm sorry to say it, but with one candle, we're all going to have to go up. I can't go up a dark basement staircase without a light. I have to call and check on my guys. I'm sure they're worried about us too."

"Yeah, I should check in on Deborah and make sure everything is okay at the store too. Let's just pack this stuff back up for now then. We can do this later." Sammy rose and crammed the yearbooks back into the Rubbermaid. She decided to bring the newspaper article along and stash it in her car.

The three slowly made their way up the basement stairs. After exiting the basement, they made their way, huddled close like a herd of three sheep, back toward the front of the house.

When they made it to the front hallway, to Ellie's delight, the crystal light was back to patterning the ceiling in design. "Hey, we got power!"

"That's good news. We must be at the tail end, or the storm passed. I don't hear thunder." Heidi rushed toward the front door and swung it open. Wet leaves stuck to the side of the screen door. "Oh boy, looks like it was a doozy." Heidi turned toward the other two and then back to the front door. "I'm going to make a run for it."

Sammy reached for her wrist before she took off running. "Text Deborah and see if she's okay. Please let her know I'll call her from the car on my drive back. And can you toss this on my front seat?" She handed Heidi the newspaper article before Heidi dashed from the front steps toward her car.

Ellie flicked the light at the bottom of the stairs, "I'm going up to grab my phone and call Randy." She left Sammy alone in the hallway, pondering her next move.

The emptiness swept over her as she realized there was no one she would call to connect with after the storm. No one waiting by a phone to hear from her, to know she was safe. If she were to admit it, it was times such as these that she wished she was in a relationship. Although she should be grateful. The two most important people in her life that *would* have concern for her safety were right there with her at Ingrid's house. But they had relationships and families of their own. The loneliness and longing struck Sammy without warning at the bottom of Ingrid's stairs. She was probably just sensing Ingrid's miserable soul. She pushed the feelings down, deep into places that were impenetrable. Her thoughts turned to Bara. She wondered if her dog had weathered the storm okay. Hopefully, she wouldn't arrive back home to find her house completely ransacked from the stress the thunder and lightning had put on him. For now, she slowly followed Ellie back to the master bedroom. What she found was her sister moving around the room, holding a cell phone up in the air, trying to get a signal.

"I only have one bar," Ellie's frustrated tone bounced off the walls toward Sammy.

"You could try the landline." Sammy reached for the phone next to the bed but when she lifted the receiver, she realized the phone was out due to the storm. "Sorry, it's out. Hey, go ahead on home if you want. I think I'm going to have to talk to Coach and revisit his idea of giving all this stuff away. There's far too much here that might bring him some needed cash. If you want to help me bag up these dresses on the bed, we can officially be done for the day."

"Are you sure? We barely made a dent?" Ellie stuck her phone in her back pocket, accepting the fact that she wouldn't get enough service to make the call.

"Yeah." Sammy dug into the front of her jeans pocket and pulled out her car keys and tossed them to her sister. "Go try Heidi's phone outside and give her the trash bags in my backseat to bring up, will you? Take the keys too; I forgot to give them to Heidi, but I think my car was unlocked anyway."

"Sure," Ellie caught the keys with one hand. "I'll send her up."

Sammy moved back inside the closet to remove the last of the dresses. The closet was still overflowing with dress pants and jackets. The woman must have kept darn near everything she'd ever bought. She could honestly say Ingrid almost bordered on hoarding. Most of the clothes had gone in, and out, of style at least twice, Sammy noted, as she placed a deep red blazer on the bed. That one might be making a comeback. She wanted to see if there was anything that could help further in the investigation before she finished packing up. But the more Deborah and Bara crossed her mind, the greater the sense of urgency to leave Ingrid's house and check on her store and furry best friend called to her heart. Ingrid's stuff would have to wait.

But as she was getting ready to close the door, something in the closet caught her attention. After removing all the dresses, the back of the closet wall revealed a hidden door in the drywall that she had originally missed. She could see how she had almost missed it, so small as it was. The compact door was about the size of a laundry chute, but Sammy doubted it could be used in that way. How would Ingrid throw dirty clothes, on her knees, behind dresses, into a laundry chute? It didn't make sense why it would be located on the back wall of the closet. Curiosity won out, and Sammy dropped to her knees and crawled into the space to get a better view. Sammy popped the compact door open to reveal an enclosed vent pipe. Inside the vent pipe was a small fireproof safe. She pulled it out, set it in her lap, and then closed the laundry chute door. A smile formed on her lips as she backed out of the closet clutching the find with both hands.

She backed up straight into the polished black shoes of a man. Her eyes flew upward to Detective Liam Nash, whose hands were planted firmly upon his hips.

"I'll take that," he said as he reached out one hand.

"What? No!" Sammy clutched the heavy safe to her chest, refusing to let go.

"You realize you are hampering an ongoing investigation." He waved his hand forward. "Give it here."

"How did you get in here?" Sammy stood upright but refused to give up the goods.

"I should ask the same of you, don't you think?" He reached for the safe, and she swung it in the opposite direction, causing him to miss.

Just then, Heidi and Tim entered the room holding hands. "Isn't he the sweetest thing coming to check up on us?" Heidi looked lovingly toward her boyfriend, and Sammy huffed in response.

"Wonderful," Sammy muttered under her breath.

"By the way, Deborah's fine, she said don't rush or worry, the store's been dead due to the weather. I told her you would give her a call on the way back." Heidi dropped her boyfriend's hand and rushed toward Sammy. "What did you find?" She dropped the box of trash bags onto the bed that was now completely covered with Ingrid's dresses.

"Fire-safe lock box, but I haven't found the key yet."

"Yes, and she's hampering an investigation by not giving it up." Detective Liam Nash crossed his arms over his chest and stood glaring at Sammy.

"What is with you two? Aren't we all on the same team?" Heidi's eyes flew toward Sammy, and now it seemed all harsh eyes were on her.

"Fine." She unwillingly handed the safe over to the detective and sat on the bed defeated. "I don't have the key, though. Good luck getting it open." Sammy huffed.

"No worries. We have tools back at the station that will pop that baby wide open in no time," Tim said.

Sammy rolled her eyes at her cousin's boyfriend.

Detective Liam Nash waved a hand from the half-filled box to the dresses on the bed. "We can come back with our warrant later to continue our investigation, Officer. We don't want to get in the way of them packing up Ingrid Wilson's clothing. We've already had the Crime Scene Unit over here anyway." He turned his head to the window. "Glad to see you all weathered the storm all right," he added in a concerned tone.

"Yeah, we're all just fine. But how's the rest of Heartsford? Any damage?" Heidi turned to Tim with a look of alarm.

"Few power lines down, trees and branches. Nothing major. You guys are lucky to have the power on here. Main street is fine—but part of the town is out." Tim rested his hand comfortably on his holster.

Sammy jumped from the bed and regarded her cousin. "Yeah. We were very lucky here," she nodded vigorously. She was not ready to share that they had been digging into Ingrid's personal belongings in the basement.

"If you find anything—and I mean *anything*—as you're packing Ingrid's clothes, please give me a call on my cell." Detective Nash tried to hand Sammy a business card, but she refused it.

"Don't you remember you already gave me your card? You should pay more attention to details," Sammy's tone was sarcastic and defensive.

"Yes. I do remember giving you a card. What I don't remember is you calling me on my cell. Ever. You always call the department and ask to be put through to my line," Liam Nash corrected. The detective turned on his heel and exited the master bedroom and called over his shoulder with his back to the room. "Officer Maxwell. Let's get a move on."

"Incredible. You really know how to yank that guy's chain!" Tim shook his head and placed a meaty hand on Sammy's shoulder. "I better get moving. He was nice enough to let me check on you three troublemakers."

Heidi leaned in and gave her boyfriend a kiss on the lips before his departure. After he left the room, she turned her focus to Sammy, "You *reeeaaally* like him!"

Sammy had a look of disdain on her face. "How do you get *that* from *this*?" She pointed to her face, which was filled with frustration.

"It's what you always do when you like someone that much, you try to push them away. It's your signature move." Heidi said as Ellie entered the room.

"What did I miss?" Ellie asked.

"You thought we had a storm outside. You should see what I just witnessed in this room." Heidi teased. "Did you get a hold of Randy?"

"Yeah." She handed Heidi back her cell phone. "Thanks for letting me borrow it. I'm going to have to go. Randy and my Ty-baby are okay, but unfortunately, the birch tree in the back didn't fare so well. Randy needs to get the chainsaw out and asked me to come home to take over with Tyler so he can safely cut it up. Sorry I can't help finish here."

Sammy moved to her sister's side. "Thanks for coming today. I really appreciate your help. If you think of anything later that we might have overlooked today, give me a call."

Ellie leaned in for a hug. "We're going to get this guy," she said firmly. "Watch your back, Samantha. I'm worried for your safety." She was already putting back on her mother hat, and she hadn't even left the room yet.

Heidi placed a hand on Ellie's shoulder. "Don't worry. Tim's on it."

Sammy eyed her cousin. "What exactly does that mean?"

"I told him about your warning. Heartsford Police Department is patrolling your neighborhood and Community Craft to look out for you."

"I seriously don't think that's necessary."

"We do." Ellie and Heidi said in unison.

"And you need to stop in at the police station and add your statement to the report. Don't forget," Heidi added.

Sammy just shook her head like the two were overreacting before giving her sister a nudge toward the door. "Go check on your family. We'll be in touch soon. Love you."

"Love you guys." Ellie straightened her arm with a clenched fist and the two others mirrored her. "S.H.E.," they all said in unison, and the three laughed like grade school children before Ellie dropped her hand and left the master bedroom.

"Alrighty then. Let's bag up these dresses and get going!" Heidi reached for a few and hung them up with one hand. "Grab a bag would you . . . and help cover these?"

As Sammy poked a hole in the upside-down trash bag to

cover the dresses Heidi put up a hand to stop her, "Whoa, hold up a second."

"What is it?"

Heidi laid the dresses back on the bed and pointed at a pin attached to the lapel of an emerald green dress. "Do you see that?"

"Yeah. What is it?"

"I've seen these on patients that have come into the hospital. It's a sobriety pin. Ingrid Wilson was an alcoholic."

Chapter
Twenty-Three

The following day, unable to focus on anything other than the investigation into the murder of The Yarn Barn owner, Sammy reviewed her notes and the newspaper article she had taken from Ingrid's house. She held the newspaper article in one hand and took a sip from a water bottle in the other. Her eyes reread a specific line in the article. She placed the paper on the counter, picked up a pen, and underlined:

Rain may also have been a factor in the accident. *According to County Police Officer, Jay Rant,* the crash is still under investigation.

Sammy stood at the kitchen counter and flipped her laptop open. Bara nuzzled at her leg to gain her attention and then moved toward the back door of the Cape house, waiting patiently for her to open it.

"You need to go out?" Sammy walked over to the door and let her dog out the back door and then returned to her laptop. She Googled the name Jay Rant, Dodge County

Police, to see what would come up in the search. Several hits came from the search, and she clicked on the first, which read:

Officer Jay Rant continues to give his time to
Dodge County long after retirement.

After scanning the article, she learned that the retired officer volunteered his time removing invasive garlic mustard from the Wild Goose State Trail. The aggressive plant was known to invade high-quality upland and floodplain forests. The county was using volunteer efforts this week to eradicate the weed on the thirty-four-mile trail. Dodge County, the next county over, was roughly forty miles from her house. If Ellie would work alongside Deborah, Sammy could pay the retired officer a visit on the trail.

Sammy quickly hit her sister's number on speed dial, and Ellie picked up the phone on the second ring.

"What's up?"

"Any chance you could work for me this morning while Tyler is at preschool? Deborah is coming into work for a few hours so you wouldn't be alone."

Sammy heard nothing but a quiet pause on the other end of the line.

"Hold on a sec."

Sammy moved to the back door and opened it for Bara to return inside.

"Yeah, Randy said he'd take Ty to preschool on his way to work. How long are you going to be? Where are you going exactly?"

"A few hours. I have a hunch, so I'm going to kill two birds with one stone. I've been so busy lately I haven't taken any personal time . . ." Sammy stretched the truth just a wee bit, as she wasn't sure she was going to learn anything anyway from her little trek through the nature trail. She chewed the inside of her cheek and then added, "I'm taking Bara with me for a long-needed walk too." She hoped this would justify the half-truth to her worry-filled sister.

"A hunch, huh? Sounds dangerous." Long pause. "I guess I'll see you at the store later and you can fill me in then. Be careful. We don't need any more warnings."

"Not dangerous. I'll have Bara with me. Thanks, I owe you one." Sammy clicked off the phone before her sister could throw more questions at her and looked at her puppy. "You and I are going on an adventure!"

She patted her leg for Bara to follow, reached for his leather leash off the peg next to the door, and headed outside to load him into the passenger seat of her car.

The drive that led to Wild Goose State Park was uneventful. Bara laid his golden head to rest on the edge of the open passenger side window, devouring every ounce of the road trip. Each mile away from their house encouraged her sense of adventure. She needed this break away from the confinement of the store sometimes. When they finally came upon the large brown sign that marked the state park, Sammy turned onto the blacktop lot, and she picked a parking spot under a budding oak tree to keep the car cool while they hiked. The sun was poking streams of light out from under a large puffy cloud. The storms had brought back cooler temperatures.

There were no complaints from Sammy. At least it was finally sunny.

A crushed stone path meandered under a canopy of trees, keeping the flat trail shaded and cool. A woman walker dressed in workout gear and a sweatshirt led a well-behaved, leashed collie off the path toward the parking lot, and Bara bolted from the car before Sammy had a chance to even turn around.

"Bara!" Sammy slammed the passenger car door and rushed after her dog to catch him and click on the leash. "Sorry about that."

"It's fine. No worries. What a handsome dog." The woman leaned down and gave Bara a pat on the back.

As the two dogs took an interest in each other, Sammy asked the other hiker. "Did you happen to see any volunteers on the trail?"

The woman jerked the leash away from Bara and led her collie closer to her leg. "Yes. I believe so. About a mile or so in? Just before you get to the marsh." She waved goodbye and then jogged away, heading toward the parking lot.

"Thanks." Sammy jerked Bara's attention from following the collie back toward the open trail. "We're going this way, buddy." Sometimes her dog mirrored her own personal behavior—very hard to control.

According to the welcome sign at the head of the trail, the state trail was built from an old abandoned railway that began in Chicago and headed northwest. Sammy had never gone as far as Dodge County to hike before and mostly stuck to the trails close to Heartsford. She welcomed this opportunity to blaze a new footpath. A chipmunk suddenly darted across the path, causing Bara to dash after it. Maybe it wasn't such a great idea bringing him after all. She jerked the leash and refocused his attention on the crushed stone trail. The smell of honeysuckle filled the canopy of trees, giving a welcoming peace. She breathed the moment in. All she could hear was the crush of stone underfoot and the occasional chickadee and cardinal singing off in the distance. She needed to take this type of time for herself more often; it was intoxicating.

A slight clearing of trees lay ahead, and she noticed the dark trash bags along the path from where the volunteers had bagged the pulled garlic mustard plants. She followed the trail of black bags until she came upon a woman in a large straw hat bent over at the waist pulling the tall white flowered weed out of the long grass.

"Hello," Sammy said kindly.

The bent woman turned and stood upright. She placed her hands behind her back to take a moment to stretch and then left them there to brace herself. "Hi there. Are you here to volunteer?"

"Not today. But I am looking for one of the volunteers. Is Jay Rant helping today?"

The woman pointed a garden-gloved finger up the trail. "He's next in line, you'll catch him around the bend." She waved goodbye, sprinkling remnants of dirt with her soiled gloved hand, and returned to plucking the hearty weed from the ground.

Sammy nodded in appreciation and led Bara farther down the trail. Her dog was not easy to walk with, as he continued to be sidetracked by any animal or scent that crossed in front of them. When she finally made it around the bend to a man in a khaki-colored fishing hat and matching nylon jacket, she breathed a sigh of relief.

Sammy placed one hand next to her mouth and yelled, "Officer Rant?"

The man stood and adjusted the sweat-filled hat upon his head, revealing a head full of lush gray hair. He turned and made his way out of the tall grass along the path and moved in her direction. "Boy, I haven't been called that in years," he chuckled. "Do I know you? If you're calling me officer, I guess this must be regarding an old case from my past?"

Sammy reached out to shake his hand. "Kind of."

He removed his glove and shook her hand. He then unzipped his jacket, removed it, and tossed it to the ground next to the trail. "It's getting hot out here. Nice to see the sun though. Guess I shouldn't complain." He fanned his brown plaid cotton shirt with his hand.

"Oh, I'm sure you do feel warm from all the tough work you're putting in. Trying to eradicate the weeds, I see?" Sammy pointed to the half-filled black trash bag.

"Yes. It's a time-consuming process. Must be done though; it's destroying our forests. My gut says that it's not garlic mustard that you're here to talk about though. Go ahead and tell me." The retired officer removed his hat again and fanned himself with it. "What's brought you out here looking for me?"

Sammy smiled at his candid tone. "I actually want to talk to you about an accident that happened years ago. I'm hoping you can help me understand a few things."

"Go on." The retired officer's interest was obviously piqued. He placed the hat back on his head and readjusted it.

"You see. I have this friend who's looking for his biological mother. Turns out, he was adopted as a baby and wants to reconnect. I have reason to believe she's deceased, and I wanted to verify with you . . . If you . . . well . . . maybe if you had any details about his mother . . . you know . . . before I share the sad news with him . . . that she may not even be alive."

The older man rubbed his chin and nodded. "Do you have any idea how many cases I handled over the years, young lady?"

"This one would have been early on in your career. Do you remember Ingrid Wilson and Olivia Dunn?

The stunned look on his face was immediately apparent.

"You *do* remember," Sammy pushed.

The retired officer took in a methodical deep breath. "Yeah, well . . . that one was personal." He shook his head and kicked a stone in the dirt with his work boot as if he didn't want to travel that part of his memory.

"Personal?"

"I went to school with those gals. They were inseparable, those two." He chuckled, "Jeez, it's funny now . . . But it wasn't at the time. I was always chasing Ingrid to go out with me. She never would," he chuckled again. "I wonder what ever happened to that gal. I still think about her from time to time," he said wistfully.

"You don't know then?"

The older man looked at her perplexed. "Know what?"

"Ingrid was murdered in Washington County recently. Inside her store in Heartsford, The Yarn Barn."

A sound of shock escaped him. "No. I wasn't aware. I don't watch the local news anymore. When you spend a lifetime being a police officer, you need to gain some peace back in your life. I need to ponder on hopeful things. Not negative news. Not tragedy. It's the way I've decided to spend my retirement. Out here in nature. And it's the only way I can survive." He shook his head. "I can't believe Ingrid's life ended in another tragedy . . . Just like Olivia. Did they get the person involved?" The retired policeman's eyes narrowed.

"Not yet."

"I can't believe it." He breathed deeply and then sighed. "Unbelievable. Just can't escape the horrible news." He took his sweaty hat off again and shook it. "Her murder happened in Washington County? That would mean Oberon's on the case. Do you know?"

"Stan Oberon retired. Heartsford has a new detective from Minnesota who just moved into town."

"Oh."

Sammy didn't want to linger on the new detective, Liam Nash. She did that enough in her own thoughts. "Do you know if Olivia Dunn had a son and if he was put up for adoption?"

"I'm not certain what happened with the baby, to be honest. Social services handled that part after the accident. I think the baby was only a month or two old when she died. He's looking for his mom, huh?" The retired officer eyed her cautiously.

"What about the father? It said in a news article she was a single mother?"

"Yeah, the father was a soldier in the U.S. Army. Came home, got her pregnant, and then was deployed overseas. To be candid, I don't even think Olivia ever told the guy. Now that I think about it, I think her older sister Charlotte dated him first or was engaged to him or something. There was some kind of scandal involved, it severed the relationship between the sisters. It's been so many years, I can't remember all the details about that. I was focused more on the accident investigation, not so much their personal business. But I do remember that there was a period of time the sisters were not on speaking terms."

Sammy leaned down and petted Bara for comfort and distraction. "Did you ever find out what caused the car accident?"

"I took Ingrid at her word. She told us a deer had run out in front of the car, she swerved, and they hit a tree. It was raining that night too."

"Were you aware of Ingrid's alcoholism?"

"Nah, we were just kids. If you're asking if the police tested her for alcohol in her system at the time of the crash, the answer is no. She was checked into the hospital where she remained for a few days and told me at the scene she was sober as a judge. I believed her. I cared deeply for her. If she drank at the time, it certainly wasn't much." He shook his head and then readjusted the hat back on his head. "Wow, that's some news you brought me here today. I can't believe she's gone."

"Do you *think* alcohol was in Ingrid's system at the time

of the accident and could have caused the crash? I guess what I'm asking is . . . Did she blame herself for the accident or Olivia's death?"

"I don't know whether she lied to me about drinking that night or not. I certainly didn't smell alcohol on her breath. I trusted what she told me happened. Look, it was an unfortunate accident. It wouldn't be the first time we had a deer-related accident off that highway. Especially in the fall when the deer are in rut. But I could see how Ingrid would still blame herself. Wouldn't you if someone was a passenger in the car you were driving?" He pointed a finger toward her. "Now that you've told me she's been murdered, I guess we'll never know. Besides, that doesn't have any relevance to helping you find your friend's biological mother, now does it?" He eyed her suspiciously, searching her face for answers.

"You're right," Sammy tried to downplay her questioning. "Don't mind me, I'm the curious type, and it gets me in a lot of trouble with my friends." Sammy chuckled. "Anyhow, thank you very much for your time. I won't interrupt your weed pulling any further."

She backed slowly away, and as she turned back toward the path she heard him say, "No problem. Sorry about your friend. I hope he finds some peace knowing his biological mother died instantly."

Sammy waved a backward hand as she retreated along the trail toward the parking lot.

The idea that Gary's biological mother had died at the hands of Ingrid Wilson continued to plague Sammy's thoughts as she walked. No longer could she enjoy the sound of the birds or the peace in the air as her mind spun, looking for answers. If Gary had been sitting with his biological aunt Charlotte at Liquid Joy, then he might know that Olivia was his mother and that she had been in an accident with Ingrid. The big question was: Did Gary know or speak to Ingrid before her murder? Or did he only discover who his biological mother was after Ingrid died? Sammy didn't know but found it all very interesting as she came to the end of the trail and then jogged across the parking lot and loaded Bara into the car. And what about the scandal? Could Gary's father have dated both sisters? Is that why the sisters had a falling out? And the reason why his aunt Charlotte didn't adopt Gary? Maybe it was too difficult for Charlotte because her baby nephew belonged to her ex-boyfriend who had left her for her sister?

On the drive back to Heartsford, her mind continued to try fitting the pieces of the puzzle together. The multiple possibilities of who could have killed Ingrid Wilson played back and forth like a tennis match in her head. She would have to start eliminating some of these potential suspects soon or she would never solve the mystery of this murder case, and the town of Heartsford would never get back to normal.

During her complete distraction, the car started to sputter and shake. Sammy tightened her grip on the wheel with both hands. She safely pulled to the side of Highway 28 and flicked on her four-way emergency lights. One look at the gas gauge and she noticed something wasn't right. It read empty. Impossible. She had just filled up the day before, after the storm. She banged both hands on the wheel in utter frustration.

Her mind flew to possibilities of how to solve her current problem. Ellie was at the store. She wouldn't be able to pick her up. Well, maybe she could leave Deborah alone at the store . . . but Ellie had refused Bara in her car on several occasions due to his long shedding fur. Her sister was meticulous in both her car and her home and refused to own a pet for that reason. Randy was at the mortgage company. She wouldn't bother her brother-in-law. Heidi was at the hospital. She wouldn't be able to pick her up either. She decided to call her last option, Tim.

He picked up the phone on the first ring: "Officer Maxwell."

"Tim, it's Sammy."

"Oh, hey, Sammy, what's up?"

"I'm in a bit of trouble. My car seems to have broken down. Any chance you can come pick me up?" She turned her head to her traveling companion. "I have Bara with me."

"I'm actually in a pinch now. But can I send Nash? He's standing right here with me."

Sammy rolled her eyes and slumped back in the driver's seat with a defeated look on her face. "You're going to make me the damsel in distress?"

"Ummm, no. I'm going to send help. Do you want it or not? You really need to settle down there, girlie."

"Fine." Sammy audibly huffed. "Thanks. I'm on Highway twenty-eight, headed east. Can't miss me."

"I'll send him over."

Sammy looked at the phone in her hand and made the dreaded call to Community Craft. She hoped Ellie wouldn't be too mad. Instead of calling her sister's cell phone, she dialed the number to the store.

"Community Craft, how may I help you?"

"Hey, Deborah, is Ellie available?"

"Oh, hi Samantha. She's tending to a customer. Can I have her call you back?"

"No, it's perfectly okay. Can you just let her know I'm having car trouble? I have someone picking me up, but I might be a little late getting back to the store."

"Sure. I'll give her the message."

"She can call me if there's a problem."

"No worries, Samantha. Just take care of your car. We got this end covered."

"Thanks, Deborah."

Sammy sighed with relief and then reached over to pat her pup. He snuggled his head into her lap and left it there, looking up at her with his round dark eyes.

"I know, Bara Buddy. Not what I had planned today either."

After what seemed like forever, Sammy noticed the familiar silver Honda Civic pulling up behind her. She breathed deep, knowing she would have to be on her best behavior. He was there to offer help, and he certainly didn't have to. She needed to keep her emotions in check and not get so easily riled, as she so often did in his presence. She carefully stepped out of the car, mindful of highway traffic, waved hello and shrugged her shoulders in defeat as he came forward.

"Having some trouble?"

Sammy and Liam Nash were now within arms distance.

"Yeah. Thanks for coming. I do appreciate you allowing me to interrupt your day."

"Not a problem." He ran a hand through his dark curls. "I do notice one problem though."

"What's that?"

"I smell gas. Can't you smell that?" He leaned closer to the car, taking a whiff.

Sammy's eye brows furrowed. "I don't understand. I did notice the gas gauge read empty, but I filled up yesterday."

The detective crouched down and then slid his body underneath the car. He poked his head from under the car and said, "Your fuel line has been cut. The pressure side of the fuel pump."

"What do you mean cut?" Sammy placed her hands on her hips as he crawled back underneath the car. "Why wouldn't there be a trail of gas behind me on the highway then?"

"Gas evaporates."

"Oh."

"That's not all," Liam said as he slid his body back out from underneath the car and sat back on his heels. He held up a small device for her to view. "Samantha, I think you may be in danger. Somebody planted a GPS tracker on your vehicle. Who knows how long it's been there. I hate to be the one to tell you, someone is very interested in where you've traveled."

Chapter
Twenty-Four

Detective Liam Nash drove Sammy back to Heartsford in his Honda Civic with Bara in the back seat, sticking his head forward between them. Her dog's tongue was panting from thirst. Sammy hadn't thought to bring a water bottle to share with the pup, and she was kicking herself for not planning in case of emergency. They had waited thirty-five minutes for the tow truck to arrive to take Sammy's car back to the local service station, where the car would get fixed and be further investigated by the Heartsford Police Department.

"Where were you coming from today?" The detective held one hand on the wheel, the other sat in his lap casually as he drove, his eyes looking forward out the windshield.

"I took Bara for a walk at Wild Goose State Trail in Dodge County."

"You are darn lucky no one came after you on that hike." His tone carried a cautionary warning. "Someone has been tracking you, looking for just the right opportunity. Now, Samantha, more than ever, you must remain vigilant. Don't be taking any more walks alone in a park. Why go so far from

Heartsford anyway?" He turned his head to face her for an instant and then turned back to the windshield.

"There were tons of volunteers out today. It was safe." Sammy only answered half the question. Then she shifted the conversation in another direction. "Are you ever going to tell me what was in Ingrid's fireproof safe? Or will I have to beat it out of you?"

Liam laughed aloud. "You are really something." He slapped his hand on his thigh and threw his head back laughing, almost hitting the headrest of the driver's seat. His eyes began to tear up, and he wiped them with one hand.

"Well? Come on! What was in it? Did you happen to find the will?" Sammy couldn't take it a minute longer. Didn't he know how much sleep she had lost over the contents of that stupid box? Obviously, he was keeping the investigation tight-lipped. As far as she knew, Heidi couldn't even get an answer out of Tim about what they found locked in the fireproof safe. Didn't Detective Nash know that she had the power to help him? If only he would share more information.

"No. The safe was filled though."

"What do you mean filled? Filled with what? Paperwork?"

He paused longer than necessary, and she wasn't sure if he was going to share what was in the safe. He had better tell her. If he left her hanging with *filled* she'd go absolutely nuts! She was just getting ready to throw a hissy fit when he opened his mouth.

"Cash." He quickly looked over at her to try to catch the expression on her face.

"Cash." Sammy took the information in for a moment

before continuing. "Interesting. How much cash?" She felt shocked he had actually shared the information. But relieved too. Maybe he did trust her a wee bit?

"All you have to know is that the safe was stacked with money. In the hundreds of thousands. But it came directly from Ingrid's bank account. I went through her financials, and she had recently cashed in an IRA. The funds are close to a match. It wasn't dirty money if that's what you think. I'm pretty sure it was honest cash."

"I didn't think it was dirty money. I was just wondering what was in the safe. I wonder why she cashed in an IRA? What was she getting ready to purchase?" Sammy knew the cash was a strong motive for murder. She kept her thoughts to herself though. She was certain the detective had come to the same conclusion anyway. Sammy wondered what the detective thought about Larry as a suspect too, but she decided to keep her mouth shut on the matter. The less she shared, it seemed, the more amiable he was. She knew the detective was smart enough to look into every angle anyway and she was afraid if she mentioned it, he would feel undermined yet again. It seemed to her that his ego took a hit every time she suggested something. She hoped she was reading that wrong, but at this point she seriously lacked clarity. Sammy leaned over and patted Bara on the head. "I have to go back to Ingrid's house and gather the rest of her clothes for donation. We didn't finish the other day. The storm kind of wreaked havoc on our plans."

"That might not be a wise choice for you right now. You ought to lay low. Someone is following you. And when they find out that we removed the device from your car, they may turn up the heat."

"Well, it's not exactly like it's my *first* warning." Sammy let the comment slip by mistake, and she immediately covered her mouth with one hand, wishing she could do a rewind like on a DVR. She really didn't want to drag that into the conversation. Especially since she hadn't talked to Liam directly about it. Instead, Heidi had filed the report with Tim and she would later revise it to add her testimony.

"I know about the report. If you think I don't know every detail going on in my investigation, you're wrong. I'm only disappointed that you didn't talk to me personally about it." Liam's eyes narrowed as they left the road to stare in her direction. "Why would you try and keep that from me?"

"Some guy in a costume, during the parade at Spring Fling. It's nothing. I'm fine. See?" She pointed to her face and, for show, gave a big, fake, plastic smile.

"Why didn't you report it directly to me, though? Especially when you know I'm the lead investigator on this case? Samantha Kane. Why don't you trust me?" The detective pulled the car in front of Community Craft, turned his body to squarely face her, and laid his hand across Sammy's seatbelt to stop her from immediately jumping from the car.

"I don't know why," Sammy answered honestly. "Maybe I didn't want you to think I was just a damsel in distress, maybe I was afraid you would keep me farther from the investigation, I don't always know why I do the things I do." Sammy surprised herself by sharing with blunt honesty. She really wanted the detective to be impressed with her, to *like her*. She removed his hand from her seat belt and unclicked it. "Thanks for the ride." She stepped from the car, walked around the back, and opened the back passenger door to let Bara out onto the sidewalk.

Liam rolled down the driver side window. "I'll let you know if we find anything else on your car. And when it's ready to be picked up."

"No rush, I don't mind walking." Sammy held Bara's leash tight. "I appreciate it, Detective. Thanks again, for the rescue."

Liam Nash winked, and it sent a flutter to Sammy's heart. *Damn those dimples.*

"No problem. Hey, one more thing? I wouldn't mind going back to Ingrid's with you when you want to go. I could do a bit of investigating there myself. Don't go over there again alone. Okay? Do I have your word?"

His eye contact was intense and direct. He reached from the window to grasp her arm, but she was too far from him. It was obvious he didn't want to let her go until he had the answer he was looking for.

"No promises," she smiled and opened the front door of Community Craft, allowing Bara to gallop inside, presumably to his water dish under the counter by the cash register. She held the door and watched Liam pull away and then stop and park in front of Sweet Tooth. The man just couldn't get enough of Marilyn's cake.

Ellie rushed to greet her. "Everything okay? What's wrong

with your car? What a bummer!" she slapped her hand to her forehead.

"You're not going to want to hear this." Sammy walked directly toward the office and Ellie shadowed.

"Oh, boy. Now what?" Ellie tried unsuccessfully to keep up with her sister's pace.

"My car is under investigation. The fuel line has been slashed, and someone put a tracking device on my car. I guess someone's interested in my comings and goings." Sammy whispered in her sister's ear as the two moved into the office. Ellie gasped and clutched her chest, just like their mother did when hit with surprise news.

When she finally caught her breath, she asked, "Who would do such a thing?"

"I guess the same person that killed Ingrid Wilson. Someone knows I'm getting closer to the truth. That's my impression. Why else would anyone take an interest in my boring life?" Sammy shrugged off her sweatshirt and flung it on a nearby metal chair.

Ellie shook her head in disbelief. A worried expression covered her face.

After Sammy had walked out of the office and past the cash register she asked, "By the way, where's Deborah?"

"Oh, right. Deborah. You just missed her. I sent her home. She got a call from the school saying her son is sick. There's a lot of crud going around right now. I'm not surprised—it's probably due to the up and down weather patterns. These thirty to forty-degree temperature jumps can't be good for our bodies."

"And Tyler? I thought he'd be here with you by now?"

"He's at a playdate with his little friend Steven. His mom owed me anyway. She picked him up after school, and he's hanging there until either Randy or I can pick him up. I'm not leaving you until I know you're safe." Ellie grabbed her sister's arm to gain her complete attention and stop Sammy from adjusting merchandise on a nearby rack. "Interesting little tidbit from Deborah this morning. You know she volunteers at the school from time to time, right? The morning that Coach was struck by the car, Assistant Coach Dave was at the school. She remembered seeing him in the parking lot and walking into the building. She said when Coach was hit that morning, the news spread like wild fire. She's without a doubt certain Dave wasn't anywhere near Main Street. I think he should be removed from the suspect list, don't you? Not to mention, he was driving a truck through the parade. There's no way he was the costume guy that warned you."

"True. He can be taken off the list . . . But what if he hired someone? He certainly had the chance to improve his son's chances of recruitment when Coach was in the hospital. That's a little hard to disregard. Isn't it?"

"I don't know. I guess so? I think it's unlikely that he would hire someone. What motive would he have for killing Ingrid? It just doesn't fit." Ellie steepled her fingers and laid them gently on her lips, her brows crinkled.

Sammy nodded in agreement. Her sister was probably right. As she turned to adjust the handmade soap back into a neat pyramid stack on the shelf, she remembered she had left a few of the bars of sugar scrub on her desk. She hurried back to the office and Ellie followed.

"Have you had anything to eat? I'm starving." Sammy's hunger sidetracked her current mission. She opened the office refrigerator door and then slammed it shut when she realized it was completely empty. Empty fridge at home. Empty fridge at work. She really needed to get organized.

"I haven't had lunch today either. How about we order takeout from the Corner Grill? Want a sandwich?" Ellie suggested.

"I'm thinking more like a juicy burger after the day I've had. *With* a side of fries!"

"Screw the diet, I'll have the same. Call it in please, and I'll go pick it up after the knitters' meeting is over. My treat for today. That sounds really good!" Ellie moved out to the display floor while Sammy called in their order from the office phone.

As Sammy finished the call, Ellie returned to the schedule in her hand. She held it out for Sammy to view. "The knitting group will be here soon for their meeting. We should try and join in to see if we can dig up any more intel. What do you think?"

"I think it's a great idea. Any information at this point that could help us dig deeper or drop suspects would be incredibly helpful. I just don't know how much gossip they'll spill with us present. Sometimes they clam up when I enter the room. I suppose I understand that though. They spend a lot of time together and share their most intimate and personal stories along the way. Sometimes it's hard for a newcomer to join in these cemented groups. Which is precisely why Ingrid didn't take part in their close, tight group."

Sammy rose from the office chair and followed her sister to the cash register. The two stood at the counter as Annabelle Larson walked toward them, her curly red head appearing out of nowhere.

"Hi, Annabelle, I didn't see you hidden among the merchandise. All ready for the knitting group to arrive? How are you today?"

"I've been better," she sniffed and wiped her wet eyes with a tissue and then blew her nose and stuffed the Kleenex in the side of her quilted handbag. "I was in the bathroom. That's why you didn't see me come in," she said in a monotone voice.

"What's wrong? Are you sick?" Sammy moved around the counter to stand next to Annabelle, while Ellie looked on from behind the counter.

"Heartsick. My husband is filing for divorce." She reached for the soiled tissue and blew her nose again. After wiping her eyes, which were rapidly filling with tears, she looked at Sammy helplessly.

Sammy pointed to Ellie who reached under the counter and pulled out a box of tissues and held it out for Annabelle to pluck a fresh one.

"Thank you," she said sadly and then brought the tissue to her eye to wipe newly formed tears. "I know it's best. I'm in love with Miles. I didn't plan any of this." Her face reddened and splotches began forming on her neck. She waved the tissue like a white flag, then blotted her eyes.

256

Sammy and Ellie stood listening, neither knowing quite what to say.

"It's just, well I've been married so long. And I depend on my husband financially." She suddenly gripped Sammy's arm desperately. "Can you hire me, Samantha?"

Sammy was caught totally off guard, "I don't have the money to pay you, Annabelle. I'm sorry. I just hired someone else, and Ellie and Carter work here from time to time. I don't have the funds for another full-time employee right now."

Annabelle nodded her head in agreement as she blew her nose again. "I understand. I'm just so afraid, I don't know what I'll do! What skills do I have besides knitting?"

"It's okay." Ellie reached across the counter and patted the crying woman's hand that rested on the Kleenex box. "Everything has a way of working itself out."

"You're right," Annabelle said as her eyes dropped to the floor.

"Can I ask you something?" Sammy knew it was a stretch, but she had to ask.

Annabelle looked up, her eye makeup, which was usually overdone to hide deep wrinkles, was now dripping down her cheeks in long black paths. "What is it?"

"Why was Miles at The Yarn Barn? Did he often pick up stuff for you?"

Annabelle stiffened. "Are you asking me about the day of the murder? Is that what you're referring to?"

"Truthfully? Yes. I'm trying to understand why Miles's coffee was sitting on the counter." Sammy's eyes searched the woman's face, looking for any hint of a flinch.

"It wasn't his coffee. It was mine. He brought it to me and then left. He wanted an excuse to see me. That's all there is to that." She turned on her heel and started and strode purposefully toward the craft room. "Thanks for the Kleenex," she said to Ellie over her shoulder.

"Annabelle . . . wait!" Sammy rushed to follow her. "Are you telling me that you were in The Yarn Barn when Ingrid was murdered?"

"Yes." She sniffed. "I was there."

Chapter
Twenty-Five

S ammy could not wrap her head around the bomb that
Annabelle Larson had just dropped.

"What do you mean you were *there*?" She swung the
woman around so hard that Annabelle had no other choice
than to face her. They both looked at each other in stunned
silence for a moment.

"Samantha Kane, I think you had better calm down."
Annabelle placed her quilted handbag on the chair inside the
craft room and then rubbed her arm where Sammy had just
tugged to turn her around. "The knitting group is going to be
here any minute. I don't think you want them to see us in the
middle of a physical altercation? Do you?"

Sammy took a deep breath. She hadn't meant to be so
forceful. She guessed the stress of Ingrid's murder and the
subsequent threats she'd received was taking a much greater
toll on her than she would have liked to admit. What she
really needed was a hot bubble bath, a full night of uninterrupted sleep . . . and a full refrigerator of healthy foods. She

was officially losing it. Barely surviving on caffeine and Marilyn's sugary treats.

Ellie suddenly appeared next to them and said, "Time out, ladies! Why don't you two go talk privately in the office. I'll start the group off without either of you." Ellie whisked the two out of the room and encouraged them to move toward the office. "Take five! Or better yet, take ten if you need it!" she strongly suggested.

The two stormed off behind the wood counter, retreating to the office where Sammy closed the door behind them.

Sammy and Annabelle stood in the office like two people who were about to engage in a fencing tournament with swords raised in a defensive stance.

"Please go ahead and sit," Sammy encouraged Annabelle.

"I'd rather not if you don't mind." Annabelle stood defensively; her deep sadness had morphed into fury. The kind of anger that was obviously misplaced. "I've already told the police everything I know. Who do you think you are? You're trying to blame me? I did not kill Ingrid Wilson! I'm innocent!"

"I'm in no way accusing you. I'm trying to understand how you were *there* and the police haven't arrested anyone but your lover! Who almost took the fall and went to jail for *you*." Sammy pointed a finger at Annabelle. "I've always thought of Miles as an upstanding and honorable man. Nor do I blame either of you for your tryst. That's between you and Miles. I'm only trying to find out who murdered this woman in cold blood!" Sammy looked down at her closed fists and released them. She really needed to calm down or she wasn't going to get any answers. "Now." She took a deep breath. "Please. Please tell me who killed Ingrid Wilson."

"I don't *know*." Annabelle's eyes were laser sharp. "If I knew, don't you think the person would be behind bars by now?"

"How can you say you were there and not know? That just doesn't make sense." Sammy shook her head, bewildered. "Can you please help me understand?"

"Since you need to know everything that goes on in this town, I'll tell you. It seems to me you think you're the town's mother hen." Annabelle brushed imaginary lint from her sleeve. "Miles wanted to see me. We can't get enough of each other these days."

Sammy could feel bile rising in her throat; she could almost taste it. There are some things you just don't want to know. The image of Miles and Annabelle together *in that way* quickly floated in front of her. *Ick.* She hoped the image popped soon. Like one of Tyler's play bubbles—here now and gone in an instant.

"Miles knew I was going to The Yarn Barn to pick up alpaca yarn, so I could work on the socks I was knitting for Spring Fling. He came into the store and brought coffee for me. You know, he's very thoughtful that way. He's an extremely attentive man. Even in the bedroom. Not like my soon-to-be ex-husband, who never even brought me one flower our whole married life—if you can imagine." She pouted like a teenager who had just had all her electronic devices taken away. "Anyhow . . . When we heard noise coming from the back of the store, we both panicked. He had just sneaked a kiss behind a rack of yarn by the counter. The most sensuous kiss." She held her hand to her heart and puckered her lips as if she was reliving the passionate moment.

Now Sammy really thought she might throw-up. It was good she and Ellie hadn't eaten their hamburgers yet. She closed her eyes momentarily to try to get rid of the images and visions that were plaguing her.

"Miles thought Ingrid might have seen us kissing and would expose our relationship, but we didn't want anyone to know. He took off out the front door like a kicked dog, and I followed him toward the front of the store. But I panicked when I realized we shouldn't both be seen leaving at the same time. Instead, I hurried upstairs toward Ingrid's office. I figured she wouldn't know I was up there because I assumed she was somewhere in the back of the store. I didn't even know she had been murdered until later that day. I didn't know where she was. I *never* saw her. I just snuck down the front stairs from her office after a few minutes and walked out the front door. I gave myself plenty of time after Miles left. Now do you understand why I didn't see who killed her? I was upstairs the entire time, hiding in Ingrid's office."

Sammy thought for a moment. Ingrid's store configuration was different than Community Craft. At The Yarn Barn, the office wasn't behind the register. Instead, it was located on the second floor, with access from the front staircase, making Annabelle's account of what occurred plausible.

"And you didn't hear a thing?"

"No, I didn't. Ingrid keeps a fan on upstairs because she must have been going through the change of life. She used to get hot flashes all the time. Didn't you know that? I swear, I didn't even know she was dead." Annabelle crossed her heart. "If I did . . . don't you think I would have called the police or exposed the killer?"

Sammy wasn't sure of anything right now. Nothing in the town of Heartsford was making sense. Even the thought of her dear friend Miles and Annabelle having romantic relations just felt plain wrong and weird. She felt like she was on the tilt-a-whirl at the summer carnival and not having a fun ride.

"The only thing I'm guilty of is leaving my green knitting needles with my partial project on the counter. The killer must have used my project to wipe away any DNA, and the other needle, according to police, seems to be missing . . ." Annabelle's face twisted. "The police told me they never found the other one . . . it's obviously not something I ever want to see again . . . I was so caught up in my escape, I forgot to go back for my stuff. The last thing I would ever think would be that my needles would end up being used as a murder weapon! I just ran out the door, and that was that."

Before Sammy had a chance to hold her words back they flew from her lips. "If it was one of your needles that killed her . . . wouldn't that make you the number one suspect?"

Annabelle rolled her eyes. "Samantha Kane. The police department cleared me after I aced a lie detector test with flying colors. Plus, Miles finally told the police the truth of our relationship when they pressed him. They know I had nothing to do with the murder of Ingrid Wilson. I can't even believe you would think that I would be capable of something so monstrous."

Sammy remained silent She didn't know what to think.

Annabelle threw one hand on her hip. "Now, if you don't mind. I want to go join my knitting friends. I'm sure they'll at least give me a little empathy for my divorce, unlike you," she said as the fat tears again began to form.

Sammy reached out, leaning forward for a hug—a peace offering of sorts—and Annabelle fell into her arms dramatically. "Can't you see how hard this has all been?"

"I'm sorry for your pain," Sammy said soothingly as the woman's mascara dripped onto her shoulder. "Things will work out. You'll see. You're just going through a rough patch."

"Still friends?" Annabelle asked as she leaned back and held Sammy at arm's length.

"You bet." Sammy reached for the handle of the office door and swung it open. "Since we're friends again, can I ask you one more thing before you join with the other knitters?"

"Sure," Annabelle sniffed and wiped her dripping nose with her finger.

Sammy retreated inside the office and reached for the Kleenex box on the desk and lifted it in Annabelle's direction. "Why didn't Ingrid fit in with the knitting group? I would have thought, with her owning The Yarn Barn, the knitting ladies would have welcomed her with open arms? I understand she could be a little difficult, but still. We all have our foibles. Don't we?"

Annabelle plucked a tissue from the box and paused a moment to collect her thoughts. "I think the biggest problem was her complete lack of humility. She always acted like she was better than the rest of us. Like she knew everything, and we didn't match up to her life experiences or finances." Annabelle rolled her eyes dramatically. "Plus, she had access to whatever natural fibers she wanted. That alone made some of the women in the group drool." Annabelle pushed wiry red curls away from her face and wiped the remainder of caked eyeliner from under her eye with the tissue before continuing. "She would even brag about things like owning a pair of antique pure ivory knitting needles. But she wouldn't show them to us. Who does that? Do you know how rare pure ivory knitting needles are? Very few even exist because they're crafted from endangered animal tusks! The knitting group would have appreciated the opportunity to touch an antique like that and see the history of their craft firsthand. Legend has it they belonged to some sea captain's wife. But I guess we weren't 'good enough.'" Annabelle said as she made air quotes melodramatically, "for Ingrid to show us! Ingrid was all talk, no action, and quite frankly it annoyed people."

"Thanks for being candid with me. I really wanted to understand. Community Craft is known for bringing people together, and I wanted to understand the separation. That's all." Sammy tried desperately to downplay what she had just heard from Annabelle. Because in her mind she had just heard another strong motive for murder: priceless artifacts.

"Well, I do feel bad talking so poorly about a woman who's dead and can't defend herself. I guess all I have right now in my life is guilt. Guilt over my marriage, guilt over Ingrid, guilt over leaving my needles behind to be used in a monstrous crime. I'm just plain sick with guilt!"

Sammy didn't know how to respond. She had her own

shortcomings to contend with. Instead, she changed the subject. "One more suggestion. One friend to another? You may want to visit the bathroom before you go join the other ladies to knit. You have a bit of mascara on your left cheek."

"Thanks, Samantha. I'm glad we had this chat. I feel much better." Annabelle rushed to the restroom to adjust her makeup before joining the rest of the ladies in the craft room.

Meanwhile, Ellie eyed her sister with a questioning expression to see if the two had made peace or were still ready for battle. "Seriously? Do we need any more drama?" Ellie's eyes searched her sister to see what had transpired.

Sammy encouraged Ellie to follow her into the office so the two could have a moment of privacy, now that the entire knitting group was comfortably assembled in the craft room. When she finally felt convinced they were no longer in earshot, she said, "Our conversation cleared up a few things in my mind. At least now I *know* that Miles is as innocent as a newborn baby regarding the murder. Infidelity on the other hand? Well . . . that's another story. That's something they are most certainly guilty of."

"Where do we go from here?" Ellie laid her hand against her face.

"I found out another possible motive for murder."

"Seriously? *Nooo.*" Ellie put her other hand on her face, so now both cheeks were covered.

Sammy looked at her sister and laughed, "You look like the kid from *Home Alone.*"

Ellie dropped her hands sheepishly and laughed along with her sister. "Okay, don't hold back. Tell me the new motive.

This just gets more interesting by the minute." She shook her head in disbelief.

Sammy became increasingly encouraged that her sister was no longer backing away from the idea of talking about the crime. "Antique pure ivory knitting needles. Could be just a rumor. Or Ingrid's way of trying to impress the tightly knit knitters. Because according to Annabelle, nobody in the group has seen them. So, I guess it's our job to find out if they truly exist and, if so, if they were in her possession before her death."

"Holy cow. I wonder what something like that is worth?"

"Priceless to the right bidder, for sure. You can't buy them anywhere. It's like finding something from the Titanic . . . Truly unique."

"I can't believe it. That woman had more secrets than the tooth fairy." Ellie sat on the edge of the office desk, bent her elbow, and rested her chin on her fist.

"Tooth fairy? You are definitely spending too much time in toddler mode." Sammy laughed and then changed the subject. "I think we should call Heidi. Don't you think another S.H.E. meeting might be in order? What do you say?" Sammy reached for the phone and pulled it closer. "Since Tyler has a play date maybe Randy can take over for a little while after that? Plus, I don't have a car. I'm going to need a ride anyway. Please don't make me beg." Sammy held up the phone, waiting for the formal approval before dialing. "We have to go back to Ingrid's house. Tonight. After the knitting club disbands."

Ellie smiled and reached her arm out in front of her with a closed fist. The non-verbal sign for their childhood club, S.H.E., presented front and center.

Before Ellie changed her mind, Sammy dialed Heidi's phone number.

Sammy pressed the speaker button, and Ellie said, "Hey, Heidi, don't make plans for tonight. We have another S.H.E. mission." Her lips curled upward in a smile.

Chapter
Twenty-Six

After dropping Bara home, Ellie and Sammy headed to the restaurant to retrieve their late dinner. Ellie parked the car while Sammy ran into the Corner Grill to pick up the takeout order. They decided they would eat their burgers on the ride to Ingrid's house, where Heidi would meet up with them to further investigate the antique knitting needles motive. As Sammy turned from the counter with a full paper bag of food in her hands, she knocked right into none other than Larry Bergeson, the Heartsford School Board President.

"Excuse me," Larry said. His blond hair was disheveled, as if he'd just woken up from a nap. "Oh, it's you. Samantha Kane from Community Craft." He ruffled his hair with one hand, which only led to an even worse appearance. "How are you?"

"Oh, hey, Larry." Sammy was standing close to the man, eyeing his height to see if it was possible he was indeed the green-faced villain. She couldn't be sure as he was leaning on the pickup counter waiting for his order of food. If only he would stand up straight!

Larry turned from the counter, leaned his arm to brace

himself, and eyed her with the bag of food, obviously suspicious of why she was still standing there. After a few moments, he asked, "Do you sell gift certificates for classes at your shop? My wife's birthday is coming up soon, and I thought a gift certificate for a craft class to get her out of the house might be a good gift idea."

Sammy was listening carefully to the sound of his voice. If only she could get him to talk with helium. Then maybe she might be able to distinguish if it was really him who had warned her. And that disheveled hair, would all of that fit in that pointy purple hat?

"Well, do you? Sell gift certificates?"

"Oh, sure. We can do that. Just stop in and ask whoever is working the counter. We have a new employee at Community Craft. She volunteers at the school. Deborah is her name. You may actually know her . . ." Sammy was desperately trying to keep the conversation going and was completely running out of things to say to the man. Her brain was on overdrive. She wished she could just hook him up to a lie detector and be done with it already.

"I don't volunteer at the school. I'm on the board," he corrected.

"Yes, of course. You probably don't know Deborah then." Sammy shook her head in agreement. "Anyhow. Stop in anytime, and we'll be happy to help you with your wife's birthday present. I think it's a lovely idea. We have so many crafts she could choose to learn. Great pastime, especially to get through our long Wisconsin winters. Well, we're coming into spring now. But she could certainly use it for next winter . . ." Why was she stumbling over her words?

Larry nodded, then turned and directed his attention to his food, which was just arriving at the pick-up counter.

Sammy walked out the door of the eatery disappointed that she hadn't been able to figure out whether Larry might have been the disguised man. Could it have been him? It was certainly plausible. But she just wasn't sure. Not only that, but could he capable of killing Ingrid? He sure had a lot to lose . . . including his reputation if she had pressed charges.

Sammy opened the passenger side of Ellie's car and handed the food inside. She slipped into the passenger seat, and Ellie pulled away from the curb while she clicked on the seatbelt.

"Well, that was interesting." Sammy plucked the bag of takeout from her sister's lap.

"Did they not have the food ready? It sure took you awhile. I figured since we were so late picking it up they gave up on us and had to throw new burgers on the grill."

"No, it wasn't that. I just ran into School Board Larry."

"Oh, boy. How'd that go? Did you ask him if he was at the parade? Did you bring up the incident?"

"No, I wouldn't dare, especially not knowing how he might react? You know, I was trying to figure out if he could have been the man in the costume that day. Maybe I should have asked him directly about the parade." Sammy pulled a burger from the paper bag, removed the paper covering and handed it to her sister while she drove.

"It's all right. Did you come to any conclusions?"

"No. Nothing definitive." Sammy pulled a French fry from the bag and said, "Sorry it took so long to pick up the food. You may not like these. They're kind of cold." She tossed the limp fry back into the bag.

"No problem. I'll skip the fries and just go for this." Ellie took a small bite of the burger and balanced it with one hand while she kept the other hand on the steering wheel. "Heidi texted about ten minutes ago while you were in the restaurant. She said she was just leaving the hospital."

"Good deal," Sammy said between mouthfuls of food. She hadn't realized how hungry she was; even the cold burger was filling the need.

The two ate in silence for the rest of the ride to Ingrid's. When they pulled into the long driveway, they noticed Heidi had already arrived and was waiting in her parked car. Sammy picked up the trash from their meal, shoved it into the paper bag, and wiped a dollop of ketchup from her mouth. She crumpled the bag and dropped the trash by her feet before exiting the vehicle. The sun had dropped in the western sky leaving a haze of pinkish purple across the horizon.

"It'll be dark soon. We should hurry. Randy's going to have a fit if I keep you out late every night." Sammy rushed to Heidi's car and knocked on the driver's side window. Heidi was in her own world, texting on her phone. She held up one finger, signaling to wait, without her eyes leaving the glowing screen.

Sammy moved away from Heidi's car and walked up to the front entrance of the Lannon stone house and opened the wooden door with the key. Ellie followed behind after giving

Heidi a "hurry up" cue, banging on Heidi's car window with her fist.

Heidi met the sisters just inside the doorway. "What did I miss? I guess we're not here this late in the day just to pack up more of Ingrid's clothes for donation?"

"You're right about that. We're officially on assignment!" Ellie closed the door behind her cousin.

"But before we get into it, how's Coach?" Sammy regarded her cousin.

"He came out of surgery and is now in recovery. Time will tell. But so far, it sounds like the surgery went well. Hopefully, in a few days, you can visit with him and bring him up to speed on things here. I'd give it a few days, though; he's pretty heavily medicated."

"Thanks for the update."

"What are we looking for?" Heidi flipped on the entryway light before following the sisters into the formal living room.

"Antique knitting needles that are apparently very rare and priceless." Sammy flipped over the folded afghans stacked on the sofa to see if there was a chance of finding them deep inside the pile.

"You're not going to find them over there," Ellie scolded her sister. "I'm sure she didn't knit with them if they're that priceless!"

"Interesting," Heidi moved to the fireplace mantel and looked at the bulky white candles flanking an intricate replica of a tall ship. The off-white mast stood a few feet tall. "I wonder how she got her hands on antique knitting needles."

Sammy looked up to see her cousin eying the contents of

the fireplace mantel. "I don't know, but you may be on to something over there! The knitting needles belonged to a sea captain's wife at one time; at least that's what Annabelle mentioned. Any chance they're in that model of a tall ship? It sure looks big enough to hold a few measly needles." Sammy rushed to her cousin's side and examined the replica with her own eyes. The two carefully lifted the ship off the mantel for a closer look. Sammy held it while Heidi craned her neck to view the underbelly of the ship.

"I don't see anywhere that she could have put them. The bottom is pretty smooth." Heidi ran her hand along the polished wood.

The two examined every inch of the ship and came up empty. "Good thought though. If I were going to hide something I think I'd put it there. We need to stay on that line of thought." Sammy tapped her index finger to her temple.

Ellie opened the side drawer of an antique mahogany desk. The appearance of brass hardware gave the impression of heirloom quality, passed down through many generations. Enclosed in the main drawer were other hidden drawers, and Ellie's excitement escalated. "Maybe they're in here!" she said as she dug into the new, hidden compartments within the desk. After several minutes of searching though, Ellie too came up empty. "It's just a bunch of office supplies. Tape, stapler, paper, a rubber band roll full of pens. Very disappointing." She huffed as she slapped a small spiral notebook back into the desk drawer.

"All right. Let's put our S.H.E. heads together," Sammy

encouraged. "If you owned something rare and valuable, where would you hide it?"

The three stood in silence and pondered.

Heidi piped up. "I'd put it with the rest of my valuables. Wouldn't you? A specific place where I kept what's most important to me."

"Okay?" Sammy asked. "Where do *you* keep your valuables?"

"My underwear drawer of course!" Heidi laughed. "I guess I don't have that much that's valuable. But my thongs are very important to me."

Ellie laughed, and Sammy said. "That's exactly *not* what I wanted to hear."

"To be honest, I already packed Ingrid's underwear drawer when we were here last time. I didn't find anything of value besides large cotton panties."

Sammy rolled her eyes. "This isn't getting us anywhere."

"Wait a minute." Ellie held up a finger. "What if the knitting needles were put in the same place where you found the safe? Do you think it's possible you missed something in the closet?"

Sammy nodded her head. "Sure, anything's possible. Let's go double check!"

The three trudged up the now familiar staircase and walked directly into Ingrid's master bedroom. When Sammy flipped on the light, a gasp caught in her throat, and she threw her hand up to cover her mouth.

"What is it?" Heidi asked.

"I didn't leave the closet door open!" Sammy eased toward the closet and dropped down to her knees. She crawled to the laundry chute door, which was ajar, which was not the way she had left it. She was one hundred percent positive she had fastened it tight. She then retreated out of the closet to face the others. "Someone else has been here."

Chapter
Twenty-Seven

The three cousins stood in Ingrid Wilson's master bedroom unsure quite how to proceed.

"Heidi, you were the last one in Ingrid's bedroom with me. You remember I closed it, right?" Sammy pointed to the closet door and then dropped her arm to her side.

"Yeah. I think so? I'm not sure, to be honest. If someone has been here though, how did they get in the house? Didn't you say Coach gave you the only key?" Heidi's manicured brows came together in a deep frown.

"Yes. That's exactly what he told me." Sammy nodded. "He was adamant. He wanted to be sure I didn't lose his only key."

"So far we haven't seen any evidence of a break-in. Are you sure you closed the door on the laundry chute?" Ellie touched her sister's arm to break her reverie. "Maybe you just forgot?"

"I'm one hundred percent positive I closed both doors. The laundry chute door *and* the closet door!" Sammy gestured toward the closet and then breathed deeply while placing her hands on her hips.

"Maybe it was the detective? Didn't Nash say they were

coming back to investigate further?" Heidi pulled her cell phone from her back pocket and held it in her hand.

"Yes, but he would have called me for the key. He knew the coach was in surgery and that he would have had to get the key from me. Supposedly I'm the only one to have one."

"I think we should call Detective Nash right away and verify that. Don't you think?" Heidi held up the phone, waiting for permission from S and E to call.

"Looks like we have no other choice," Ellie said in agreement.

"Crap." Sammy threw her hands up in surrender. "Fine." She plucked her own phone from her pocket and hit the detective's number on speed dial. After he had suggested that she never dialed his cell, she had programmed his number into her phone.

"Nash."

"Hey, yeah, hi . . . This is Samantha Kane calling."

"Ohhh, so you *do* have my cell phone number," he teased. Sammy could tell by his tone he was smiling and she was glad she had caught him in a good mood. "Yes, your car is ready for pickup. Unfortunately, it wasn't ready before the service station closed because we still had a bit more work to do. Sorry about that. You can pick it up tomorrow when they open. I was just going to call you and let you know there was nothing major found in our investigation of your car other than what you already know—the tracer and cut gas line. I think it could have been a lot worse. We did have some concerns about the emergency brake line. There were minor cuts, as if the perp wanted to cut the line but it was too much effort. It's fixed, and it should be safe to drive. I'd be happy to give you a ride to the station in the morning if you need it?"

"Believe it or not, my car is not the reason I'm calling."

"Pardon?"

"Any chance you've been over at the Wilson property? Like recently?"

"Ingrid's house? Nope. Not a chance. The coach said if I needed to get the key I should contact you. We spoke before his surgery. However, you promised you would call me if you were going over there again. I'm guessing you didn't do a very respectable job of keeping that promise."

Sammy could hear his annoyance, so she decided to get right to the point, "Never mind that. I think we have a problem." Her eyes bounced from her sister to Heidi. She clicked the phone to speaker. "Ellie and Heidi are with me. Say hello if you want. I just put you on speaker so everyone can hear what you have to say about this." She held the phone out so everyone could take part in the conversation.

"Good evening, ladies. To what do I owe the honor of the call?"

"We're here at Ingrid's, and it looks like someone has been in her bedroom," Heidi said.

"Besides us," Ellie added.

"Why? What have you observed to make you think that?"

"The closet door was open, and the door to the laundry chute where I pulled out the safe was open. Both were closed tight when we left last time. I'm positive I shut them." Sammy nodded.

"I'll be right over. I might bring Tim with me. I think he's on duty tonight."

"He is," Heidi confirmed.

"Be there in a bit. Don't touch anything and keep your cell phones close." He clicked off the call, and as an act of defiance, Sammy tossed her cell phone on the expansive bed.

"Now what?" Ellie asked.

"I think we continue to search while we wait," Heidi suggested. "Better than just sitting around."

"Good idea. Ellie, you stay in here but keep out of the closet in case the detective needs to dust for prints or something. Heidi, you check out the craft room, and I'll search the doll room," Sammy directed.

Ellie gave an audible sigh of relief. "Yeah, I'll stay in the master bedroom. I'll take anything over that creepy doll room! Good luck with that."

The three fanned out into the various rooms to continue their search for the elusive knitting needles.

As Sammy stepped into the doll room, she began to understand Ellie's apprehension. *A certain creepiness* was a nice way of putting it. The way the dolls were displayed on the shelves made it feel as if hundreds of eyes were watching her. All the dolls stood on rows of what appeared to be bleachers rising in multiple levels; there had to be hundreds of them. Some of the dolls were clothed in handmade dresses. Sammy recognized as the work of a local seamstress who sold her creations at Community Craft. It was about the only thing in the room that brought Sammy comfort. She took a deep breath and then stepped forward. The closet on one end of the room caught her attention. She walked over and snapped open the door. Boxes of brand new dolls, still in their packages, stuffed the closet full. Empty boxes, from the dolls that stood on display, were stacked on the left side of the closet. Sammy couldn't believe her eyes. The woman was an organized hoarder. At that moment, she decided she would talk to the coach about the collection. So many less fortunate children could receive a new doll still in the box for Christmas. She was sure he would agree. This was a complete waste. Sammy dropped to one knee and dug through the closet, but from what she could see, it seemed like it was only filled with doll boxes. Could it be a suitable place to hide the antique needles? She didn't think anyone had taken the time to empty the closet to look. It was too perfectly packed. She decided to abandon the doll room for the moment and return to the others. Doll eyes followed her as she shuffled quickly out the door.

Sammy hurried down the hallway when she heard the song of an old-fashioned doorbell. "I'll get it!" she hollered in the expansive hallway so that Ellie and Heidi would be sure to hear.

After skipping quickly down the stairs, she threw open the wooden front door.

Detective Liam Nash and Officer Tim Maxwell were standing on the front stoop. Tim was waving his hand to rid himself of mosquitos. "Darn humidity after the storms the other day brought the bugs out already. Seems early in the season to me," he said, obviously annoyed. "Hurry up and let us in."

Sammy opened the screen door and the two entered.

"Didn't I specifically tell you to call me if you were coming over here?" Detective Nash eyed Sammy while he crossed his arms over his chest.

"We didn't ask you guys over here for a scolding. If that's what you're after, you both can just go and I'll call another officer of the law."

"Where're the other two troublemakers?" Tim asked.

Sammy pointed toward the stairs.

"I wish you two would kiss and get it over with," Tim said as he shoved his way past them, made his way to the staircase, and started climbing.

Sammy's face instantly flushed, and the detective stood in stunned silence. The two stood close, eyes locked. When her feet no longer felt like she was standing in concrete, Sammy pushed past the detective and shadowed Tim up the staircase. She could hear Nash following close behind her.

After they had all piled into Ingrid's master bedroom, Detective Nash moved to the closet to assess the situation. "You're absolutely sure this was all closed up when you left?" He turned from the closet and rested his eyes on Sammy.

"Positive."

"Officer Maxwell, call in the Crime Scene Unit. We're going to have to dust for prints and take some photos. Please tell me you three didn't touch anything."

"Only the first time we were here. We didn't touch anything in here today." Sammy confirmed.

Tim leaned into the radio on his shoulder and called it in. In the small town of Heartsford, the Crime Scene Unit consisted of two additional deputies from the station. They weren't a large enough operation for a separate unit and van.

The detective ushered all of them out of the room with his hands. "Don't touch anything else. This is now an official crime scene. You ladies have no choice except to go home at this point."

Sammy threw up her hands in defeat, and none of them moved.

"I'll give you a ride home. I realize your car is still at the service station. Tim, would you mind waiting here for the Crime Scene Unit?" he asked Officer Maxwell.

Tim placed his hand on his holster and leaned on one hip. "No problem."

"That's okay, Detective. My sister or my cousin can give me a ride."

Ellie signaled Heidi with her eyes before regarding her sister. "Why don't you let the nice detective take you home. I've had a long day away from the family," she faked a yawn. "I'm sure Randy and Ty are anxious for me to get home right away. Heidi, didn't you say you have an errand to run before going home?"

"Yeah, can you have Nash take you home?" Heidi gave Ellie gave a thumbs-up behind her back.

"Fine."

"It's always an adventure with you! Get some sleep tonight, okay?" Ellie kissed her sister on the cheek. "Good night all," she said before heading down the hallway.

Heidi reached for Tim's hand, pulled him close, and kissed him quickly on the lips. "I'm going to say good night as well. I have an early shift tomorrow morning. Maybe we can meet in the morning for a coffee?"

"You bet, babe." Tim released Heidi, who waved to everyone before heading out the door.

"I'm going downstairs to wait for the unit." Tim left, leaving Sammy and the detective alone in the master bedroom.

For a few moments, the room was silent. The detective broke the quiet by asking, "What brought you out here so late at night? It must have been something good. I guess you weren't out here to pack Ingrid's things."

"Very perceptive of you."

"Well? Are you going to tell me?"

"I found out today that Ingrid may have been in possession of some very rare antique knitting needles. I guess I wanted to know if it was true."

"Knitting needles?"

"Yeah. Pure ivory. Extremely rare and priceless."

"So, you are looking for another motive?" his eyes narrowed, and he moved uncomfortably close.

"I guess I am." Sammy held her ground. Even though he was unnervingly close to her, she refused to adjust her stance.

He stared her down for a moment and then turned toward the door and gestured. "Whenever you are ready, I can give you a ride home."

Sammy moved toward the door and stepped out into the hallway. She turned to the detective for a moment before walking farther. "Do you have another suspect you're closing in on to make an arrest?"

The detective just laughed and directed her forward.

Sammy play-punched Tim on the arm on the way out the front door of Ingrid's house.

"Hey, Sam, good night!" Tim's words followed her: "Thanks for keeping my job interesting."

"No problem." Sammy waved a backward hand as she walked out into the indigo night.

The detective moved to the passenger door of his silver Honda Civic and opened it for Sammy. She slipped into the seat, and he closed the door behind her. *I bet he can't wait until I'm out of his hair*, she thought.

When Detective Liam Nash started the engine, he turned to her and gave an innocent reminder. "Click it or ticket."

Sammy pulled the seatbelt across her chest and clicked it tight.

They retreated out the driveway and headed left on Old Lannon Road. Once they were comfortable riding down the street, Liam turned to her and said, "If you have anything else to tell me about this investigation, now would be a perfect time."

"I'm not keeping secrets, Detective," she assured him. "Right now, I can't think of anything that would be beneficial to your investigation. If I think of something, you'll be the first one I call. How about that?"

"I doubt that. I'm sure you'd call your sister and cousin first." He huffed.

"Is that jealousy I'm hearing?"

"No. It's frustration." He kept his eyes on the road and didn't look in her direction.

"Do *you* have anything about the investigation that *you* could share? Maybe I can help *you*?"

The detective chuckled. "There might be. Want to hear something interesting? I think Ingrid was under the impression that someone was going to try and steal the money from her." His eyes left the windshield for a second and looked in Sammy's direction.

"What makes you say that?"

"That safe you found?"

"Yeah?"

"There was a handwritten note inside."

"A note? What did it say?" Sammy leaned in closer. As close as the seatbelt would allow.

"'For the one who tries to steal, all eyes are upon you.' Can you believe that? She was instituting guilt right from the get-go."

"For the one who tries to steal, all eyes are upon you," Sammy repeated. "For the one who tries to steal, all eyes are upon you." Her mind instantly recalled something her sister said when she had left the doll room. "Liam. Stop the car! Stop the car!"

The detective eased to the side of the road. "Are you okay? What's wrong with you?" His head turned in her direction, and his hand instinctively reached for her.

"Turn the car around! Turn the car around! We have to go back to Ingrid's! Right now!"

"What are you talking about?" He rested his hand on her arm to try and calm her.

"Just trust me. Would you please turn around?" Sammy's eyes bore into his.

The detective huffed a breath. "Like I have another choice." He turned the car back in the direction from which they had come. "Do you want to explain?"

"No. I'll *show* you."

Chapter
Twenty-Eight

When they were back in Ingrid's driveway Sammy dashed out of the detective's car as soon as his foot hit the brake. The detective threw the car in park, slammed the driver's side door, and chased after her. Tim was standing at the front door and opened it for them. The Crime Scene Unit had arrived just minutes before.

"What are you two doing back here?" Tim asked as Sammy dashed past him and ran for the stairs.

"I have no idea." The detective answered over his shoulder as he tried to keep pace with her.

Sammy took the stairs two at a time until she reached the top landing where she tripped forward and fell on one knee. She picked herself back up and kept running until she reached the doll room. After a flick of the light switch next to the door, she moved quickly to the tallest dolls on the shelves and began flipping them over and looking underneath their clothing.

The detective stopped in the doorway and caught his breath. "What *are* you doing?"

"I'm looking for the antique knitting needles! Come help me!"

The detective took a doll in one hand and flipped it over, revealing the underside of a dress. "This is wrong on so many levels."

"Just keep looking!"

"You realize that even if we find something, we've contaminated the crime scene."

Sammy stopped dead in her tracks for a moment. "I hadn't thought of that."

"I know," he said in a belittling tone. "That's the problem with you, Samantha Kane. Although I appreciate your enthusiasm for investigating the crime, you don't know the law and what's required to get the job done and bring the perpetrator to justice."

Sammy frowned and placed the doll that was in her hand back on the shelf. She backed a foot away and stood like a child placed in time out.

"Well, you might as well keep looking now," he encouraged. "We're already into it. What makes you so sure we'll find the knitting needles here anyway?"

"All eyes upon you. Isn't it creepy coming in this room? All the doll eyes staring in the direction of the door? Ellie couldn't stand it!"

"I guess. I don't know." He threw up his hands. "I've seen a great deal of horror in my line of work. I guess, to me, doll eyes are rather harmless."

"Touché. It's all in the perspective." Sammy reached forward and pulled the next doll off the shelf. She flipped it over and gasped. Without removing or touching anything under-neath, she placed the upside-down doll under the investiga-tor's nose. "*Boo-yah*! I think we just found what someone was searching for."

Detective Liam Nash plucked a glove from his jacket pocket and placed it on his right hand. He pulled out two antique ivory knitting needles, and his eyes met Sammy's. "You know what? You are pretty good at this, I must admit. Samantha Kane, you are full of surprises."

Sammy smiled and then frowned.

"What's wrong?"

"Well, if *we* found them, I guess it may *not* be the only motive for murder. The cash in the lockbox must be another motive."

"Not necessarily. Someone has been in the house recently. They obviously weren't as smart as you to find what they were looking for."

"True." Sammy shrugged. "But I wouldn't have found them had you not shared what Ingrid wrote in the note which was left enclosed in the safe? Funny how that note was meant for a warning, yet it tripped my memory as to what my sister said about the doll room."

"I guess that makes us a good team. Don't you agree, Ms. Kane?" his lips turned upward in a half smile.

Sammy returned the smile. "I guess I'd have to agree with that."

"I'm going to give these needles to CSU to pack in an evidence bag. I'm not comfortable leaving them here. Espe-cially since someone has obviously been inside the house and they may come back. I'll have to figure out how the perpetrator got in Ingrid's house without a key. A quick search before I take you home. I'll meet you downstairs?"

"Sure. Hey? Do you think the killer took Ingrid's keys from The Yarn Barn after he killed her?"

"He?"

"Yeah, of course. A woman wouldn't have been capable of that kind of murder."

The detective just smiled and shook his head as he left Sammy in the doll room. She bowed at the waist in front of the dolls, saying, "Well, thank you, ladies!" and then quickly shuffled out of the room, hopefully never to return except to pack the creepy dolls up and ship them out.

The first few minutes of the car ride home were quiet. Both Sammy and the detective were deep in thought. Finally, Detective Nash broke the silence. "I do appreciate your insight into the investigation. I know your heart's in the right place."

Was he asking her to surrender or urging her to continue to help? Sammy waited for the other shoe to drop.

"I just wish you weren't so impulsive."

And there it was.

Sammy didn't respond. She was emotionally and physically exhausted. Ever since coming across the body of Ingrid Wilson at The Yarn Barn, she had thrown herself into investigative mode. She guessed it was her way of coping, so she wouldn't have to relive the horror of it all.

"I'll try and mind my own business," Sammy said finally.

"I'm just trying to protect you. You don't make it easy. Do you understand that?" He reached for her hand, but she tucked it underneath her thigh, so he wouldn't have the opportunity. It felt like he was just appeasing her. Didn't he know she could help him? Sammy didn't know what else to say. She'd survived all these years without a man protecting her. Why should she stop now?

"I can stop by in the morning if you need a ride to pick up your car from the service station," he offered.

She felt like now he was trying to make nice and she was too tired to argue. "Sure, I would appreciate that. I left a note on the door at Community Craft that I would be opening late due to unforeseen circumstances. Whenever you can come and pick me up in the morning would be great. That's very kind of you."

The detective pulled into her driveway and put the car in park. "I can walk you to the door."

"Not necessary. Thanks for the ride." She slid out of the passenger seat and hauled her weary body to the front steps of her home. She turned and waved before slipping the key into the lock and moving inside.

Bara at once came and greeted her at the door. It was late, and she felt bad that she hadn't taken her pup for a walk. Sammy clicked the leash before he barged past her. He was so desperate to get outside, he nearly pulled her arm out of the socket as he tried to push his way out the front door. Immediately, Bara headed to his favorite oak to finally get relief. Out of the corner of her eye, Sammy saw a car's headlights approach from the rear. The car slowed, and she turned her head and gasped. It was the dark blue car. Her stomach tightened, and her heart hammered in her chest. The window opened, and the driver leaned over to the passenger side. It was the man. The stranger she had seen before. Her mind flashed to him standing watching the coach's accident and to the time she had secretly followed him when she was on her way to the flower shop. Her eyes darted to the car, so she could get the make and model number. It was a dark blue Chevy Malibu. The car had pulled next to her, so she couldn't get the plate. The driver motioned for her to come closer, and although her intuition told her to make a run for it and see if she could make it safely to the front door, her curiousity, unfortunately, won the battle. She moved a half-step closer.

"Can you tell me how to get to Brady Street?"

Sammy's heart beat fast. "What? No GPS? No cell phone?"

The man shook his head no.

She squinted in an effort to see his face more clearly and pick out any unique features. It was so freakin' dark outside, making it difficult at best.

"Your best bet would be to turn and head back to Main," Sammy suggested. "Stop at the gas station on the corner of Sumner. They should be able to tell you." She backed away from the car and gripped Bara's leash tight, causing her knuckles to turn white.

"Pretty young ladies shouldn't be out with their dogs this late at night," he warned, before pulling slowly away from the curb.

Sammy felt a shiver tickle down her back. She wanted to run to the safety of the Cape Cod, but first, her eyes darted to the license plate. Her heart thumped in her chest making it hard to breathe. The back of the car was shadowy, but she made out the first half. *Illinois plate GR7.* She jerked Bara's leash. Her eyes followed the car as it drove farther away and the taillights dimmed. She hurried to the front door. After they had made it inside, she closed the door and dead-bolted it. She leaned against the front door and breathed heavily, hand against her throat, while Bara retreated to his dog bed beside the fireplace. Without turning on any indoor lights, Sammy sneaked to the front window and pushed the curtain aside to get a clear view. She scrutinized the road for a long time to be sure the dark blue Chevy Malibu wasn't going to return. It was obvious to her he wasn't really looking for directions. He had come as a warning. Despite removing the GPS tracker, the stranger knew where she lived, and he was still following her.

Chapter
Twenty-Nine

S ammy stepped out of her morning shower refreshed and
renewed. Before fully dressing, she slathered her arms and
legs with Mrs. Brown's handmade lavender lotion. Instantly,
the soothing scent calmed her nerves. When she had finally
succumbed to sleep the preceding night, it was the soundest
sleep she'd had in weeks. Even considering the encounter with
the strange man in the dark blue Chevy Malibu, her body
must have just given in to the exhaustion. He had come to
taunt her. Not to ask directions. Intuitively she felt convinced
of that. But she refused to let him have the upper hand and be
bullied by his scare tactics.

She slipped into her most comfortable pair of faded Levi's,
the ones with a slight tear in the knee, but she didn't care.
Today was about comfort and confidence. After stepping bare-
foot into the closet, she pulled her favorite pale pink and white
muted plaid cotton blouse off the hanger and slipped it over a
pastel pink tank. After a stroke of rose blush to her cheeks and
some cinnamon lip gloss, she covered her feet in a pair of low
ankle white cotton socks.

Sammy padded down the stairs where Bara came to attention at the sight of her, lifting his head from his water bowl. "Hey, sweet Bara," she cooed and then opened the back door, where he took his cue and headed outside. She slipped into her Sketchers that idly waited by the matt.

The doorbell rang and instead of following her dog out into the back yard, Sammy instead turned in the other direction and headed toward the front of the house to open the front door. Her hair was still wet from the shower, so she shook it out like Bara after a swim in the lake, and combed her fingers through it. Then she opened the door.

"Come on in," Sammy held open the screen door, and Detective Liam Nash stepped inside. "Coffee?" she asked over her shoulder, as she moved toward the kitchen. He followed her and nodded his head in agreement.

"Sure. I'll take a quick cup." He stood at the kitchen island and searched around his feet. "Where's the Golden?"

"Out in the backyard." Sammy jutted a thumb in the direction of the back door and then handed the detective a steaming cup of black coffee. "Did you want creamer? I only have French Vanilla."

"I'll take a squirt."

"Help yourself." She handed him a spoon and gestured to the creamer that stood atop the center island.

As he was stirring the coffee slowly in the mug, he asked. "Sleep well?"

"Yeah, considering."

"Considering what?"

"My encounter last night."

"Encounter?" He blew into the steaming cup of java and then took a sip, making a slurping noise.

"Remember that guy I told you about? The guy I wanted you to have sketched? You know . . . The one with the blue car?"

"Ahh, yes. Where did you go last night after I dropped you off? I mean, where exactly did you see him?"

"I was here, in the front yard with Bara just after you left. He stopped and asked directions to Brady Street. Who does *that* so late at night?" She handed him a piece of scratch paper. "Here's a partial license plate, anyway."

His eyes narrowed as he read the paper and then looked up. "Why didn't you call me?"

"Because you said it was no big deal! I've told you about him before, and you basically blew me off and called me ridiculous." Sammy took a sip of her coffee and then set the mug down on the counter top.

The detective rolled his eyes. "Samantha Kane. Whatever am I going to do with you?"

Sammy shrugged her shoulders and then moved to the back door and opened it. Bara bounded into the kitchen, filling the tiny space between them.

The two finished the remainder of their coffee in silence, and then Sammy snatched her leather purse from the counter top. "Whenever you're ready?" She was anxious to get going, not only to have her car returned, but also to have the freedom of using her vehicle for solitary investigation.

Liam Nash leaned his head back to retrieve the last drop of his coffee, moved to the sink, and rinsed out the mug. He set the rinsed cup neatly inside the sink. For some reason, this amused Sammy. She grabbed his arm and shook it to encourage him to hurry up and move along toward the front of the house. She patted her puppy goodbye and then closed and locked the front door behind them.

What a joy it was to step outside no longer needing a jacket. The warm spring sun was streaming in the morning sky, sending bright reflections off the detective's silver car. Sammy plucked sunglasses from her purse, placed them on her face, and pushed them up on her nose with her index finger before sliding into the passenger seat. His car was beginning to feel familiar. As if Liam Nash had been in her life forever. She wondered if they would ever see each other after this case was closed. She brushed the thought aside as she wasn't sure exactly how that would make her feel.

A comfortable quiet hung between them as the detective drove toward the service station. "You seem to be learning your way around the town pretty quickly," Sammy noted as she watched the ease and comfort with which the detective was taking side roads to reach their destination.

"It's pretty easy to find my way around town. I love the fact that I don't have to drive in heavy traffic anymore. Heartsford is a nice little community."

"Yeah. We're spoiled here as far as that goes. I don't miss the traffic of Madison either."

Liam Nash pulled up to the service station and put the car in park but left the engine running. He turned to Sammy. "I'll keep an eye out for the partial license plate—see if I can get any information on who owns the car. Stay safe. You hear me?"

Sammy nodded and smiled. "Thanks for the ride. I do appreciate it."

After paying the bill for the car repair and retrieving the keys to her car from the service manager, Sammy was on her way. Only she wasn't going to Community Craft. Not yet.

Instead, Sammy pulled away from the repair shop and headed in the direction of Brady Street. She retrieved the Google Map on her phone to familiarize herself with that part of town. Why would the strange man ask for directions to *that* road? She took a left at the next traffic light. After passing the high school, something about the direction she was taking seemed vaguely familiar. She veered right . . . past the bend in the road.

Sammy had been down this road before, but it had been a long time ago. Years to be exact. She passed the house that looked like it was made out of gingerbread, like something out of a nursery rhyme. The familiar landmark Kate always mentioned she wanted to someday own. Suddenly it dawned on her. This was the direction she and Kate had traveled when they had driven to Gary's parents' house. The few times Kate had picked Gary up to go to school and Sammy had been a passenger, they had taken these exact roads.

Finally, Sammy took the last turn onto Brady Street. As she drove closer to Gary's parents' house, she was surprised to see a bit of commotion. Cars lined both sides of the road. It appeared a rummage sale was taking place. She pulled her car to the curb and jammed the gear shift into park when she noticed the strange man walking from the sale about five cars ahead—to the dark blue Chevy Malibu. He slipped into the car and pulled from the curb before Sammy even had a chance to shut the driver's door and retrieve the rest of the numbers and letters from the license plate.

Sammy noticed Greta organizing items behind a long twelve-foot table. She rushed over to her to see if she knew the unidentified man. She didn't waste any time for fear the car would disappear again.

"Do you know that guy?" Sammy pointed to the taillights of the Malibu, which was stopped at the end of the street before turning right, away from Brady Street.

"It's Dustin Briggs. A friend of Gary's from rehab. Why?"

"Just wondering. I've seen him around town. He stopped me for directions recently. Like anyone wouldn't know how to get from point A to B in our small town," Sammy added lightly, trying to downplay her interest in the man. "I'm assuming he's been to your parents' house before?"

Greta nodded in agreement. "Yes, he's been here many times."

Sammy knew he hadn't been asking for directions last night! But she eased her breathing and calmed her voice. The last thing she wanted to do was tip Greta off that she was still nosing around into her brother's business. "So . . . having a big sale?"

Greta eyed her curiously before answering. "We're having an estate sale. The house is going on the market in a few days. Mom and Dad have decided to move."

"Where are they moving? Are you moving too?" Sammy felt a jolt of surprise at the news she had just heard.

Greta didn't answer because an impeccably dressed woman,

wearing a muted, stylish sundress with a perfectly made-up face to match, interrupted with a bread maker in her hands.

"Would you take ten for this?" she asked Greta.

"I don't know . . . it's only been used a handful of times. I'll go ask my mother, she's inside the house. It belongs to her." Greta rushed from the table. By the look on her face, she was happy to have an escape so she could dodge Sammy's question about where they were moving.

The woman stood with the bread maker and defended her cause to Sammy. "I can't believe they want fifteen dollars for this," she said as she rolled her perfectly shadowed eyes.

Sammy was silently amused at how the well-dressed, wealthy ones always had to haggle their price down. She smiled at the woman but didn't respond. Instead she searched for Gary but didn't see him among the shoppers.

Sammy's eyes traveled to a craft area inside of the garage where it looked as if Greta was selling all her knitting items. Skeins of multicolored yarns, patterns, and needles were all laid out on one long table. She wondered why Greta would give this stash away for pennies on the dollar? Unless she was giving up the craft? Sammy decided to take a closer look. Before walking over to the table, she craned her neck to see if Greta was back outside, so she could confront her about why she was selling it all. Greta had returned and was standing with the bread maker lady consumed in deep conversation.

Sammy moved to the table and confirmed that it had to be every knitting supply the woman owned. One large stack of aluminum knitting needles held together in a rubber band was selling for much less than their combined worth. Sammy rolled them in her hand. Each knitting needle had a pair. Except one. One lonely green aluminum needle stood out alarmingly from the pile. Sammy's stomach tightened, and her heart hammered in her chest. She felt light headed as if she could faint any moment. Beads of perspiration formed on her forehead. She was positive. She knew exactly where the other half of the green aluminum pair was. In Ingrid Wilson's neck.

"What are you looking for?" Gary had stepped out of the house, into the garage, and slipped uncomfortably close behind Sammy. So close, she felt his breath on her neck. The shock of his voice made her legs feel like rubber bands. She braced herself by gripping the table with one hand but turned to him showing a big smile. "Just browsing."

"Find anything you like?" His dark eyes traveled sensuously from her feet to her face before finally meeting her eyes.

"Nothing I like. But something I don't understand." Sammy said politely.

"What's that?" Gary ran a hand through his straight dirty blond hair. He shifted his weight and rested one narrow hip against the table with casual ease.

"Why anyone would sell one knitting needle amongst a group of pairs? Greta wouldn't do that? It's useless. Unless, of course, the person who put it there knew nothing about knitting. Someone like you. You don't know that knitting needles are only sold in pairs. You put it there. Didn't you? That green knitting needle doesn't belong to your sister. It came from The Yarn Barn. And you put it with Greta's things to hide it. Not a smart move." Sammy pointed to the lone green needle sticking out—in her mind—disturbingly from the rest.

Gary visibly stiffened. "I'm actually quite smart. I pulled that one out of the yarn with my bare hand and, knowing it was now covered in my DNA, I took it with me and just dumped it in with my sister's craft junk. I used the other one, which was all covered in some stupid knitting project, to do the deed and not leave a trace." Stunned by the sudden confession, he tried to retract his statement, but it was too late. "I mean *if* I was there that's what I would have done."

Gary's teeth came together hard. His jaw flexed and his nostrils flared. He grabbed Sammy tightly by the arm as he said through gritted teeth, "I think you've taken this far enough. Dustin warned me you wouldn't stop. In fact, he knew you would show up on Brady Street. He knew you would take the bait. But I didn't listen. I wanted to spare your life, but you're leaving me no other choice." He led her quickly outside the garage, sharply around the corner, out of the eyesight of the other shoppers before she even had the chance to refuse. Part of her wanted to scream. The stronger part though wanted answers.

"This friend of yours . . . Dustin. He helped you, right? He drove you from the scene of the crime. I know you murdered Ingrid Wilson . . . what I can't figure out is why? Why would you do such a thing?" Sammy searched his face for answers. The scar along his jaw line was pulsating. He pushed her deeper into the back yard, toward impenetrable woods, farther from earshot.

"It wasn't intentional. She wouldn't listen to me! It was my money! It belonged to me. She cashed the IRA for me and was holding out! The old bat wouldn't give me what was *mine*."

"What do you mean by that? Why would Ingrid have *your* money?" His grip was progressively tighter on Sammy's arm, feeling instantly familiar. The way his slender fingers dug into her flesh. Her mind rapidly triggered back to the costumed man with the green painted face and purple pointed hat. "It was *you* wasn't it? You were the one in the costume who attacked me during Spring Fling!" As soon as the words were out of her mouth she was sickened by them. How could Gary do such a thing to her? They had gone to school together, for heaven's sakes.

"I was trying to warn you. You never could keep your nose out of it. Even when I was dating Kate you had to stick your nose in." Gary moved them deeper and farther away from safety.

"I just don't understand who you've become, Gary. I guess I was right to try and break you and Kate up in high school. You're a horrible person." It was the first time since Kate's passing that Sammy was glad her best friend wasn't alive to have to witness this. Kate would have been absolutely horri-fied to find out her ex-boyfriend was involved in such a hei-nous crime.

"Ingrid killed my biological mother! She *owed* me!" The venom in his voice sent a ripple of fear down Sammy's back. They were getting closer to the thick woods. Closer to being hidden from sight. Closer to no return.

"Who told you that? It was your Aunt Charlotte, wasn't it? She still blames Ingrid for her sister's death. Well your aunt Charlotte is wrong. It was a horrible accident, Gary. Ingrid didn't mean it. Olivia was her best friend. Ingrid didn't cause the car accident on purpose, she wasn't drunk. It was the deer that put fate in motion." Sammy tried to keep her voice calm. She knew that being hauled into the dense pine forest with Gary was a dangerous proposition. She tried to wriggle from his grasp, but he only gripped tighter. So tight, in fact, her hand began to tingle.

"Ingrid knew the accident was her fault," he spat. "Why do you think she moved back to Heartsford? She was looking for me. My aunt Charlotte found me first, though, then Ingrid saw us together, and it made her angry. Ingrid wanted to get to me first and convince me of her side of the story. I told Ingrid to cash the IRA, and she did. But then she changed her mind. My aunt Charlotte said I should file a civil case against her for killing my mother! Ingrid Wilson had family money to spare, and I was going to sue her for every last nickel of it. That is my money! And the old bat knew it and wouldn't give it to me unless I went back to rehab. Who does she think she is? She is not my *mother*! She doesn't get to make the rules! I grabbed the first thing I saw on the counter and let her have it. Dustin and I were close to finding the cash—until you started butting in," he said, spitting saliva as he spoke.

"So, you decided to exploit the woman's guilt for being the driver that took the life of your mother? It was an accident. I know your life could have been different knowing your biological mother. But your adoptive parents love you, Gary. You've had a good life here . . . What about them? And your sister loves you too. What about Coach? Why would you hurt him?" Sammy's eyes darted along the ground to find an escape. They were now tramping through the thick pine, and she knew if they went deeper into the forest she would not return unharmed.

"I didn't do nothing to the coach. That was Dustin. He thought the coach would find the cash first after Ingrid died. My money! She cashed the IRA for *me*!" he jabbed his chest with his free finger.

"And you broke into her house to find it. Didn't you? Actually, you stole her keys after you killed her. That's why there was no evidence of a break-in. But I beat you to it! I found the money first." Sammy seethed. "That's why Dustin has been stalking me!"

Gary didn't respond, he just pushed her deeper into the copious trees.

Finally, after some thought, Gary mumbled out of the side of his mouth. "Dustin has been following you because he wants his money. He's my drug dealer, and I owe him big time. If I don't pay up . . ." Gary let the assumption hang in the air. And Sammy filled in the blanks. Gary's safety and that of his family would be at risk.

"You owe Dustin a lot of money and now he's not only threatening you, he's threatening your family too. That's why your parents are putting the house up for sale, isn't it?"

"You really need to learn how to mind your business," Gary spat. "Always sticking your nose where it doesn't belong. When are you going to learn? I guess I'm going to have to teach you the hard way." Gary pinched her arm a little tighter, making her squeal out in pain.

Sammy eyed something along the path that might help her escape. Abruptly, she pulled her body sharply to the right, practically pulling her own arm out of its socket. Her plan worked. Gary tripped over a tree root that jutted above ground from a large maple, and for just a moment, he lost his grasp on Sammy.

Sammy's adrenaline kicked into overdrive. She leaped over the tree root with an athletic ease she didn't know she had and took off running in the opposite direction of the expansive woods. Branches slapped her face and tore at her flesh as she fought to retrace the path back to the edge of the forest and the open field of grass. She ran as fast as her five-foot legs could carry her. But Gary had caught his balance and was chasing her, making considerable progress. There was no way her short legs could ever outrun his long ones. Her heart was beating like a speeding freight train from the exertion, and she thought she might collapse and suffer a heart attack. He was gaining on her, and just when she thought he might be able to reach her, Sammy found herself running right into the arms of Liam Nash.

Detective Liam Nash must have seen the alarm on Sammy's face because he looked at her with deep concern before shoving her aside to chase after Gary. "Stop! Police!" he yelled. But that was not going to stop Gary Dixon. Gary's fear of capture sent him fast and furious in the other direction as he galloped for the thick pine woods at full speed.

Sammy felt she could cry or heave at a moment's notice. She wasn't sure which would come first, the tears or her partially digested coffee. She leaned forward, bent at the waist, and rested her hands on her knees as she tried desperately to catch her breath. When she finally stood upright, she noticed her cousin's boyfriend had appeared from the other direction. Gary, cornered between Tim and Detective Nash, threw up his hands in defeat. She watched as Tim tackled Gary to the ground. Tim's solid frame covered the perpetrator as he cuffed his hands behind his back and instantly lifted him back on his feet with such ease it made Gary look like a ragdoll.

Sammy followed the officers to the front yard and maneuvered her way through the rummage sale tables and the newly formed rubber-necking crowd to stand alone on the sidewalk by the police car's flashing lights.

Innocent bystanders dropped their items for purchase and followed the offender with their eyes as Tim briskly escorted Gary to the squad car. Many stood with their mouths agape as the arrest of one of the townspeople unfolded right in front of them.

Detective Liam Nash stood beside Sammy on the sidewalk. She reached for the detective's hand and laced her fingers through his. His face lit in surprise from the sudden intimacy. But she didn't care.

Sammy led the detective away, to the safety of his parked Honda. Before they crossed the street and reached his car, she dropped his hand and turned to face him. "How did you know I was here?"

"Brady Street. I knew you wouldn't let that go." He winked. "Tim was on patrol, so I sent him over to check on you. He saw your friend with the Chevy Malibu and ran the full license plate. There's a warrant for his arrest in Illinois, for not sticking to his probation rules—we had him picked up already."

Sammy noticed Gary's parents gathering with Greta on the front lawn, where they were watching the events unfold with deep sadness. The Dixon family's lives were about to change forever. Sammy breathed in the fresh air, knowing Gary wouldn't be breathing it for a very long time.

Before Tim had a chance to place the perpetrator into the backseat of the police car, Gary's eyes searched out Sammy and lasered in on her. "Samantha Kane," he yelled. "I know you think Kate's death was an accident. It wasn't!" he spat before Tim put his hand atop the man's head and encouraged him, with a shove, to get inside the vehicle.

Sammy glared at the squad car. "Did you hear what he said?" She flung an irritated hand in Gary's direction. "He said that Kate's death was no accident!" Sammy's sadness for the Dixon family instantly shifted into hot anger.

Detective Liam Nash turned Sammy to face him. He rubbed up and down her arms gently to encourage her. "Don't listen to him. Perps say this kind of garbage all the time to get people riled up. Don't let him. Don't let him under your skin. Don't let him steal your power." He leaned her back a step to affirm she had heard and understood his words and then pulled her close in an embrace. Her head rested safely on his chest as they watched the blazing lights of the squad car pull away.

Chapter Thirty

S ammy slid across her favorite red leather seat in the corner booth at the Sweet Tooth. The smell of sweet sugary treats tantalized her senses. Marilyn rushed to the table balancing a work of culinary art—a layer cake covered in creamy white frosting with thick curls of rich dark chocolate and one enormous fresh strawberry to top it off.

"For you, darlin'! Let me tell you! This latest masterpiece has four chocolate mousse cookie crumb layers underneath that top layer of icing. I think you're really going to like it!" she placed chubby swollen fingers, on which a silver ring looked like it was being suffocated, to her overflowing bosom.

"Oh, no doubt I will! Looks delicious." Sammy licked her lips in anticipation. "Thanks for hosting the gathering for us." She waved a one-handed hello toward her sister and cousin, who had just entered the bakery. Then she directed her attention back to the head baker. "It's very kind of you, Marilyn. You are sweeter than the cakes you serve."

"Sweetheart, you three deserve it." Marilyn slapped her hands on her apron, sending a cloud of powdered sugar into the air. "You gals restored our community and brought it back to order. Why, if it weren't for you, your sister, and cousin, we'd all still be on edge!" She shook her head in disbelief. "I think the police department should hire you three as consultants, that's what I think." She turned the cake so the strawberry faced Samantha, as an act of appreciation. "I'd better get back to the kitchen. We're going to have a full house tonight, and I want to be prepared!" She blew a quick kiss to Sammy and turned on her heel, heading back in the direction of the kitchen.

"That doesn't look like it will fit in with my diet." Ellie approached the table and looked at the cake with eyes filled with longing. If Sammy didn't know any better, she thought her sister might shed a tear.

Heidi followed behind her. "Screw the diet. Tonight, we celebrate!" Heidi encouraged Ellie to slide into the booth, and she scooted in behind her. "What a gorgeous cake. Almost looks too good to eat. *Almost.*" Heidi's smile widened.

"Marilyn's an amazing baker, that's for sure."

Sammy snuck a dollop of frosting with her index finger and shoved it in her mouth, hoping the other two hadn't noticed. Ellie caught her, though, and tried to slap her sister on the hand, but she was too late. Sammy retracted her hand and smiled.

"Who's coming to celebrate with us?" Ellie asked.

"Carter, Mayor Allen, and Connie. Coach is going to try and come. Annabelle, Miles, and some of the girls from the knitting club, Deborah, and her husband. Randy, Tim, and maybe . . . a few others from the police department . . . it's all very informal. If people want to stop by they can."

Heidi smiled. "I know Tim will be here soon and so will Detective Nash." She elbowed Ellie next to her in the booth as they both waited for Sammy's reaction.

"I'm warming up to the guy," Sammy smirked and kicked Heidi lightly under the table. "I kind of figured he'd come. I know for a fact he has a serious addiction to Marilyn's cakes! If he keeps at it, he'll soon be joining overeaters anonymous." The three laughed in unison.

"Okay, Sammy, you have to fill us in on everything we missed in the investigation." Heidi leaned her elbows on the table and clasped her hands together.

"What do you want to know?"

"What details did we get wrong? What did us three S.H.E.s miss?" Ellie nodded and leaned in closer.

"After many hours of interrogation, Gary made a full confession to police. You want to know the funny thing? He had no idea knitting needles came in a pair. He had watched Greta crochet with one needle and assumed knitting was the same! He thought just tossing it in with her pile of craft stuff was a good plan. If he hadn't been so dumb we might never have caught him."

"What an idiot!" Heidi exclaimed.

Gary gave up more details too. His friend from court-appointed rehab, Dustin, was his co-conspirator. Rehab didn't stick with either one of them. Dustin was also Gary's drug dealer and Gary owed him a lot of money. When Gary tried to appease Dustin by telling him Ingrid was cashing an IRA for him and he'd be able to pay-up soon, Dustin dialed up the heat and kept pretty close tabs. Unfortunately, it sounds like both their addiction to drugs and money won out."

Sammy shifted in her seat and rested her arms in front of her on the table. "We did get a few minor details wrong. Liam said that during the police interrogation Gary shared a lot of details. Ingrid wasn't an alcoholic, but his own birth mother Olivia Dunn was the heavy drinker. Addiction seems to run in the family genes. Apparently, Ingrid wore her deceased friend's pin to try and meet with Gary at the biker bar. She wanted to win him over by pretending she too had addiction problems. It was her way of getting to know Gary, to see if he was still struggling with drugs. The money from the IRA did belong to Gary's biological mother. Ingrid kept it in a trust all these years to give to Olivia's son one day, and boy did the money accumulate! I think Ingrid had thrown in a few thousand of her own—out of guilt for the accident. She wanted to find Gary earlier, but it was a closed adoption and it took her a while to track him down. After seeing Charlotte and Gary together one day on Main Street, Ingrid put two and two together, did some digging, and found out Gary was indeed Olivia's son. When she realized he was an addict though, she wouldn't give him the cash as he requested. She found it strange that he wanted the IRA in cash and not transferred into his name. That tipped her off that he wanted to use the money for something untraceable. Ingrid was afraid he had plans to shoot-up all the money. But it was too late. Gary found out that she had already cashed the IRA one day when he watched her leave the bank, so he knew she had it in her possession. He felt entitled to it. It was messy."

"Wow." Heidi and Ellie echoed in amazement as they took in the added information.

"And I can't help but notice that you're now referring to the detective by his first name. That's a bit less formal, isn't it?" Heidi and Ellie shared a look of amusement. "What about the aunt? The woman who owned the locket . . . right? Why didn't she adopt Gary and keep the money safe for him all these years? I would have thought a family member would have taken care of those things after Olivia's death," Ellie questioned.

"Well, that's where it gets interesting. There was a scandal in the family. Olivia's sister Charlotte was involved with a man in the military. On one of his military leaves, he had an affair with Olivia. Apparently, news of the affair was the talk of the town at the time. Charlotte found out when she overheard someone at the restaurant where she worked gossiping about it. After the betrayal, she felt nothing but disdain for Olivia and the baby."

Sammy paused a moment before continuing.

"Gary's aunt Charlotte met with him only recently to discuss why she hadn't taken a greater role in his life and to explain his past. When she was younger, she'd had a tough time seeing him, knowing his connection to her ex-fiancé . . . and the affair that had taken place with her sister. But now, aging rapidly and close to the end of her life, she wanted to meet her nephew and make peace."

"Wow. So, they really are related. You were right!" Ellie said.

"Unbelievable," Heidi finally added.

"So why did Greta have the locket? Where did she get it? And how did it end up at Community Craft?" Ellie asked.

"She found it in the glove compartment of Gary's car. I assume his Aunt Charlotte must have dropped it in Gary's car during one of their recent visits together. The clasp was broken. Gary just shoved it in his glove compartment to return later. Greta found it though and thought he had stolen it to pawn off for drug money. She was hoping to get it back to the rightful owner, so he wouldn't get in any more trouble. But before she could take it to the pawn shop to see if anyone had been looking for it, Greta accidentally dropped it in the craft room when she was digging through her quilt bag. When Charlotte saw it in the lost and found box, she must have assumed she dropped it herself at the store. What she didn't know was that it was found in the craft room, where she'd never been. That's what tipped me off, to be honest . . ."

The three sat silently for a few moments, taking it all in.

"Dustin was the one who saw me walking to The Yarn Barn as he and Gary screeched out of the parking lot after the murder. He also overheard Greta tell her parents I was digging into her brother's business by asking about the locket. And he assumed I was nosing around the investigation. He was the one who was following me via the GPS tracker on my car. I guess I was next in line to be killed if I didn't back off."

Heidi and Ellie shook their heads and held hands to their hearts like mirror images of each other. "You could have been murdered!" Ellie finally said as she reached across the table for Sammy's hand.

The three sat in silence for a moment, the full danger of the situation sinking in.

"What about Larry?" Ellie finally broke the silence and removed her hand from her sister's and placed her hands back in her lap, far away from the tempting cake.

Sammy shrugged. "He must have missed Spring Fling because he was sleeping off a bender. He definitely got away with something. With Ingrid no longer around, there's no one to press charges or prove he ever groped her at a bar."

"Let's not ever tell him we thought he might have killed Ingrid," Heidi said. "Let's keep it our little secret."

The three nodded in agreement.

"What about the antique knitting needles that you found in the doll room?" Heidi asked. "What will happen with those?"

Sammy smiled. "Coach is donating them to the Heartsford Historical Society in his Aunt Ingrid's honor. Isn't that generous? He could make a mint off them but decided they would be better off staying right here in our community. A lawyer came forward with a copy of Ingrid's Last Will and Testament. He was on vacation in Aruba at the time of the murder and when he got back home he contacted the coach. Coach inherited all of her estate; he's now officially a wealthier man!"

"Wow," Heidi said. "I guess he felt the community gave to him in his time of need with the brat-fry and he gave it right back . . . enormously. That's really something."

"Hey, I almost forgot. Did you hear the good news?" Ellie touched Heidi on the arm to get her attention. "Go ahead. Tell her, Sam. Tell her about Annabelle."

"Annabelle Larson is taking over The Yarn Barn. Since her

pending divorce, she decided she needed to go back to work full-time. She's working out the deal with Coach to keep the shop open. Isn't that great?"

"Wonderful news! I'm sure the knitters and crochet gals will be super happy about it too." Heidi agreed.

"Wanna hear even better news than that?" Sammy pointed to the door where her honorary little brother had just stepped inside. Heidi and Ellie turned their heads to see who had just entered the bakery. "Carter was scouted at the basketball game by Wisconsin, a full scholarship and he'll be playing for their basketball team! Woot! Woot! My alma mater. Isn't that cool?"

"Wow! That's amazing! We'll have to drive out to Madison and catch a few games," Ellie said.

"Boy, we're starting to sound like the biggest town gossips!" Heidi slapped her hand on the table and threw her head back in laughter.

"You know what?" Sammy laughed along with her cousin. "Kate was right about one thing. It feels good to be home. Where the small-minded gossips might be big . . . But the people's hearts are bigger . . . In our little ole town of Heartsford.

Ingrid's suggested yarns for various purpose:
Knit or Crochet
Always use the most natural fiber you can attain
in your price point.

The YARN BARN specializes in the following
NATURAL Fiber Yarns

Alpaca Yarn: Suri Alpaca and Huacaya Alpaca. Suri is the rarer of the two (Suris have longer hair)

Warm, yet lightweight

A lot of drape (great for shawls; not so good for some sweaters because of the stretch factor)

Soft and not scratchy or prickly like wool

Stronger than wool

Resists pilling

Alpaca/Llama Blend: 80% llama, 20% alpaca fleece

Splurge yarn $$

Machine washable on cold-gentle cycle

Not shedding or pilly

Naturally hypoallergenic

Soysilk Yarn: A fiber spun from soy proteins

Soft, thick texture

Warm

Wicks moisture

100% Hemp: Produces more protein, oil, and fiber than any other plant on earth

Very strong, long-living fiber

Cool in summer & warm in the winter

Corn Yarn: A flat-strand yarn created from the fibers of corn

Machine wash friendly (washes and dries well)

Great for summer projects as it's light

Bamboo Yarn: Created from the fibers of bamboo (grows very fast)

Cool and silky to the touch

Beautiful drape (perfect for sweaters, shawls)

SeaSilk Yarn: A unique yarn made partially from seaweed (70% silk and 30% SeaCell derived from seaweed)

Looks like silk

Can be hand-dyed

100% Cotton: A cotton yarn spun only from organic cotton (grown without any chemicals)

Perfect for cable knits

Washable

Durable

100% Organic Wool, Undyed: Most commonly spun from local organic sheep farm (sheep were raised without pesticides, hormones, or GMOs) and then the fiber processing is also organic.

Perfect for natural dying with vegetables like onion skins, spices such as turmeric, or fruit such as plum

Organic Merino Yarn: Locally spun from ancient breed of sheep—Merino sheep (softest wool of any sheep)

Gorgeous for both knit and crochet projects

Breathable for summer/insulating for winter

Soft and lightweight / hand-wash only

A very special note of thanks for the two *originial* sock patterns added to this book especially for you readers:

Maria Leigh who created the Vanilla Pod Socks pattern (Amigurumikr on Ravelry)

And Kay Nitschke who created The EASY sock pattern (a friend of Betty who owns and runs *Loose Ends* in Mayville, WI)

Vanilla Pod Socks

Finished Measurement:
8¼"/ 21cm from cuff to heel and 9½"/ 24cm from heel to toe. Woman's shoe size medium foot circumferences.

Materials:
Yarn Knit Picks Imagination Bare [50% Merino wool. 25% Superfine alpaca. 25% Nylon; 438yd (400m) /100g]

Needles US size 1(2.25mm) 32"/80cm circular for magic loop method. Feel free to change to smaller or larger size needles for narrow or wide foot.

Notions Tapestry needle, stitch markers.

Gauge:
18sts and 22 rounds in St sts over 2"/5cm.

Note:
This is a very simple sock with eye-catching eyelets in the center of leg and instep. If you prefer a fitted cuff, please use one size smaller needle for the ribbed band

Cuff:
CO 64 sts used preferred method. I used old Norwegian CO in this pattern. Join in the round, be careful to not twist.

*K1, p2, k1; rep from * around. Work 2×2 rib pattern 1¼"/3.5cm from CO edge.

Leg:
Rnd1 K48, yo, k16.

Rnd 2 Knit around.

Rnd 3 Knit around.

Rnd 4 K47, 3rd st over 2nd and 1st st on the left needle, k1, yo, k1, k15.

Rep Rnd 2–4 6"/15cm from CO edge.

Single eyelet stitches on center of front leg and instep has 3 rows (rnds) rep

Divide 32 sts for sole and 33 sts for instep.

Heel Flap:
Work back and forth first 32 sts as follows;

Row 1 * Sl1, k1; rep from * across.

Row 2 Sl1, p31.

Rep Row 1 - 2 14 times more.

Turn Heel:
Row 1 Sl1, k18, ssk, k1, turn.

Row 2 Sl1, p7, p2tog, p1, turn.

Row 3 Sl1, knit to previous slipped st (aka gap st on RS), ssk, k1, turn.

Row 4 Sl1, purl to previous slipped st (aka gap st on WS), p2tog, p1, turn.

Rep Row 3–4 5 times more. 20 sts rem.

Next row Sl1, k19, turn garment clockwise, pick up 16 sts on chained edge, place marker (pm), work in patt next 33 sts for instep, (pm).

Gusset Decrease:
Pick up 16 sts on chained edge right side of heel flap, k36, (sm), work in pattern next 33sts for instep, (sm). There are 52 sts for sole and 33 sts or instep. Total 85 sts rem.

Rnd 1(dec rnd) K2, ssk, knit 4 sts before marker, k2tog, k2, (sm), work in pattern, (sm).

Rnd 2 Work in pattern.

Rep Dec every other rnd 9 times more. 32 sts for sole and 33 sts for instep, total 65 sts rem.

Keep working on single eyelet patt.

Foot:
Work in pattern for foot 2"/5cm shorter then desired foot length.

Total 65 sts rem.

Toe:
Knit next 4 rnds.

Dec rnd *K2, ssk, knit 4 sts before next marker, k2tog, k2; rep from * once more.

Dec 4 sts every 3rd rnd 3 times, every other rnd 4 times, every rnd 5 times. 13 sts rem. Remove markers.

Finishing:

Cut yarn. Use a tapestry needle to draw the cut yarn through rem stitches. Pull tight to close. Tie off.

Block lightly.

Abbreviation:

CO Cast on

K Knit

P Purl

YO Yarn over

Ssk Slip 2 sts individually, knit them together

K2tog knit 2 sts together

P2tog Purl 2 sts together

(pm) Place marker

(sm) Slip marker

The EASY Sock

Materials:

Naked sock OR exchange berroco ultra alpaca and misty alpaca hand paint sock

Size 2 sock needles

Crochet hook darning needle for Kitchner St.

Sizes 56, 60, 64

CO, 60

Cuff:

Join and k2, p2, continue for 2 ins. 20 sts. on each needle. Making sure that the sts. are pointing toward the middle.

Con. Knitting for 7 in or the length before you start the heel

Heel:

Divide sts. On three needles. Knit 32 sts. Knit 16 sts. Knit 16 sts. This will bring you back to the 32 sts for the heel. Slip 1st st. knit across, turn slip 1t st. knit across. Do these two rows until 30 rows.

Turning Heel:

knit 16 sts. Place marker (pm) knit 3 sts. Slip 2 sts. and kit, knit 1. (ssk2) TURN knit to marker, slip marker (sm) knit3, knit2, together (K tog.2) purl 1, Turn. Purl back slipping marker purl to break and turn. These 2 rows will form the heel. You should end on the wrong side. Purl back. Next row: Slip 1ˢᵗ st. knit 8 st. to marker. Leave these st.8 stich on the needle and remove marker. Knit the next 8 st.

Instep. Pick up 16 st. With your working yarn and with your crochet hook pick up 16 sts. Poke the crochet hook under the slipped sts. Along the heel and pull the working yarn through and slipping it onto the needle. Continue until you have 16 new sts. on the needle. You should now have 28 sts. on that needle. Knit the next 16 sts. Knit the next 16 sts. You are on the other side of the instep. Pick up 16 sts. In the same manner that you did for the other side, knit the 8 sts onto that needle (28 sts) You should now have formed what looks like a boat. Pin a marker to indicate beginning of round.

Row 1, knit around

Row 2, knit around

Row 3, knit to 3 sts to the end, K2tog, knit 1, knit 16, knit16, knit 1 ssk, knit to the end.

Row 4, knit around. Continue row 3, 4 until you have 16 stitches on the instep needles. You have completed the instep. You should have a total of 16 sts on each needle.

Foot:

At this point you may put 20 sts on 3 needles and continue to knit 7 in. or until you have reached the length for the heel to the beginning of the big toe. Everyone measures differently, and this may be longer.

Toe:

Divide 16 st. on 4 needles making sure that you have a top, bottom and sides. Place a marker on one side for the beginning of the round Row 1: K1, K2tog. K to end, K 16, K to 3 st ssk, K1. This completes around. Row 2: Knit, continue these 2 rows until you have 10st. on each needle. Next, work row 1 until you have 5 st. on each needle on the last round. Next row: Knit 5 st. knit the next 5, you now have 10 on the needle, do the same for the next 2 needles. You now have 2 needles with 10st. each.

Now you may use the Kitchener stich to close your sock. Visit YouTube for a demo if not familiar.

Acknowledgments

T hanks readers! Considering the abundance of text we
are inundated with on a daily basis, I feel honored and
blessed that you took the time to read my work. I hope as you
spend time in the fictitious town of Heartsford you're enter-
tained, it's a place you've come to love, and everyday stress
takes a back seat to a curious escape.

It takes many helpful hands to bring words from a laptop
to a finished cozy mystery that you now hold in your hand.
Please indulge me while I gush over a few that have helped
along the way.

Sandy Harding; my agent and confidant. Thank you for
your insight in those early days and guiding me like a beacon
of light to take a shot when I was ready to quit. Your profes-
sionalism and years of skill have brought us here. Also, my
editor at Crooked Lane Books: Faith Black Ross, who sharp-
ened my pencil and added invaluable insight, it's been a privilege to work with you. Jenny, Sarah, Ashley, and the rest of the
team at Crooked Lane Books, your work has not gone unno-
ticed in this author's eyes . . . Thank you team! And to the
cover artist: Ben Perini-awesome job. Because books really are
judged by their covers!

Acknowledgments

Those at Spencerhill Associates and Crooked Lane Books who have worked behind the scenes on our behalf. Thank you.

A very special note of thanks to: Maria Leigh / Vanilla Pod Socks and Kay Nitschke / The Easy Sock for creating unique knit sock patterns just for you readers! Their patterns are included in the back of this book. Please feel free to send me pics of your final creations to pass on to them.

Wendy and Jason. What you do for the public and how you motivate others has been true inspiration for the sense of community in this book. Sharing yourselves and loving others. You guys are just full of Faith and Giggles. Keep shining your light!

Jared, Sara, Jesse, Aubrey. How I miss you and wish we all shared life closer.

My sweetheart of a husband, Mark. Your continued support and encouragement amazes me. Only you would put up with our imaginary book friends this long and enjoy them as much as I. When I think of love, I think of you.

Finally, the original S.H.E. Yes. Those were the best of times . . .